ACCUSED

Patience closed her eyes the ceiling. She stretched slowly at first, then faste so suddenly that her bill back and forth around h now pointed toward the brethren, apparently singling out Andrew and Wilhelm.

"And you!" Patience said, her voice deepening as if speaking now for a male angel. "You have sinned in deed."

Patience's arms dropped to her side and hung limply. Her head slumped toward her chest as if a puppeteer had dropped the strings. "Patience, are you ill?" Rose asked. "Do you need help?" Patience shifted her gaze to Rose's face. Her eyes were dark as loam.

"Mother's angels would never harm me," she said. "They know my strength. And they will use me to tell the truth."

PRAISE FOR DEBORAH WOODWORTH AND SISTER ROSE CALLAHAN

"Woodworth does an admirable job
of opening up the world of these peaceful
and industrious people to the reader."
Post (Denver, Colorado)

"Bits of Shaker lore add a fresh slant to a historical novel
that also offers a neat plot. But it is Rose herself—
intelligent, compassionate, and very strong—
whom readers will especially want to see again."
Star Tribune (Minneapolis St. Paul)

Other Sister Rose Callahan Mysteries by
Deborah Woodworth

A DEADLY SHAKER SPRING
DEATH OF A WINTER SHAKER

DEBORAH WOODWORTH

Sins of a Shaker Summer

— A —

SISTER ROSE CALLAHAN
MYSTERY

AVON
TWILIGHT

This is a work of fiction. Names, characters, places, and incidents either are the product of the author's imagination or are used fictitiously. Any resemblance to actual events, locales, organizations, or persons, living or dead, is entirely coincidental and beyond the intent of either the author or the publisher.

AVON BOOKS, INC.
1350 Avenue of the Americas
New York, New York 10019

Copyright © 1999 by Deborah Woodworth
Published by arrangement with the author
Library of Congress Catalog Card Number: 98-90922
ISBN: 0-380-79204-4
www.avonbooks.com/twilight

First Avon Twilight Printing: April 1999

AVON TWILIGHT TRADEMARK REG. U.S. PAT. OFF. AND IN OTHER COUN-TRIES, MARCA REGISTRADA, HECHO EN U.S.A.

Printed in the U.S.A.

WCD   10 9 8 7 6 5 4 3 2 1

40943334

For Norm, with love

ACKNOWLEDGMENTS

As always, my gratitude goes to my writers' group: Tom Rucker, Peter Hautman, Mary Logue, Becky Bohan, Marilyn Bos, and Larry Rogers; to my editor, Patricia Lande Grader; my agent, Barbara Gislason; and, of course, my family.

AUTHOR'S NOTE

The North Homage Shaker village, the town and the county of Languor, Kentucky, and all their inhabitants are figments of the author's imagination. The characters live only in this book and represent no one, living or dead. By the 1930s, the period in which this story is told, no Shaker villages remained in Kentucky or anywhere else outside the northeastern United States. Today one small Shaker community survives, Sabbathday Lake, near Poland Springs, Maine. The Pleasant Hill Shaker community (near Harrodsburg, Kentucky) closed in 1910, but the village has been restored and is open to visitors who wish to see how Believers lived during the nineteenth century.

Deborah Woodworth
1999

pile next to her and placed it on a broken white plate in front of Betsy. Next to the new flower sat a white one, with several bites missing, nestled in a bed of nibbled leaves. Nora licked her fingers as if savoring juices.

Betsy was not to be convinced. "The other flower tasted bad. I don't want any more." She scooted back against a tree and pulled her knees up to her stomach.

Nora clucked her tongue with impatience. "I keep telling you, this is a magical salad, and it tastes wonderful. What's wrong with you, Betsy? You're not any fun at all today."

"Nora, I want to go back now. My tummy really hurts. I want Sister Charlotte." Her voice rose to a tearful wail. She hugged her knees tightly and began to rock. "We're not supposed to be here," she added, her small voice starting to quiver. "Charlotte will be mad that we sneaked off."

Nora frowned, but she sensed defeat, and her own stomach felt queasy, too. "All right," she said, "but we have to clean up first." Her insistence had less to do with neatness than with hiding evidence of their unsanctioned outing. She gathered the two cracked cups and the broken plate and slid them into their hiding place, a pile of leaves. The flowers they had used for their meal, she dropped into the nearby undergrowth. Betsy did not help her. She clutched her knees against her stomach as if the pressure was a relief, and beads of perspiration appeared on her pale forehead.

"Mama," Betsy said, her voice soft and breathless. "Mama, the boys are pulling my pigtails." She grabbed at her short hair. "Make them stop, make them stop."

"What? Betsy, your mama is . . . She isn't here anymore, remember?" Nora clutched Betsy's shaking shoulders. The younger girl's mother, and father as well, had been dead for two years, which was why the Shakers were raising her. Nora slipped her arm around the smaller girl and urged her to her feet. "Come on, I'll get you home, don't worry." Betsy shivered and moaned. Nora felt none too well herself, and she was close to panic. If they didn't get back, she thought, Sister Charlotte would blame her, and that would be awful. All the children adored Charlotte; she was firm but kind. Sneaking off to the woods for a play tea party would earn her wrath.

"Come on, quickly," Nora urged. By now, Betsy was gasping for air. The two girls staggered out of the woods, past the herb fields and the old cemetery. Betsy's legs wobbled, and she tripped over a tree root. Both girls fell to their knees. Nora struggled to her feet.

"Please, Betsy, please get up," she begged. She hooked her elbows under Betsy's shoulders and yanked her upright. Nora felt her strength ebbing and wished she could curl up in a ball to soothe her own stomach. But the image of Charlotte's anger kept her going, especially when she thought about Charlotte telling Eldress Rose how disobedient they'd been. To be in the bad graces of both women was more than Nora could bear to contemplate. She tightened her grip on Betsy and forced her feet forward.

They cleared the herb fields, and the Center Family Dwelling House came into view. At least, she thought it was the dwelling house. It seemed to be moving, rippling like a lake in the wind. Betsy crumpled in Nora's arms. Whimpering with fear and her own pain, Nora let Betsy slide to the grass, then stumbled toward the building. The thick grass seemed to clutch at her feet, pulling her down. The sky began to twirl around her head, then turned green, and she was dimly aware that she had fallen. Her stomach lurched. She curled into a tight ball.

From somewhere nearby, Nora thought she heard a voice call her name. She lifted herself on one elbow but could push no higher. Through half-closed eyes, she looked toward the sound. She saw a movement, and the movement became an angel in flight. Voluminous robes billowed around the hovering figure. It was carrying something. More tea? Yea, it must be more magical tea, Nora thought. The tea. They shouldn't have sneaked away, shouldn't have had the tea. She squinted again at the creature, now leaning

TWO

"Best get over here fast, Rose," Sister Josie Trent barked into the phone. "We've got two very sick little girls here at the Infirmary, and I'm not certain they'll make it."

Rose Callahan, eldress of the dwindling North Homage Shaker community, dropped her notes for Sunday's homily and raced out the door of the Ministry House, stuffing errant red curls under her cap as she ran. She found Josie in one of the Infirmary's larger rooms, tending the girls in two adult-sized cradle beds. Josie scurried between the beds as fast as the heat and her plump, eighty-year-old body would let her.

"What happened? Any idea?" Rose asked. She grimaced at the rank smell of sickness in the room, but forced herself to concentrate. She bent over a narrow bed containing a pale girl who moaned and jerked as Rose touched her cheek; it felt clammy.

"Gretchen was carrying some clean laundry to the Trustees' Office when she found them lying in the grass. Betsy was barely conscious, and Nora seemed to be hallucinating before she passed out."

"Have you alerted Wilhelm?"

"Nay, haven't had time. The girls came to long enough for me to give them some Ipecac to empty their stomachs and some valerian to calm their convulsions. I think they are done being sick for now, but I haven't dared leave them

5

alone.'' Josie sloshed some rose water into a bowl to sweeten the air, but it did little good.

"I'll stay with them," Rose said. "I can shout for you if there's a change for the worse."

Josie nodded. "I'll call Brother Andrew, too."

Rose tossed a questioning glance at her.

"I suspect they ate something they shouldn't have," Josie said. "Andrew has studied pharmacy much more recently than I. He might have some ideas about what on earth we should do for these children. There's no point in calling to Languor for help, with Doc Irwin recovering from that heart attack, and it would take too long to get a doctor from another town."

When Josie had left, Rose opened all the windows. Even a sticky breeze was better than the fetid, oppressive air in the hot room. A rocking chair with a faded woven seat waited in the corner for visitors. She placed it between the two cradle beds. She was just able to see over the sides of both beds, so she could watch for changes in the girls' conditions. She rocked herself and began to calm down—until Nora cried out. Rose hurried to her side. The child's body shivered and writhed, pulling loose the sheet Josie had tucked around her.

"Quiet, now, Nora. It's all right," Rose said, placing a calming hand on the girl's chest. Nora muttered a few syllables, and Rose bent near her.

"Angel," Nora whispered. "Bad angel . . ." Rose could hear the girl's shallow breathing and felt her neck for a pulse; it was weak. Nora's eyelids flew open, and her dilated pupils fixed Rose with a haunting stare. Just as suddenly, the girl's eyes closed, and her body convulsed.

Rose sensed someone behind her and turned. Brother Andrew Clark, North Homage's new trustee, stood a few feet from Nora's bed. His tall, thin body was motionless, shoulders hunched forward with tension. Damp and disheveled dark brown waves fell over his forehead as if he had just run through the wind. He muttered something under his breath, stared briefly at the ceiling, then approached the shivering child.

"Wilhelm's out in the far fields," Josie said from the doorway. "I've sent one of the boys for him. What has happened? Has Nora taken a turn for the worse?"

"She seems to be semiconscious and hallucinating again," Rose said. She was not surprised to hear the girl mention an angel. Indeed, the spirits of long-dead Believers were known to visit living Shakers, especially during dancing worship, trances, and funerals. If Nora was dying, surely an angel Believer would come to be with her. But why a "bad angel"?

Rose stood well back as Andrew bent over Nora's bed. He drew a long finger gently across her dry lips as she muttered "bad angel" again and again. His jaw tightened, and he sighed. He straightened, staring over Nora's bed, apparently absorbed in the apothecary jars that lay scattered on the pine dresser next to her. With his right hand, he rocked the cradle bed in short, fluid movements as if the rhythm helped him think.

"What is it, Andrew? What do you think might have happened?" Rose asked.

Andrew's head jerked toward her as if he had forgotten her presence. He opened his mouth, took in a breath to speak, but let the breath out in another sigh. Without a word, he went to Betsy's bed and repeated his examination.

"You say they've been hallucinating?" Andrew asked.

"Yea, indeed," Josie said. "Gretchen said Nora seemed quite terrified of her, kept calling her a monster, which is nonsense, of course. We all know how gentle Gretchen is." Josie's voice trailed off as it became apparent that Andrew was not listening.

Rose watched him with irritation. Clearly he had a theory about what was wrong with the girls; why wouldn't he say what it was? She forced herself to give him a few more moments of silent thought. His narrow face expressed a series of emotions—Rose was certain she saw some fear, possibly anger, and a hint of vigilance in his brown eyes.

She knew very little about Andrew yet. He had been with them only since the late spring, sent by the Lead Ministry in Mount Lebanon, New York, to take over as trustee. In her confessions to her friend and mentor, the former Eldress Agatha Vandenberg, Rose had admitted a nagging resentment against Andrew. Something about him bothered her, though as Agatha wisely pointed out, the problem might merely be that Rose had loved being trustee and regretted letting go of the job.

Certainly Andrew had been a welcome addition to the dwindling brethren. He was still no more than forty, with a quick mind and able body. Using his training in pharmacy and his business experience, he already had begun to reduce their debt by expanding the Shakers' tiny medicinal herb industry. Perhaps having to give up sole control over herb production also helped explain Rose's irritation with Andrew. When her duties as eldress allowed her, she still found herself drawn to the Herb House to help dry, press, and package tins of culinary herbs. But now Andrew was growing new, experimental herbs and taking over much of the culinary harvest to create patent medicines.

Rose snapped back to attention. Was that what Josie had been thinking about when she called Andrew to look at Nora and Betsy? Did she suspect they had gotten into some of his concoctions? Or worse yet, might he or one of his helpers have tested some new product on the children? *Goodness*, she thought, *I am growing sadly mistrustful.*

Andrew continued to stare into space, so Rose drew Josie aside. "Do you have any idea where these girls might have been when they became ill?" she asked in an undertone.

Josie shook her head. "Nay, I haven't had even a second to question the other children, and these two haven't been lucid enough." Her eyes strayed over to the small forms. "I have my suspicions, though."

"Which are?" Rose asked, with a swift glance at Andrew.

"Well, you know what children are like. I'm sure we'll find they sneaked off and got into something they shouldn't have. Gretchen found them in the grass between the Trustees' Office and the Center Family Dwelling House. Either building would contain all sorts of cleaning compounds, and then there's the kitchen and the medic gardens, and who's to say what those two girls might have taken a notion to nibble on."

"It's hard to believe they evaded Charlotte's eyes."

"That little Nora is a clever one," Josie said with a half smile. "She'll have thought of a way."

Without a word to the sisters, Andrew strode from the room, his face pinched.

"Such an odd man," Rose said before she could stop herself.

"Oh, do you think so, my dear? I think he is a godsend, truly a godsend. He knows so much, I wouldn't be at all surprised if he solved this mystery in no time. He already has an idea, you could see it on his face." Josie's round face returned to its normal cheerfulness. Rose, on the other hand, felt unaccountably annoyed.

Rose cut across the unpaved road that ran down the center of North Homage and headed for the Children's Dwelling House. With a twinge of guilt, she ignored the path and angled through the trim, thick bluegrass. Her loose cotton work dress stuck to her back, heavy as winter wool. The thin white cap that covered her head, indoors and out, felt like a metal helmet, and the fluffs of hair that escaped from its edges were plastered to her face with perspiration. The heat wasn't helping her mood, which was part worry, part impatience.

Elder Wilhelm Lundel would be expecting a report from her soon, and she wanted to piece the puzzle together before she talked to him. Wilhelm had trouble accepting that they were now equal partners in the ministry, the Society's spiritual leadership. Since Rose had been eldress for less than a year, she was aware of her inexperience and felt a need to prove herself worthy. It certainly would have helped if Andrew had shared his suspicions with her, she thought with renewed irritation. Never mind, she'd ask him later.

The Children's Dwelling House felt cool after the intense sunlight. Charlotte and the children had worked in the gardens all morning and again after the midday meal. They would all be tired. Normally Charlotte had them rest awhile in midafternoon, sometimes for several hours, on these steamy summer days.

Rose climbed the staircase to Charlotte's second-floor retiring room and knocked gently. After a second, louder knock, a groggy voice beckoned her in.

Charlotte slumped in a ladder-back chair at her small pine desk. A geography book and some notes were spread open in front of her. She had removed her white cap, and her short, dark blond hair fell forward over her face. A crease across her forehead revealed that her study session had turned into a nap.

"Oh, Rose," she said, with a self-conscious laugh. "The girls are resting, and I thought I'd get a head start on my teaching for the fall. But I must have fallen asleep. I'm so sorry. This heat . . ."

Rose laughed, too—a welcome moment of release. "I believe I speak for Mother Ann and all Believers," she said, "when I assure you that you are forgiven."

Charlotte grinned as she ran her fingers through her tousled hair and pushed it back into her cap, which she tied at the nape of her neck.

"What is it? What has happened?" she asked as Rose's smile dissolved.

"Nora and Betsy sneaked out of their rooms."

"Those two! This isn't the first time, you know. I'll give them a good talking-to, you can count on that." Charlotte stood and shook out her wrinkled dress.

"I fear it might be some time before you'll be able to

have that talk. They've gotten into something and made themselves ill.''

''Oh dear. Very ill?''

''I'm afraid so.''

''It's my fault,'' Charlotte said, dropping back in her chair. ''I should have known; I should have watched more carefully. Are they going to be all right?''

''I don't know.''

''Dear God.''

''Indeed. Charlotte, I need to know what those girls might have touched or eaten. You said they've sneaked off before. Do you have any idea where they've gone?''

''Nay, I've never been able to catch them at it, the clever little creatures.'' Charlotte's stern tone held a hint of admiration. ''Each time they've 'just been to the bathroom' or 'down in the kitchen,' and I haven't been able to disprove it. But it's always the two of them at the same time, so I know they're up to something.''

The hall telephone jangled, and Rose heard a young voice answer.

''Are the children finished with their naps?'' Rose asked Charlotte.

''Yea, it sounds as if they're up and about.''

''Then let's ask them if they know anything about Nora and Betsy's adventures, shall we?''

As Rose turned to the door, a girl of about seven, clutching a corncob doll, peeked inside. ''Sister Charlotte? Sister Josie says to tell Eldress to get back over to the Infirmary right away.'' She smiled shyly at Rose.

''Thank you, Marjorie. Did she say why?'' Charlotte asked.

The girl shook her head. ''Nay, I think it was a secret.''

''Why do you think that?''

''Because she was whispering.''

Leaving Charlotte to question the children about Nora and Betsy, Rose rushed back to the Infirmary. As she

crossed the central path, Elder Wilhelm's muscular body
and shock of white hair disappeared through the Infirmary
door. She felt her jaw tighten as she wondered how Wilhelm would turn this tragedy into a criticism of her com-
petence as eldress. He hoped to replace her with someone
who thought as he did—someone who would support his
efforts to take the Society back to the early nineteenth century, when novitiates signed the covenant and crowded into
dwelling houses as fast as the brethren could build them.
It was because of Wilhelm that North Homage Believers
wore traditional dress, which other Shaker villages had
modernized or even abandoned.

Rose assumed that one or both girls had taken a turn for
the worse, and she expected flurried activity around their
beds, but what she saw when she entered the sickroom sent
a flash of fear through her heart. Three sisters had joined
Josie on one side of Nora's bed, while Andrew and Wilhelm stood on the other side, their backs to Rose. She
rushed forward, convinced she was viewing a deathbed
scene. But when she reached Nora, she saw one sister bent
over the bed, both hands covering the child's face.

Sister Patience McCormick's deep voice half-sung what
sounded like a prayer. At least, to Rose it seemed to have
the rhythm of a prayer, though she heard only an occasional
word in English. Rose had finished the Shaker school system and left the Children's Order by the age of fourteen,
more than two decades earlier, so she had little experience
with other languages, except what she had learned from
visiting businessmen during her ten years as trustee. She
thought she recognized a few French words, a little
German, and some Latin.

Startled by a familiar clumping sound, Rose glanced toward the entrance to the sickroom. Sister Elsa Pike planted
her sturdy body just inside the doorway. Her round, flat-
featured face exuded suspicion.

"I heard one of them girls got into something she
shouldn't've," Elsa announced, "so I come right over. If

it's anything grows around here, plant or animal, I'll know what to do.'' She brushed past the sisters to the foot of Nora's bed.

Rose clenched her hands around the sides of the cradle bed. Perhaps her reaction was instinctive—whenever Elsa entered a room, Rose prepared for battle. This battle, she feared, would be fought over a helpless eight-year-old child. She was certain that Elsa had somehow heard about a healing in progress and raced over to interrupt. Elsa considered the gifts of the spirit to be her own private domain.

Ignoring the drama unfolding next to her, Elsa grabbed Nora's foot and shook it, as if she were awakening the child from slumber.

Patience did not flinch, but her tone became louder, more insistent. A drop of perspiration traveled down the side of her flushed face. Her eyes flew open and she began to tremble as if electric shocks pulsed through her body. Wisps of gray-streaked black hair pulled free of her cap.

''Mother Ann is among us,'' she said in a raspy voice. ''She has come to heal this innocent child. From our Mother's heart through my hands, may this child be healed!'' She stroked Nora's face over and over. Now not even Elsa stirred. When Rose became light-headed, she realized she had stopped breathing.

Nora twitched violently, then grew still. She seemed to have fallen into a deep sleep.

''She is healed,'' Patience whispered, stepping back from the bed. The slow blinking of her eyes betrayed her own exhaustion. Without another word, she left the room.

After a few moments of silence, Josie drew her hand across Nora's forehead, then felt for her pulse.

''She does seem better,'' Josie said.

''Can you be certain she is truly out of danger?'' Rose asked. Wilhelm narrowed his eyes at her, but she ignored him.

''Well, her pulse does feel a bit stronger,'' Josie said.

''But you can't be sure?'' Rose asked.

THREE

"WALK BACK TO THE FIELDS WITH ME," WILHELM COM-
manded. "We must discuss how to proceed."

A private chat with Wilhelm usually gave Rose an aching
head, but she was curious about his reaction to Patience
and her apparent healing of Nora. Certainly healing was
one of the gifts of the spirit possessed by their foundress,
Mother Ann, and by many early Shakers. Wilhelm longed
for the gifts to reappear in North Homage. His longing was
so ardent that he had allowed himself to be duped in the
past.

They walked in silence down the village's central path,
past the Meetinghouse and the Ministry House. The Shakers frowned upon private conversations between men and
women, but as elder and eldress, Rose and Wilhelm were
expected to consult often about Society concerns. Even so,
Rose took care not to walk too close. In truth, she felt more
comfortable at a distance from Wilhelm.

"We must find ways to cultivate this gift that Patience
has shown," Wilhelm said as they passed the barn and
stepped into the first fields east of the village. A narrow
path ran through the half-grown rows of sweet corn to allow workers and horses quick access to farther-flung acres.
Rose walked behind Wilhelm to keep enough space between them.

"If her gift is true, then surely it will simply emerge,"
Rose said.

"Nay, we must encourage it, give it opportunities to
grow and mature."

"Are you suggesting we poison a few more Believers so
Patience can practice her technique?" Rose knew at once
that keeping such thoughts to herself would be wiser, and
she vowed to curb her tongue next time. Or at least to try.

Wilhelm did not turn to glare at her, but she saw the
muscles in his neck bunch. "Thy levity, as usual, is ill
timed," he said. "But then, the future of the Society has
never been of great concern to thee, has it?" Wilhelm and
Elsa were the only North Homage Believers to use the archaic "thee" instead of "you," and to Rose it seemed the
word was always couched in an insult.

"Even if Patience has the gift of healing, the Society's
future does not depend on her; it depends on us all and on
God," she said in a clipped voice.

"Yea, it depends on us, on our ability to listen and understand when God speaks. God is speaking through Patience. He has given her healing hands, and maybe other
gifts as well. It is up to us to hear the message and welcome
the messenger."

Rose kept silent. His words had meaning for her, though
she was unconvinced as yet about the reality of Patience's
gift. Wilhelm seemed unconcerned about the girls' survival,
because he believed in the healing. Rose required more evidence.

"We shall have Patience lead the dancing at Sunday
worship," Wilhelm said.

"Certainly I have no objections to that," Rose said, ignoring the fact that Wilhelm had not asked her opinion.
"But I wonder how Elsa will react."

"She will be glad for the Society, naturally," Wilhelm
said.

Rose held her tongue this time, though she suspected that
Elsa's prideful nature would balk at letting another sister

gather too much attention during dancing worship. As if reading her thoughts, Wilhelm stopped and faced her.

"Now that I think of it," he said, an unsettling gleam in his eye, "watching Patience develop her gifts might help Elsa refine her own. Furthermore, I believe we should open the worship service to the world again."

"Wilhelm, I think that is unwise."

"It is time," Wilhelm said. "It is time we showed ourselves again to the world." He left Rose standing amidst the young corn, an all-too-familiar dread rising in her chest.

By midafternoon the steamy air in the Laundry felt heavy enough to sweep aside. Rose decided to make her visit quick. She found Gretchen, the Laundry Deaconess, pulling wet clothes out of a large washing machine. Her loose sleeves were rolled high above her elbows, and perspiration formed dark patches on her cotton dress.

"Where are the others?" Rose asked. "Surely they aren't upstairs, not in this heat."

"Nay," Gretchen said, "I've sent them all to deliver clean laundry and then to their retiring rooms for a rest. We'd had one fainting already, and I didn't want to risk more."

In the summer, laundry was done as simply as possible, without benefit of the upstairs ironing room, where clothes were hung on steam-pipe drying racks and exposed to pumped-in heat from the downstairs boiler. On sultry days such as this one, temperatures in the ironing room soared to levels neither God nor Wilhelm would expect Believers to endure.

"Let me help you with that," Rose offered.

"I won't object," Gretchen said. "This is the last load for today, and the sooner we get these hung up, the sooner I can splash some cold water on my face."

Together they carried the heavy basket through the back door to the rows of clotheslines.

"I suppose you want to ask about Nora and Betsy?"
Gretchen asked.

Rose nodded as she accepted a handful of clothespins
and pulled a damp brown work shirt from the basket.

"I found them right between the Center Family house
and the Trustees' Office. They were both lying in the grass,
and Nora was babbling something about angels and mon-
sters and tea."

"Could you tell where they'd come from?"

"Nay, but I wondered if they'd been in the Center Family house. With no one there, except in the kitchen, they
could have sneaked into the root cellar to play. I'm sure
it's lovely and cool down there." Her clothespin hovered
above a blue sleeve, her eyes faraway as if imagining the
coolness.

"When we've finished here, go straight to your retiring
room and rest with a cool cloth on your forehead," Rose
ordered.

"On any other day, I'd argue with you," Gretchen said,
"but today I'll just say a fervent thank-you."

"Not too fervent," Rose said, "or you'll melt."

The Society's root cellar was a large room under the
Center Family Dwelling House. Two stairways led down
to it—one from the kitchen and another from a storage area
at the north end of the building. Since the kitchen garden
surrounded the north and east sides, Rose thought it possible that the children might have picked some herbs and
taken them down to the root cellar to play. She couldn't
imagine what culinary herb could have made them so ill.
Perhaps they had risked sneaking into the nearby medic
garden, but surely someone would have seen them.

Rose walked all the way around the large limestone
building, looking for telltale bits of discarded plants, but
she saw nothing. Of course, anything out of place would
be cleared away by passing Believers. She returned to the
front of the dwelling house and entered by the sisters' door-

way. Her gaze on the floor, she walked between the separate staircases for sisters and brethren, past the kitchen entrance, all the way to the back of the building. No leaf or clump of dirt marred the neatness of the floor or the stairs down to the root cellar.

The cellar itself would need a more thorough cleaning before the fall, when potatoes and squash would be brought in for storage and winter use. By this time of the year, most of their stores had been used up. Much of what remained had withered or rotted and been tossed out. Despite the earthy air, the coolness tempted Rose to tidy up for a while. But she resisted. She saw no sign that children had used the room as a play area, and Nora's and Betsy's lives might depend on identifying, as quickly as possible, what they might have ingested.

On her way to the stairs, Rose peeked into a side room lined with shelves. Two areas held canning jars. One section contained dwindling rows of string beans, beets, and pickles in dusty glass jars. The other area, on the opposite side of the room, was beginning to fill with jellies in pale hues. Rose went closer to read the labels: rose-petal, violet, and peppermint jellies. Just reading the names made her tongue tingle. Was this more experimentation? She had certainly lost contact with work assignments since leaving the trustee position in Andrew's hands.

Rose emerged from the staircase leading back to the kitchen, startling the kitchen sisters hard at work beginning preparations for the evening meal. The huge cast-iron stove was unlit; given the heat, the meal was to be cold and light—a large salad, iced potato soup, pickles, and bread.

"Sorry, Gertrude, I didn't mean to pop out at you so suddenly," Rose said, as the Kitchen Deaconess squeaked and hopped backward at seeing her.

"Goodness," Gertrude said, fanning her flushed face with a large hand. "Goodness, goodness. What were you doing down in the root cellar? There's almost nothing down there now but blessedly cool air. Honestly, I've been wanting to move the kitchen downstairs before we all melt into puddles on the floor.'' Before the last words were out of her mouth, Gertrude had spun back to the large worktable and begun ripping chunks of greens into a bowl. The lettuce had bolted in the heat, so she was using mustard greens and young cabbage. Rose selected a cabbage and began to help.

"I wondered if Nora and Betsy had by any chance been playing downstairs, perhaps with some herbs from the medic garden or something else that might have made them sick."

"Nay, I don't think so," Gertrude said. "At least, we've never seen or heard them. Someone would have told me."

"Will you ask the others for me?"

"Certainly."

Rose gathered a handful of curly mustard greens and ripped them into bite-sized pieces. "I noticed some interesting new jellies downstairs," she said.

"Aren't they lovely?" Gertrude said.

"Andrew's idea?"

"Certainly not! Andrew has no interest in culinary herbs. He's even using more of the herb crop for medicines and leaving us less for cooking than we used to have, and I, for one, am quite disappointed. We Believers are known for our cooking, and we've always sold wonderfully flavorful herbs to hotels all over, haven't we? Well, I just thought I'd show him a thing or two about our cooking herbs. Those new jellies came from us, the kitchen sisters. We all put our heads together and came up with some very tasty ideas, if you'll forgive us our pride." The last was said with a quick glance at Rose, who smiled to show there was nothing to forgive.

"Has Patience shown any interest in culinary herbs?"

"That one? Not likely. She isn't interested in anything but her precious experiments. And those so-called gifts of hers, of course." Again she darted an uncertain glance at Rose, who was in a quandary. She wanted all the information she could get about the Medicinal Herb Shop workers, but she would be condoning gossip. With reluctance and a stinging conscience, she decided that information, just now, was more important than living as the angels.

"You think her gifts are false?" she asked.

Gertrude sniffed. "I shouldn't judge, I know, but it just doesn't seem right to me. She isn't the sort of person Holy Mother Wisdom would endow with gifts, that's my opinion. She's . . . she's mean-spirited."

"Why do you say that?"

Gertrude's lips hardened into a straight line, and she ripped away at her cabbage as if it had to be killed before it could be eaten. To Rose's surprise and dismay, a row of tears gathered along her bottom eyelids. "I'm very proud of this kitchen, and my kitchen sisters, and all the work we do. Why, without our work, this Society wouldn't even survive, would it?"

"Nay, it would not."

"Well, I was so proud of the inventive new recipes the sisters and me came up with, and I was telling Patience about them, and you know what she said? She said we were using up too many of the herbs, and we had to stop! Well, I said, 'The herbs are ours, too, you know, and they were ours before they were yours, and where would you be without the kitchen sisters, anyway?' And she said she could live on plain water and bread, which she could easily make herself. She said herbs are wasted on cooking and that . . . that we were just a bunch of gossipy old hens." The tears had spilled over, and Gertrude was trying to mop them up with her sleeve without letting go of her cabbage.

Rose put an arm around her shoulders. Dealing with tears was not her strength, but she had learned from Agatha that sometimes a touch is better than any words, so she said none. As Gertrude settled down, Rose considered the hints she was gathering about Patience. An unpredictable woman—blunt, judgmental, harsh, arrogant, perhaps gifted. But was she anything else? Was she unthinking enough to

FOUR

ROSE HAD NOT ENTERED THE TRUSTEES' OFFICE FOR WEEKS. It had been her home and her workplace for ten years. Leaving it, moving to the Ministry House to live and work as eldress, had been a wrenching change. She had thought it best to throw herself into her new role and to cut her ties as fully as possible with her old one.

She sat in a ladder-back chair in the office that used to be hers, facing Brother Andrew, the new trustee. Everything looked the same, yet strange somehow, like her retiring room seemed after she'd returned from visiting another Shaker village. The strip of pegs encircling the wall held a man's blue Sabbathday surcoat and a broad-brimmed hat. The aged pine of the double desk had the same orange glow, but was perhaps not quite as tidy as when she— Rose stopped herself before her thoughts went beyond uncharitable to prideful.

Andrew Clark watched her in silence as she drew herself back to her mission. He seemed to know when she had returned.

"Have you brought news of the children?" he asked.

"Nay, there is little news. I was hoping that you could shed some light on this mystery," Rose said.

"Me?" Andrew's dark eyebrows arched in surprise.

Rose regarded him for a long moment. "Surely you realize that Josie asked you to examine the girls' symptoms

23

because she hoped you might recognize them. In fact, it seemed to us that you did. Yet you said nothing.'' Rose gazed at him with an expectant tilt to her head. The gesture had often extracted information from hesitant informants, but Andrew only frowned.

''I'm sorry, Rose, but I could not identify what the girls might have eaten, if that's what they did. Certainly there are several plants or medicines that could cause such symptoms if eaten or taken to excess, but . . . It seemed to me that Josie did the best thing possible for them—she gave them an emetic. That's all I would have recommended.''

''Andrew, I apologize for being so insistent, but if there's anything, anything at all that you suspect, we can't afford not to know.''

''Truly, I would never keep knowledge to myself if it would help those children. You must believe me.''

Andrew leaned toward her in what felt like familiarity, though Rose told herself it was only supplication. She wanted to believe him. Despite his aura of secretiveness, she liked him. He was a refreshing change from Wilhelm. Andrew wore his dark hair fairly long so that brown waves brushed the stand-up collar of his work shirt. His trim beard challenged Wilhelm's edict that the brethren be clean-shaven. Though his clothing resembled the loose, plain work clothes of the nineteenth-century brethren, his brown shirt and trousers had a cleaner, updated line. These casual displays of defiance pleased Rose as much as they irritated Wilhelm.

Still, she couldn't shake the sense that he knew more than he was saying. She decided to try a different approach.

''We have been so busy since you arrived here that I've had no time to chat with you about your business plans. Perhaps we might do so now? I'd love to see the gardens you've developed and find out how you are using them to make medicines.''

''Right now?'' Andrew tensed and glanced at the office door as if hoping for an interruption.

"Now would be perfect," Rose said. "Nora and Betsy could become more ill, of course, but for the moment they seem stable. Perhaps a discussion of herbs will trigger an idea for one of us." Without waiting for help, she swung her chair upside down and hung it from several wall pegs so the seat would be free of dust for the next visitor. She led the way to the door, and Andrew followed without further objection.

In silence they exited the front door of the Trustees' Office and descended the long row of front steps. They approached the Medicinal Herb Shop and circled to the right of the building, where Andrew had created a new medicinal herb garden. Here he experimented with varieties of herbs not normally grown in the medic garden behind the Infirmary.

A young man crouched before a row of plants with orange flowers, which Rose recognized as pleurisy root. The man's earth-stained hands worked quickly, nipping small weeds from between the plants. When he heard them approach, he raised a round face with translucent green eyes.

"This is Willy Robinson," Andrew said. "We hired him from Languor to help out in the gardens and the shop. He has a special interest in medicinal herbs."

"Glad to meet you, ma'am," Willy said. He held out his hand and withdrew it quickly, darting a glance at Andrew. His hands were rough, smeared with brown and green stains, the nails chipped and dirty. A musty smell wafted toward Rose. She would mention to Andrew to allow the boy to bathe here and bring his clothes to be washed.

Rose had not spoken with Willy before, which did not surprise her. Hiring extra help and directing work had been her responsibility as trustee, but for some time now she had distanced herself from the day-to-day operations of the Society's businesses. She felt a surge of longing as she remembered the pleasure of bargaining for real estate and developing new business ideas. If she had not become eldress, it would have been she who watched over these strange, new plants and— Nay, she knew little of medicinal herbs. Without Andrew, none of this would be here. She promised herself a thorough confession to Agatha very soon; these jealousies would lead her far from the path of Mother Ann.

"As you can see," Andrew said, "we keep a small patch of pleurisy root going all summer. Josie doesn't bother with it in her own medic garden, and we needed some for our experiments."

The young hired man picked one of the orange flowers and held it up to Rose. A shy smile spread across his face, revealing badly stained teeth. Rose hesitated. Believers did not waste flowers on ornamentation, but she did not wish to scold the boy after such a kind gesture. She decided to leave it to Andrew to explain their ways to him. She thanked him and took the flower.

Andrew did not seem to notice the interchange. He knelt before a wilting plant, shaking his head as he examined the large, pleated leaves. "I was hoping this would make it," he said. "It's green hellebore. Wonderful plant. We use the rhizomes to make a tincture that works as a sedative and painkiller. But this really needs cooler, damper soil. Willy, are you keeping it wet? The soil seems dry." He pushed a finger into the ground near the roots.

"Yes, sir, I was just about to water it, just thinkin' about it as you folks come up." With a quick movement, he grabbed a nearby watering can, splashing over the side as he hurried to the suffering plant. He began to slosh water on it before Andrew had time to stand and step aside, and globs of dampened dirt splattered against the trustee's work pants. When he saw what he had done, Willy jumped backward, and his wide, frightened eyes darted toward Andrew's face, as if searching for signs of violent explosion.

Andrew's eyebrows knitted in mild irritation, and then he laughed. "This is why my work clothes are dark brown," he said. "No harm done, Willy."

Instead of relaxing, Willy narrowed his eyes in suspicion,

and he clutched the watering can in front of him with two hands, like a shield.

"Willy, Andrew tells me you have a special interest in herbs used as medicine," Rose said, hoping to break through the boy's fear.

Willy darted a glance at her and nodded once before staring again at Andrew.

"Yea, indeed," Andrew said. "Willy is quite knowledgeable about all the plants in this garden. He has seen uses that I've only read about."

Willy relaxed. He lowered the watering can but continued to hold it with both hands. He ventured a longer look at Rose.

"Granny taught me," he said. "I lived with her when I was a kid, after my ma and pa left."

"Was your grandmother a healer?" Rose asked.

"Yes, ma'am," Willy said. "We didn't have no doctor, so she was the one folks come to when they was hurt or sick. She used to take me all through the hills hunting wild herbs for her tonics, and she talked to me the whole time about how you could take slippery elm bark and make it into a poultice that was good for healing burns and suchlike. She knew more'n anybody in those parts. I reckon I could've took over when she died, if I'd a mind to."

"Once you've learned what Andrew can teach you, perhaps you can go back and help your people," Rose said.

Willy reddened and shrugged one thin shoulder.

"It sounds as if they could use your knowledge," Rose said.

Willy shot a wary glance at Andrew. "Don't reckon they'll be much interested in taking me back," he said. He turned his back on Rose and began to pull fine blades of grass that had sprung up where they shouldn't.

"Shall we continue?" Andrew asked from behind her shoulder.

Rose waited until they were out of Willy's hearing before

asking, "Has Willy something in his past that I should know about?"

Andrew clucked in annoyance. "I told him not to talk about that," he said. "People will misunderstand. As you probably noticed, Willy is good with the herbs but lacking in . . . Well, he isn't stupid, certainly, but he doesn't seem to know how to present himself."

"Surely awkwardness is no sin. With help, he will learn the niceties in time, but I am more interested in his past," Rose said with a firmness that was meant to yank Andrew back to her original question. She glanced sideways at him and saw his jaw tighten. However, he answered in a calm voice.

"Apparently when his grandmother was growing sickly, she let him take over much of the healing. She had taught him well, but there was a mix-up of some kind, and a young man died."

"You mean he poisoned someone?"

"Nay, I'm sure he did no such thing. It was an unusual case, some sort of breathing problem, I believe. He said that his grandmother had to teach him a new formula, one she hadn't used for years. It's likely that, given her weakened state, she remembered it wrong. Or the young man may not have been able to tolerate the tonic for one reason or another. Anyway, the family blamed Willy and came after his grandmother for revenge. Willy took responsibility for the error."

"Noble of him," Rose said, "but however did he escape punishment? Surely the grieving family arrived fully armed and ready to take vengeance." She glanced at Andrew and saw him chew his lower lip.

"Yea, that was a bit unclear to me, too," he said. "Hugo might know more of his story. They talked together quite a bit before Hugo became so ill. At any rate, Willy's knowledge of herbal remedies is phenomenal."

Rose said nothing. She feared Andrew's devotion to the medicinal herb industry might have blinded him to potential problems with his people. She decided to keep an eye on Willy Robinson.

FIVE

"THIS IS THE AREA WE HAVE CONVERTED INTO THE MEDIC-inal Herb Shop,'' Andrew explained as he and Rose entered the old Broom Shop.

Since only brethren had been broom makers, the building had a single entrance. Andrew stood well back as he held the door open so Rose would not accidentally brush against him. She stepped into one large room that she remembered from her early childhood, when bits of broom straw had littered the floor. During those days, half a dozen brethren would fasten batches of straw onto handles and stitch them into the flat design invented by a long-ago Shaker brother in New York. Now the room looked more like a laboratory. Several tables and rows of shelves held dozens of apothe-cary bottles containing herbal infusions, tins and bags of dried herbs, and bunches of drying stems hanging from wall pegs.

On one side of the room, Rose recognized Andrew's assistant, an intense young brother named Benjamin Fulton. Benjamin was slim and darkly handsome, with masses of curly hair and long black eyelashes. Rose found herself thinking what a pretty girl he would have been. His full lips puckered in concentration as he examined what looked like glass infusion equipment. He called Andrew over for a consultation. A third brother bent over a journal, making painstaking notations. Sister Patience worked by herself on the other side of the room, measuring dried herbs and grinding them in a mortar and pestle. Before adding another ingredient, she consulted a large book that lay open on the table, as if she were following a recipe. Curious, Rose approached. Patience glanced up and made a quick protective gesture, as if to hide the page. The gesture seemed odd for a woman who had so recently displayed spiritual gifts. Patience must have sensed Rose's surprise, because she kept her arm moving in a smooth arc until it was no longer near the book.

Rose moved alongside her. "Is this an experiment of some sort?" she asked. "Anything promising?"

Patience smiled, but her dark eyes remained serious. "Nay," she said, her mellow voice sounding out of breath. "Nothing of great interest. Just a very old medicine formula that I was hoping to update."

"Oh? Which are you trying out?" Rose asked, looking at the two open pages containing four recipes.

"This one." Patience pointed to a formula for a painkiller, at the bottom of the second page. The original recipe contained opium-poppy juice.

"How interesting. I suppose you are hoping to replace the poppy juice with something more benign but equally effective?"

Patience gave a curt nod but no further explanation.

"How did you first become interested in the medicinal properties of herbs?" Rose kept her voice interested, though part of her attention was occupied as she skimmed through both open pages. Just above Patience's finger was a recipe for reducing fever. One of its ingredients was extract of monkshood root, which Rose knew to be poisonous. Patience's arm partially obscured the two recipes on the facing page, but what Rose could see looked harmless.

From the corner of her eye, Rose saw Andrew approaching. Patience went back to her work, pulling the book away from Rose's view.

"As you see," Andrew said, "we are all experimenting

with new and revised patent medicine formulas. Everyone except Thomas, of course. He is our salesman and does a good job of keeping informed about our progress."

Rose glanced at Thomas Dengler, another of the small band of new North Homage Believers who had arrived with Andrew from the East. All had been willing to uproot and move west so they could continue their work with him. Thomas was a husky man in his early thirties, with a ruddy complexion and pale blue eyes. Rose had been curious about him since his arrival but had left his initiation to Wilhelm. She knew only that he had been a husband and father in the world and that his wife, Irene, and their two children had come together to Mount Lebanon, the Lead Society in New York. They had separated and given their children over to the care of the Children's Order, as required, completed their novitiate period, and signed the covenant. For reasons she didn't know, the entire Dengler family had made the move to North Homage. In Rose's perception, Irene seemed content as a Believer.

"Is the business doing well, Thomas?" Rose asked.

"Yea." Thomas nodded once, and his pen continued down a column of numbers.

"Perhaps you could show me the figures sometime soon," Rose said. She was itching to delve into business affairs again, and she felt uncomfortable knowing so little about the medicinal herb venture.

Thomas paused and looked up, his face screwed up in disapproval. "Why? There's nothing wrong. I keep very good records."

"I'm sure you do," Rose said. "I merely hoped to learn more about the business." Andrew insisted that Thomas was a superb medicinal herb salesman, but Rose wondered how that could be, given his combativeness.

"It's complicated." Thomas's gaze wandered around the room. "Tough to understand, unless you're a salesman."

Rose felt her cheeks flush.

"The eldress will have no difficulty understanding, Thomas. Remember that she was trustee for many years before you and I arrived." Andrew's mild voice conveyed a gentle but clear rebuke. Thomas flashed a look of disdain at Andrew, but the trustee had already turned back toward his assistant.

"Benjamin, show the eldress what you're working on. It's quite intriguing," Andrew said, excitement seeping into his voice. "He's trying to develop a treatment for asthma that doesn't use the poisonous ingredients we used once, but that will work more effectively than what is currently available. As I'm sure you are aware, ever since Congress passed the Pure Food and Drug Act in 1906, we've had to adjust our recipes for curatives to avoid poisonous ingredients and exaggerated claims of curative properties."

Benjamin snorted in derision. "People can be so foolish. Just because they see a poisonous herb listed in the ingredients, they think a medicine will kill them. All they have to do is follow instructions."

"In this part of the country," Rose said, "many people cannot read. And they are sadly susceptible to wild claims that a remedy can cure them, whatever their illness."

Benjamin shrugged one shoulder and turned away.

"Thank you for the tour, Andrew. I'm glad to get to know all of you better," Rose said with forced cheerfulness. Only Andrew listened to her; the others had buried themselves in their work.

"If you have any more questions, I'd be glad—" Andrew said.

"Indeed, I do. I must head back to the Ministry House. Walk with me a bit." Rose noticed Patience pause and stare in her direction. No one else seemed to take notice.

"I didn't want the others to hear," Rose said as she and Andrew walked away from the Medicinal Herb Shop. "Do you . . . ?" Rose spoke slowly, searching for the right phrasing. "Does it seem to you that your little work group is somewhat . . . strained?"

Andrew glanced over at her, his face open with surprise.

"Strained? Nay, I can't say that I'd noticed it. They seemed quite themselves to me."

"Really." Rose walked a few steps in silence.

"Was there something in particular . . . ?"

Rose stopped, forcing Andrew to look at her. "Andrew, those people were disrespectful to both of us, and not just once. You can't tell me that you didn't notice at least when Thomas implied that I would not understand his sales figures."

"Oh, that. Thomas signed the covenant shortly before we left Mount Lebanon. He is still partly in the world, I'm afraid, and his attitudes show it. He hasn't yet absorbed our belief that sisters and brethren are equal in the eyes of God. I mean, he understands Mother Ann's chosenness, but somehow he slips up in his day-to-day life."

"He should have learned more thoroughly before signing the covenant."

Andrew's angular chin tightened. "I'd have to say that I agree with you. In fact, when the time came to decide whether he and Irene might sign the covenant, I was a dissenting voice. He has superb sales skills, which the Society values, but I felt he was not yet ready to commit his soul to the community."

"I see," Rose said. "And so he resents you."

"Perhaps, though my opinion was ignored. At any rate, his disrespect to you was not personal; it was a reflection of his worldly attitude toward women in general. I will take him to task for it."

"Nay, you did so already. But please keep an eye on him. I want him to treat the sisters as equals, and you are most likely to catch him doing otherwise."

"Shall I bring the issue up with Wilhelm?"

Rose pursed her lips to stop a cynical retort from escaping. "Nay, I wouldn't bother. Tell me, do you find Thomas trustworthy?"

"Trustworthy." Andrew rolled the word around in his

mouth and it came out as a statement. "I have no reason to believe him otherwise."

Rose noted the careful wording, but instinct told her that she would get no unsupported guesses out of Andrew. She could sense him closing up.

By unspoken agreement, they had strolled into the herb fields north of the Herb House. Rose stooped to snip a basil leaf, which she rolled between her fingers to release the spicy fragrance. The rush of pleasure distracted her, and she veered too close to Andrew. He did not seem to notice as she quickly sidestepped away from him. After a year in the world as a young woman, as well as serving her Society for ten years as trustee and dealing daily with the world's people, she felt none of the discomfort with men that some of the other sisters developed. She really should watch herself more carefully. As eldress, she wanted to set a good example.

"Tell me about the others," she said. "I'm intrigued by Patience and her gifts. Did she display them in Mount Lebanon?"

"A little. I believe they were beginning to emerge, but I remember only an occasional gift song or perhaps an inspired dance. Her dancing is remarkable. But spiritual healing, nay, I saw no sign of that. It does not surprise me, though—she is so interested in healing. She begged to become a medicinal herb worker, even though she is the only sister in the group. It took a full year to gain permission from the Mount Lebanon Ministry, and I had to promise a separate working space for her."

"Does she get along with Thomas and Benjamin and Willy?"

"She keeps to herself, as she should, surrounded as she is by brethren. But she is well able to work on her own. I do little supervision, with her or with the brethren. They are all quite gifted and hardworking, and that leaves me free to develop new business ideas."

They had reached a row of gray-green sage. Rose

brushed the bottom of her work dress against the fuzzy leaves to release the pungent fragrance.

"Has Benjamin worked with you for a long time?" she asked.

"Since he first appeared on our doorstep, three years ago. In fact, he signed the covenant only shortly after I did."

"And yet you have become trustee, and he is still an assistant."

"I am no more talented than he, I assure you. Less so, in fact. Perhaps it is God's plan to keep him at his experiments, doing what he does so well."

Rose let a few moments pass. Andrew had given her some tidbits, but mostly she had learned that he was protective of his workers. She admired that, even if it frustrated her search for information.

"And what about you?" she asked, as they stepped over a row of low-growing thyme, recovering from its first harvesting. "What is your story?"

"A very boring one, I assure you," Andrew said with a small laugh.

Rose felt a flush of embarrassment, as though she had delved on too personal a level. "How did you become interested in medicinal herbs?"

"When I was in the world, I trained in pharmacy," he said. He cleared his throat. "I'd planned to find work in a drugstore, but then I became a Believer, and . . ." His voice grew quiet as it trailed off.

"So you joined us just over three years ago?"

"Three and a half."

"But . . . Forgive me, but I guessed you to be only a few years older than I. Surely there were some intervening years, between your training and becoming a Believer? Did you work in business?"

Andrew's breathing grew audibly jerky, as if he was holding back emotion. Watching him sideways, Rose saw his tall, straight back hunch forward as if a sack of bricks had been lowered onto his shoulders. Her wish to protect his privacy struggled with her need to know everything she could about each of the medicinal herb workers, including him. Her kindness won.

"I believe I've stumbled onto a painful subject, Andrew. You do not need to answer me, if you do not wish to."

"Thank you," he said. "Perhaps later."

"I understand." Rose walked quietly with him a few more moments, feeling the air heavy with heat and painful secrets. She hoped he would someday trust them all enough to lighten his burden by sharing them.

SIX

DRIVING THE EIGHT MILES OF RUTTED ROAD BETWEEN North Homage and the town of Languor gave Rose a chance to sort through her thoughts. The open window of the Society's black Plymouth sucked in the heavy afternoon heat along with the dust that coated her face and the leather seats. The car would need a good cleaning when she returned, but she couldn't bear to close the window.

She had decided to pay a visit to her former protégée, Gennie Malone, now eighteen and on her own in the world. Something was askew in the Medicinal Herb Shop; Rose felt sure of it. The disrespectful attitudes, the odd secrecy . . . She suspected the shop was connected with the apparent poisoning of Nora and Betsy. The girls were still floating in deep sleep, so she couldn't question them, but she'd found no evidence of their being anywhere near cleaning compounds. It was far more likely that they had ingested some dangerous plant. Yet North Homage took special care to avoid growing poisonous plants and to teach the children to recognize and stay clear of the few the village still grew. To help sort out this mystery, Rose needed another pair of eyes and ears, and Gennie's were sharp and reliable.

Fields of half-grown corn sped by, and she entered the poorest section of town, shanties that lined the eastern outskirts. A few tanned and ragged children drew in the dirt road with a stick, the heat slowing down their movements so they seemed to be playing in their sleep. The other inhabitants must actually have been asleep, because the scraggly yards and front stoops were empty. Rose was relieved; driving through this section of Languor always saddened her and reminded her why the Society always planted extra crops to be harvested by hungry neighbors.

The sweltering air cooled a notch as she entered a more well-to-do section of town, where elm trees canopied the streets, giving welcome shade. Here the children were better fed and well clothed, and they played with more energy. Rose parked on a side street and walked the short distance to a narrow shop nestled in a line of attached buildings surrounding the town square. A sign showing a painted red rose advertised the tiny flower shop where Gennie Malone worked.

A bell tinkled her entrance as Rose opened the door. A young woman with auburn curls poked her head out of a back room, and her face lit with pleasure.

"Rose!" Gennie rushed forward and threw her arms around Rose, standing on tiptoe to do so. "What perfect timing. Come on back, I've got something to show you." She took Rose by the hand and led her through the salesroom, with its neat bundles of flowers soaking in vases of cool water. Rose recognized carnations and black-eyed Susans. The workroom was a startling contrast. Fragments of stems and leaves, snippets of ribbon, and twisted lengths of floral wire littered the floor and a large worktable. At one corner sat a slender glass vase holding a tall floral confection, a riot of pinks and purples.

"What do you think?" Gennie asked.

"Well, Gennie, I must say, I'd hoped that we had taught you better," Rose said, trying to keep herself from laughing.

"I know it's using flowers for adornment, but, Rose, I'm in the world now, and really, don't you think it's just lovely?"

"Nay, what I meant was that I'd hoped we had taught you to keep a floor swept."

"Oh, you—you're teasing me. Well, you also taught me not to waste my efforts, so I give the place a good sweeping when I've finished my work for the day. Now, tell me what you think of my creation."

Rose stepped up close to the bouquet, ran her hands over velvety petals, and sniffed the variety of fragrances. "I must admit," she said, "the colors are luscious. And you've used some unusual flowers, haven't you? Isn't this foxglove?" she asked, fingering a stalk of bell-like pink flowers with freckled centers.

"Yes! I mean, *yea,* it is." Gennie giggled. "I'm starting to sound like Elsa."

Rose smiled. Elsa tried to speak in the old way, like Elder Wilhelm, but she tended to slip back into hill-country vernacular. "We will always be friends, no matter how you speak. As you said, you're part of the world now." She turned back to the bouquet. "How did you think of using foxglove?"

"I remembered them from the medic garden, and I always loved them. I thought they were every bit as pretty as the roses."

"You know, they are poisonous. Will you warn customers not to let children nibble on them?"

"I hadn't thought of that. This bouquet is for a centerpiece. Grady's family is giving a big dinner party tonight. No children will be there, but I'll warn Grady anyway. And I'll be there, so I can keep an eye on it," she added, shyness softening her exuberant voice.

Rose swallowed hard. She had so hoped that Gennie would sign the covenant and become a Believer, but each day took her deeper into the world. She couldn't worry about that now, though.

"Gennie, I've come to ask a favor of you," she said. "Something has happened in North Homage, and I need your help." She told Gennie about the children's illness, the "healing" of Nora, and the confusing behavior of the Believers in the Medicinal Herb Shop.

"So you want me to spy," Gennie concluded, with a sparkle in her eyes.

"Within reason, of course. I want you to remain safe always. But with your knowledge of herbs, I think you'll fit in without arousing suspicion, and then all you have to do is keep your eyes and ears open. There may be no foundation for my fears, of course, but I want to be certain."

"Are you sure I won't seem suspicious? After all, I didn't remember that foxglove was poisonous, and they will surely know that we are friends."

"I've thought of all that. I'll tell them that times are tough and you lost your job here, so I've hired you to keep you going until you can find another position. They will understand that. And I'll tell them of your expertise in the culinary uses of herbs and your interest in learning about their medicinal aspects so you can look for a job in a drugstore. We can ask Emily to give you a leave of absence and back up our story, if anyone asks her." Emily O'Neal was manager of the flower shop and Grady's sister.

Gennie's small face puckered and cleared as she thought through the proposal. "I suppose it could work," she said finally. "It would certainly be an exciting change for me. Grady won't like it, of course, but I'm an adult, and I can do what I want. Anyway, it wouldn't hurt to have Grady aware of what's going on and maybe keeping a watchful eye on North Homage. Okay, I'll do it! I'll talk to Emily when she gets back this afternoon. I know she won't have any problem letting me go for a while; business is slow in the summer. And I'll tell Grady tonight. I can arrive sometime tomorrow afternoon. Is that early enough?"

"Perfect."

A tinkling sound announced the arrival of a customer, so Rose gave Gennie a quick hug and followed her out to the salesroom. Now that her plan was going into operation, Rose felt torn. She was relieved to have Gennie's help. But she hoped and prayed that she wasn't placing her young friend in danger.

Rose parked the Plymouth next to the Trustees' Office just as the bell rang for the evening meal. Before leaving, she had sent a message to Elder Wilhelm that she would be absent for a time, doing errands in Languor. He wouldn't expect her at the Ministry House, so she decided to dine at the Center Family Dwelling House, a short distance away. She joined the line of sisters gathering at the women's entrance to the house. In a quiet interchange with Gretchen, Rose discovered that Nora's and Betsy's conditions had not changed and Josie would be staying with them through the meal, until Patience went back to relieve her.

The Believers' subdued chattering resolved into silence as they entered, single file, and stood at their places in prayer. Meals were always taken in silence, the sisters at one end of the room, brethren around one table at the other end. The cold meal looked surprisingly good to Rose, who relished the creamy iced potato soup as it cooled her throat.

Rose seemed to be the only sister, besides Elsa, with any appetite. Gretchen, after working in the heat of the Laundry, passed up the soup altogether, and the others took only small servings. No Believer would dream of putting more on her plate than she could finish. Patience took the smallest portions of all, just a few leaves of lettuce and a spoonful of soup. She lifted one lettuce leaf on her fork, nibbled a corner, then put it back down again. She merely touched her lips to the soupspoon, and Rose wondered if she was swallowing anything but air. Between each tiny bite, she bowed her head for several moments of silent prayer. Her cheeks flushed a pale pink, as if she might be overheated.

Rose chewed on a bite of salad and let her gaze roam around the long table. Elsa ate hungrily, the next bite waiting on her fork before she'd finished chewing the last one. Most Shaker sisters remained fairly slender from long hours of physical labor. Elsa had been plump when she'd joined them a couple of years earlier, and now she was even huskier. But for all her unpleasant characteristics, she worked hard, and it wasn't as if anyone in the Society were starving.

Sister Irene Dengler sat toward the end of the table, so Rose could see only her profile. Irene had approached Rose a few times for brief confessions, but she never revealed anything about her past—or, in fact, about herself. Andrew had questioned Thomas's calling, but Irene seemed a devoted Believer. Did she suffer, giving up her children? She had come with Andrew's group to North Homage, yet she did not participate in the medicinal herb industry. Might she still be bonded to her husband and children by affection, despite her vows?

Rose finished the last of her salad and laid her used utensils and white cloth napkin over her empty plate. As if she had given a signal, the other sisters imitated her movements. They all rose from their benches and filed out. As Rose walked the length of the table, heading in single file toward the sisters' door, she glanced down at Patience's plate. The napkin crumpled on top did not hide the lettuce leaves and spoonful of soup left to be thrown away. It looked very much as if Patience had eaten nothing.

Believers often went back to work after the evening meal, before settling down for prayer and an early bedtime. But tonight was Thursday. For the past year, at Wilhelm's insistence, the North Homage Society had reinstated the Union Meeting. With the exception of the leaders, sisters and brethren were required to keep their distance from one another at all times. Most of the buildings had two entrances and two staircases, to ensure the separation between men and women. A brother and a sister might greet one another briefly in passing during their workday, but extended conversations were forbidden. In such a small community as North Homage, this restriction grew tiresome, and over the years, compliance had loosened. The Union

Meeting was a time-tested way for brethren and sisters to meet their need to converse socially with one another, to get it out of their systems for another week.

In the old days, when Shaker villages were larger, small groups had met in retiring rooms to chat. But North Homage contained only thirty-four full members, including the new souls from Mount Lebanon. So they all met together in the family meeting room in the Center Family Dwelling House. Two double rows of ladder-back chairs faced each other down the length of the room. One side of each row held fewer chairs. These were for the eleven remaining brethren, who had to stretch out and talk to more than one sister at a time.

Rose entered with the rest of the sisters and made straight for an empty seat next to Irene Dengler. Even though they would be talking to a brother, not to each other, Rose was certain she could learn much about Irene from listening to her. As Rose approached her quarry, she was startled to see Benjamin Fulton bypass several empty chairs to sit across from Irene. *Ah, so I have learned something already,* she thought, *and I'm afraid it does not bode well.*

A grimace of irritation crossed Benjamin's handsome face as Rose took the seat next to Irene. Rose glanced to her side. Irene's impassive expression told her nothing. Either Irene did not feel toward Benjamin as he seemed to toward her, or she was skilled at subterfuge.

Neither of her companions rushed to speak, so Rose asked, "How are your experiments in the Medicinal Herb Shop coming along, Benjamin?"

Again irritation flashed across his face, but it cleared almost instantly. "Quite well," he said, "as you know, of course, since we spoke of them only this morning."

Rose smiled as if he had said something charming. She heard a small intake of breath from Irene. *Good,* Rose thought. Such rudeness would surely prevent Irene from feeling tempted by a forbidden relationship with Benjamin. At least, she hoped so.

"We never really spoke in depth about your work," Rose said. "Have you a special interest you are following, or do you simply conduct the experiments Andrew chooses for you?"

Benjamin reddened as the gentle jab hit its mark. "Andrew knows nothing about my work," he said. "He's got some pharmacy training, book learning, but that's about it. He's a businessman."

"I see. So you must have a more extensive background in medicinal herbs?"

"Indeed I do," Benjamin said, arrogance marring his smooth voice. His gaze flickered to Irene and back to Rose. "I've studied the ancient uses of herbs as curatives, both in Europe and here among the Indians. I'm building on all that, and I'm close to developing some remarkable medicines."

Rose nodded, momentarily speechless in the face of such pride. Had he confessed it to Elder Wilhelm? She thought not. He probably did not recognize hubris in himself. Moreover, she was sure this display was meant to impress Irene.

"Have you found anything that can help those poor little girls?" Irene asked.

"My guess is they don't need anything else besides what Josie already did for them—a good, old-fashioned emetic and a sedative. They'll come around when they've had enough rest, and maybe they'll remember the emetic next time they're tempted to get into the cleaning supplies." Benjamin's face softened as he spoke to Irene, but Rose thought she heard wariness in his voice.

"So you think that's what happened?" Rose asked. "They sampled a cleaning solution? Those solutions are hardly appetizing, I'd think. Why would they do such a thing?"

"Why do children do anything?" With a wave of his hand, Benjamin dismissed the rationality of all children. "They probably did it to get attention. They need to be watched more carefully."

"Those girls have suffered dreadfully, and I hardly think they knew what they were doing!" The forcefulness in Irene's voice grabbed the attention of several Believers seated around her, who interrupted their own conversations to glance over with interest. Benjamin was too startled to speak. Rose settled back against the slats of her chair and waited a few moments before breaking the impasse.

"I was wondering, Benjamin," she began when the interest around them had waned, "could the girls have gotten into something in the Medicinal Herb Shop or garden?"

"Nay, impossible. Their silly . . . I mean, their adventure took place in the afternoon, when all of us were in the shop. We can see the garden through the east window. The door and all the windows were open to let in some air, so we would surely have heard if children were giggling away outside." He grimaced and glanced at Irene as he realized that more harsh words about children would likely displease Irene. Irene sniffed but did not speak. Rose tried to keep from smiling.

"When Gretchen found the girls, she said Nora thought she was a monster," Rose said, "and at the healing—"

Benjamin's lip lifted in a cynical arch, which hardened his attractive features.

"At the healing, Nora kept talking about a bad angel. Does any of that mean anything to you, Benjamin?"

"Nay, why should it?"

"I just wondered if, in your extensive study of the medicinal properties of herbs, you might have run across anything that might cause such a reaction."

"Nay." Benjamin's gaze wandered off into the distance. He fidgeted with the round collar of his clean work shirt. He was hiding something; Rose could sense it. But she also knew this was not the time to push the issue.

SEVEN

THE RINGING OF THE BELL OVER THE CENTER FAMILY Dwelling House told Rose it was 4:30 A.M. Time to get up. She was already awake, though groggy after a restless sleep. The air had barely cooled through the night. Rose had longed to toss off her cotton nightgown and let her bare skin breathe in what little breeze fluttered through her open windows, but that would have been far too immodest. After all, she never locked her retiring room door. What if an emergency brought another Believer barging into her room while she was unclothed?

She slid out of bed and to her knees for a few moments of prayer, which she directed to Holy Mother Wisdom, the female aspect of God. Rose asked for insight as she sought to solve the riddle of Nora and Betsy's illness.

Her work clothes hung on one of the wall pegs encircling her room. She eyed them with misgiving. They'd be hot, she knew, despite the loose fit and the light weight of the blue cotton. She pulled the long dress over her head and tied the white apron around her waist. Selecting a large white kerchief from a drawer, she arranged it over her shoulders and crossed the ends in a triangular pattern over the bodice of her dress. She pinned the ends under her apron, making sure to keep the kerchief loose over her bosom. The ensemble was designed to hide the female form to keep the brethren from temptation.

Though she was now eldress, Rose worked at daily chores, as did all able-bodied Believers. To consider herself above physical labor would be the height of hubris, and neither Rose nor Wilhelm would have entertained such a thought.

Already the room felt oppressive. Rose was grateful to lift her thick red hair off her neck and stuff it into her thin white cap. Folding the sheet at the end of her bed for airing out, she faced her morning chores, which had changed once she'd moved to the Ministry House. In the Trustees' Office, she had shared a large building with a few other sisters, so mornings were spent in general tidying. Now she shared a small dwelling house with Elder Wilhelm, who lived on the ground floor. By now he would be out helping the rest of the brethren to feed the farm animals.

Rose slipped downstairs and entered Wilhelm's empty retiring room. Her responsibilities included doing his cleaning and mending, as other sisters did for the brethren in their building. Being in Wilhelm's room always felt uncomfortable to Rose because their relationship had been strained for years. Although she did not question her duties, caring for his clothing seemed like a step back to the time before she was eldress, when Wilhelm made sure she never forgot her lesser place. Shaking off her discomfort, she swept and straightened the two rooms and swiftly reattached a button to a work shirt. As she knotted and snipped the thread, the bell rang for breakfast.

She quickly turned down the sheet of Wilhelm's bed. As she did so, Rose noticed a book open and facedown on his bedside table. Submitting to a twinge of curiosity, she picked it up and turned it over, rather than leave it or simply close and reshelve it. Wilhelm had been reading the *Testimonies of the Life, Character, Revelations and Doctrines of Mother Ann Lee.* This was not unusual reading for a serious Believer, and Rose would have thought nothing of it, but the chapter he'd been studying was entitled "Prophecies, Visions and Revelations." Again, if Wilhelm had been any other Believer, such reading would have been natural, especially for a spiritual leader. However, this was Wilhelm. In his longing to return to the past, he had become increasingly obsessed with a period one hundred years earlier, known now as Mother Ann's Work. It had been a time when Mother Ann's spirit had often been among them, inspiring almost constant trances, hundreds of new songs and dances, and scores of new converts. In her heart Rose wished she could have been part of that era, a time of growth and vibrancy in the Society. But she knew that, practical in nature as she was, she would probably have been more observer and recorder than participant. She served her people in other ways.

Wilhelm's soul lit up at any hint that Mother Ann had returned to do her work again among Believers. Because Elsa had exhibited such gifts of the spirit, Wilhelm protected her from Rose's legitimate authority over her. And now Sister Patience seemed to demonstrate these same gifts, but in more depth and abundance than Elsa. Despite the growing heat, Rose shivered with both fear and excitement. She replaced the book as she had found it. With relief, she left Wilhelm's room and headed for the Ministry dining room.

"I've sent two of the brethren to spread word throughout Languor that our worship service will be open on Sunday," Wilhelm said as he smoothed a small portion of raspberry preserves on a thick slice of brown bread. "And I want to add a dance or two to the service—with Patience leading the sisters."

Rose's hand hesitated as she reached for her water glass, but she said nothing.

"Does this disturb thee?" Wilhelm took a large bite and watched Rose as he chewed.

Feeling his eyes on her, Rose spooned some preserves onto her plate, then began to spread it evenly across her bread. The silence thickened the already heavy air in the sunny room.

"I do not need to remind you that normally the eldress leads the sisters in the dancing," Rose said.

Wilhelm sliced himself more bread. "Nay," he said, "I need no such reminder."

"I am not required to agree, as you also know," Rose said, after enduring more moments of silence.

Wilhelm nodded once without looking at her.

"And why should I agree?"

Finally Wilhelm glanced at her, one bushy white eyebrow high over an ice-blue eye. "Because," he said, "in the end we have the same hope, do we not? Is it not thy wish, as well as mine, that the Society thrive?"

"If it is God's will," Rose said.

"Of course." Irritation tinged Wilhelm's voice. "But we cannot sit by passively waiting for perfect understanding. We must push forward with all our might to know God's will for us and to accomplish it. We know quite clearly that Mother Ann put herself in mortal danger to help the Society form and grow. She willingly let herself be imprisoned and starved for us." Wilhelm's eyes flared with blue flame, and his half-eaten bread lay forgotten on the plate before him.

"Wilhelm, Mother's world isn't our world. What we are meant to do may be quite different now."

"Nonsense. Our mission is timeless. We are called to live as the angels, chaste and apart from the world."

"Yea, indeed, but must we grow in number to fulfill this purpose?" As trustee of the North Homage Society, with her mind on practical matters, Rose had been exhausted by discussions such as this one. But lately, as she grew into her role as eldress, spiritual matters intrigued her more and more. She could feel herself rising to Wilhelm's challenge.

"Of course we must grow," Wilhelm said. "How else can we show the world a heaven on earth? Without our example, the world's people will be hopeless slaves to their carnality."

"And without their carnality, there would be no new Shakers," Rose said, "and we could not grow." She leaned back in her chair and tilted her head at Wilhelm, waiting for the powerful response she knew would come.

Wilhelm's already ruddy complexion reddened. "Perhaps," he said, "that would be for the best. I would welcome our own demise if it meant the end of carnal relations in the world."

"But, Wilhelm, not everyone is called to—"

A swishing and panting sound drew their attention to the open entryway to the dining room. Elsa Pike steadied herself against the doorjamb, one hand spread across her neckerchief as if to hide the immodest heaving of her ample chest. Her cheeks flushed with exertion. She opened her mouth to speak but gasped in air instead.

"What is it, Elsa? What has happened?" Rose rushed to her side and reached an arm around her shoulders. "Steady now. Sit down and catch your breath."

Elsa dropped into the chair Rose had just left. Ignoring Rose's ministrations, she spoke directly to Wilhelm.

"It's bad spirits," she said, leaning her elbows on the table. "False spirits."

"What do you mean, Elsa?" Rose asked, not sure she wanted to know. Wilhelm leaned forward, his face alight with eagerness.

"Elder, you gotta come stop her," Elsa said. She'd caught her breath and was beginning to relish the drama she had created. Rose decided not to encourage her with any more questions; they were unnecessary anyway.

"It's that Sister Patience," Elsa continued, her voice hushed, as if she were speaking of the unspeakable. "She's a witch. Those gifts of hers, they ain't from Mother Ann or Holy Mother Wisdom or no one you'd ever want to know."

Wilhelm's eyebrows inched together over worried eyes, but otherwise he sat rigid, waiting. "Explain thyself," he said.

A warning tinge to his voice seemed to quell Elsa's dramatic tendencies. Rose, ignored by both of them, watched their faces. Wilhelm did not want to hear that Patience was evil—that much was clear—and Elsa was getting the hint. Yet she had always hungered to be the most gifted of Believers, and Patience was usurping that position. If she was wise, she would change direction instantly. But her craving easily overpowered her modest wisdom.

"Come and see for thyself, Elder," Elsa said, remembering finally to use the archaic language Wilhelm preferred. "Patience is alone with them poor girls. She's supposed to be taking her turn watchin' them while Josie has breakfast, but sure as I'm sittin' here, what she's really doing is putting spells on them."

"There! See what she's doing?" Elsa pointed to Patience, who leaned over Nora's cradle bed. Rose approached the bed close enough to see over the sides. The top of Patience's hand lay across the girl's cheek as if she were stroking it.

"They are still deeply asleep," Patience said, glancing up at them without apparent concern.

"Ha!" Elsa said. "Josie said they was starting to come to, but now suddenly here they are sleeping like the dead again, and the only difference is, it ain't Josie with them. Explain that!" With her sturdy legs planted apart and her fists on her plump hips, Elsa glared in triumph at Patience.

Rose was prepared to intervene, but one look at Patience stopped her. Patience straightened her back with catlike leisure and faced her accuser. The folds of her dark work dress seemed to elongate her tall body so she towered over the shorter, fuller Elsa. Her face remained impassive, though her dramatic dark coloring gave her a smoldering look.

"I wonder," she said, "why you had such need to hurry over here when you heard the girls were awakening. Were you perhaps worried about what they might say?"

Flame spread across Elsa's cheeks. "Me?!" She sputtered a moment, confused by the attack. Darting a worried glance at Wilhelm, Elsa drew herself as straight as she could. "I got no call to be worried," she said. "Unlike some. Nay, I just wanted to help. I know a lot about herbs and such; learned it all growing up. I figured if the girls could tell me what they got into, I'd know how to help them."

"They no longer need help," Patience said.

"Why? What have you done to them?" Elsa asked, rushing toward Nora's bed.

"I believe you saw that for yourself." Patience's voice had grown softer, as if she were calming an overexcited child. "Nora is healed. She has been near death, and she needs a long rest."

Not satisfied, Elsa leaned over the sides of the cradle bed and touched Nora's forehead. The girl stirred and moaned in her sleep. Betsy moaned in answer from her bed. Elsa straightened and turned to the group, her plain face lit with cunning.

"We saw something, all right," Elsa said. "But about it being a healing, well, that's what you told us, but that don't make it so. I don't believe it."

"Why?" Wilhelm barked out the question. After his long silence, the force of his voice jolted Rose. For Elsa, it seemed to be the question she'd been waiting for.

"Because, Elder, if it was really Mother Ann and Holy Mother Wisdom working, why'd they send Patience to Nora and not to Betsy? I don't believe they'd do that— pick one little child out as better than the other for healing. They'd save both girls. Right, Elder?"

In the moment of silence that followed, Rose looked from face to face. Wilhelm said nothing, but he watched Patience with intensity. Elsa's triumphant stance held a hint of uncertainty; she wasn't used to engaging in logical reasoning. Patience herself relaxed; her generous mouth curved in a slight smile. She reminded Rose of Humility, the Society cat, when she knew she had a barn mouse cornered.

"Mother Ann was here indeed," Patience began, her low voice silken, "with all the eldresses that followed her path and crowds of lovely angels dressed in white and gold." Intensity deepened her voice. She closed her eyes and began to sway, as if reliving her trance. "All the sisters who have gone before us came to the aid of these innocent children, and Holy Mother Wisdom watched over us all. Every one of them guided my hands, sent healing through my hands." She held her hands out in front of her, fingers spread apart.

Elsa looked worried. Her voice faltered, but she stood her ground. "Why'd they guide your hands only toward Nora, then? Why not poor little Betsy?"

With her arms still extended, Patience opened her eyes wide and stared at Elsa. "Because Betsy did not need healing," she said. "Holy Mother Wisdom told me herself. She blew the message into my ear like a gentle wind, and I knew that Betsy would be well without my help. She was never as ill as Nora." Patience lowered her arms and gazed around the small group. "Although none of you could have known that, of course."

Elsa opened her mouth to object again, but Wilhelm cut in. "Thy experience has clearly been Mother Ann's Work among us again," he said. "I have complete faith that the children will recover. We are deeply pleased. Are we not, Sisters?" He glanced from Rose to Elsa, who glared at the floor. "And now I have an announcement. On Saturday we will begin again a ceremony that has fallen into disuse."

Rose's heartbeat picked up speed. Wilhelm should have discussed the idea with her first; he often forgot—whenever it was convenient—that they were now equal partners in spiritual guidance for the North Homage Believers.

Wilhelm's rough, thin lips rarely smiled, but now they did so as he said: "On Saturday afternoon, immediately following the noon meal, we will conduct the sweeping ritual.''

Rose was thrown off balance. The sweeping ritual? What could that possibly gain for him? The sweeping gift had come and gone so quickly a century earlier, during Mother Ann's Work, that few Believers even knew about it.

"Wilhelm, you and I should discuss this," Rose said quietly. "The sweeping involves the sisters, so—"

"I would have done so at breakfast, but remember that we were interrupted."

Rose was reasonably certain that he'd had no such intention. His plan had the feel of a sudden inspiration.

"Elder, what's a sweeping? I been clear through my novitiate, but no one said nothin' about it."

"That is understandable," Wilhelm said. "The cleansing was a regrettably short-lived gift given during Mother Ann's Work. It is most appropriate now, I believe. After all, it is thy own assertion, is it not, that there are evil spirits at work here. Remember what Mother Ann said: 'Good spirits will not live where there is dirt.' We will cleanse and purify ourselves and our dwelling places with brooms and sacred fire delivered by the angels. And then we shall see." For the second time, he smiled, which redoubled Rose's discomfort.

"How's it done?" Elsa asked.

"I'm sure thy eldress will prepare thee and the other sisters for thy roles in the ceremony, as I will prepare the brethren. The sweeping used to take all day, but we have too much work to do, and too few hands, so we will set aside only the time between the noon and evening meals. And we must work doubly hard today to spare even that time. So 'hands to work' . . ." Wilhelm turned and left the room.

Elsa looked confused but intrigued. Patience absently rocked Nora's cradle bed and began to hum a haunting tune. Though her face was unreadable, Rose felt certain she was delighted by Wilhelm's announcement. Rose herself thought frantically. She knew about the sweeping gift and could easily prepare the sisters—but why? To cleanse them of evil spirits? The explanation rang false to her. As she watched the two eager women before her, the answer slipped into place. The ritual, though performed—separately, of course—by both brethren and sisters, took the sisters' task of cleaning into the realm of the spiritual. It was the ideal setting in which to trigger a competition between two sisters who exhibited spiritual gifts. During such a battle, who knew what could happen? That was what Wilhelm wanted—a powerful spark to relight Mother Ann's flame, a century after it had died away. And never mind the consequences.

EIGHT

IN TIMES OF CONFUSION, THE HERB HOUSE BECAME ROSE'S sanctuary. She almost ran toward it now. She had dispatched Elsa to pass the word among the sisters to meet together briefly after evening meal, when Rose would explain the sweeping ritual to them. She would lead it herself, both because she was eldress and in hopes of keeping either Elsa or Patience from taking control. In the meantime, she wanted to pursue the other problem weighing on her mind—the apparent poisoning of Nora and Betsy, and any possible link, accidental or not, between that episode and North Homage's medicinal herb industry.

The Herb House, a white clapboard building, stood well back from the unpaved path that ran through the center of the village. Rose had spent many happy days working in the upstairs drying room, hanging bundles of herbs to dry, pressing crumbled dried herbs into round tins for sale to the world, and recording production figures in her daily journal. Since she'd become eldress, those days had dwindled to a few hours here and there. This afternoon she had a good reason to capture more of those pleasurable hours.

Irene Dengler, Thomas Dengler's wife, was working her rotation in the Herb House. Though not legally divorced, the couple had agreed to separate upon joining the Shakers. What better way to find out more about Thomas, Rose thought, than through Irene? She would have little contact with him now, of course, but perhaps she could offer some insights into his character.

As she entered the front door, Rose expected a wave of fragrances, sweet and earthy. She inhaled deeply to capture that first moment. But the predominant odor turned out to be machine oil. Several sisters were working on the first floor, hovering around two large herb presses, which had been gathering dust for years. During her times in the Herb House, the ground floor had been used mostly for storage, and the sisters had generally worked upstairs in the herb-filled drying room. Andrew had taken over the unused area. Had he reported this change to her? She couldn't remember his mentioning it in any of their conversations. He didn't have to, of course; he had undoubtedly discussed it with Wilhelm, his elder. But he might have thought of telling her—after all, she was former trustee, and she had asked him about the medicinal herb industry.

One of the sisters smiled a greeting, and Rose approached the machine. A pungent aroma greeted her as a large batch of sage was pressed into a hard pack.

"Is this the early perennial harvest?" Rose asked.

"Yea, Patience said we were to press it for Andrew's medicines."

"What about the culinary herb business? Will there be enough for our regular customers?"

"Andrew said we'd be cutting back on culinary herbs, but we did save some. Irene is upstairs working on the tins."

Rose nodded her thanks and headed for the stairs. Her cozy mood had soured—no doubt, she thought, because her nostrils were disappointed—but it wouldn't do to let the sisters feel the pinch of her annoyance.

As she reached the top of the stairs, Rose heard a mellow soprano sing a lighthearted Shaker dance song about making merry like the birds among the trees. She recognized Irene's voice, often part of the a cappella chorus at Sabbathday worship.

"Irene," Rose called out as she entered the drying room, hoping not to startle the sister.

The singing stopped, and the same cheerful voice answered, "Rose, is that you? I'm working at the table, though you'll hardly see me behind all these piles of herbs." There was a lilt in her voice, as if it were about to bubble into joyful laughter. Rose smiled in anticipation of the chat; she had liked Irene from the moment of her arrival.

The drying room held the fragrances Rose had expected downstairs—the sweetness of lemon balm, the apple scent of chamomile, powerful oregano, and the freshness of parsley. Her good humor was fully restored by the time she located Irene, only her head showing above a mountain of serrated lemon balm leaves. She was tying a length of string around a clump of branches, preparing them to be hung from the pegs and hooks spaced around the walls and across the ceiling beams.

Rose scooped up another batch of sprigs and began to help. Irene did not question this sudden appearance of her eldress. She hummed quietly and continued her work. Irene was a few years younger than Rose and a head shorter, with a delicate-boned face and china-blue eyes that crinkled often with laughter. She had no special skills but a joyous faith that made her a welcome addition on any work rotation. Rose was surprised to find her working on her own.

"Was no one free to help you hang the herbs?" Rose asked.

"Nay, they're needed on the presses, what with Andrew wanting to send out a shipment soon, so I said I'd take care of the culinary herbs myself. Besides, I enjoy hanging the herbs much more than stuffing them into those machines."

"I'd have to agree with you," Rose said, pinching a lemon balm leaf under her nose to release the fragrance. "Are you particularly interested in herbs?"

"Oh, I enjoy them certainly," Irene said, "but, then, I enjoy all the rotations."

Rose would not have believed this coming from some of the sisters, but Irene possessed the gift of contentment with whatever her task might be. "So you have no special fascination with medicinal herbs?"

At this, Irene's expression clouded. "Nay, I have no interest at all in such things."

"I was only wondering why you elected to come to North Homage with the medicinal herb group," Rose asked.

"It was not because of Thomas, if that's what you are trying to ask me."

So there is fire behind the sunny disposition, Rose thought. She offered a disarming smile and reached for a bit of string to tie up her bundle of lemon balm sprigs. "If I thought you'd come for anyone, I'd have assumed it was your children," she said quietly.

"It was."

"You could have stayed with them in Mount Lebanon. You needn't have uprooted everyone." Rose was pushing hard, digging for the person underneath the perpetual happiness. Much as she believed in conversion, she couldn't help but wonder if there was more than one reason for a young wife and mother to give up her family. Her less-than-complete separation from her children, and perhaps her husband, hinted at an ambivalence that had not yet surfaced during her enthusiastic confessions.

"It seemed best," Irene said. "For everyone." She scooped up a pile of herbs, tied in bunches with string, and began to hang them from wall pegs which she had to stand on tiptoe to reach.

Rose did not offer her superior height as assistance; it would be insulting. She busied herself cutting lengths of string until Irene returned to the table.

"Did you not wish to separate the children completely from their father?" Rose asked. "Even though they would have little contact with him?"

"Sometimes I wish we had never come here!" Irene bit

her lip and grabbed a pile of wilting oregano sprigs. Rose waited.

"Thomas . . ." Irene dropped the oregano back on the table and stared out the window. "Thomas was not eager to become a Believer. Not like I was. I was sad not to be raising my children, of course, but I knew they would be treated well, fed and clothed and educated, and I wouldn't be far away. We couldn't give them all that. Thomas was a salesman, and he was good at it—he can sell anything, truly—but with this Depression and all, he lost his job and couldn't find another." Irene lifted the corner of her apron and dabbed perspiration from her forehead. The afternoon heat was reaching its peak, and Rose put down her own work, as well.

"We had a little house that my parents had left me, but we hadn't enough money to eat, and what little savings we had went for Thomas's . . . Well, he started drinking, you see."

"Did he hurt you or the children?" Rose had heard this sort of story so many times in recent years.

"It was so frustrating for him." Irene picked at the leaf bits littering the worktable. "But I couldn't let it go on, could I? If it had been just me, maybe . . . But I had the girls to think of. I couldn't let them suffer."

"If you are saying that Thomas was violent with you, I certainly understand your separating from him. But did you tell the Ministry at Mount Lebanon?" Rose knew the answer to her question when Irene avoided her eyes.

"He took his vow of nonviolence," Irene said. "And he doesn't drink anymore, so I have no reason to suspect he is not a good Believer."

"And you, Irene—do you wish to be with him again, as husband and wife?"

"I have been true to my vow of celibacy."

"That is not what I asked."

Irene's dimpled chin jutted out a fraction more than usual. "I wish to be exactly where I am—a Believer, doing the work of the Mother and the Father. As soon as I heard about Mother Ann losing her four children in childbirth, I knew. I lost two little ones, my last two. Soon after, I went to a Sabbathday service at Mount Lebanon, and the elder preached about the price of carnal sins, and I felt he was talking right straight to me. I brought Thomas the next week. He wasn't so convinced, but really, how could he disagree? He'd done everything possible to make sure those two babies were born healthy, and they weren't, so it had to be the will of God.''

"What do you mean? What did Thomas do to ensure healthy births?"

"Oh, I thought I'd told you. He used to do just what he is doing as a Shaker—he sold all sorts of patent medicines. He made a good living because the medicine from doctors was so expensive. Thomas could offer curatives for much less money because he and his brother could mix it all up by themselves, and then they didn't have to fuss with that law—what's it called?"

"The Pure Food and Drug Act?"

"Yea, that's the one. Thomas said it was just meant to make medicine expensive so doctors and pharmacists could get rich from selling it, and only the rich could afford it. He wanted to do something good for the poor. So you see, even though we had our bad times and I couldn't live with him anymore, I thought he would make a good Shaker.'' Irene's clear eyes searched Rose's face with worried hope.

"And he fed you some of these medicines while you were carrying your last two babies?" Rose asked.

"Yea."

"Do you remember what was in any of them?"

"Something that had the word 'apple' in it, I think." Irene's expression darkened as her doubt overshadowed her hope.

"Thorn apple?"

"I think so."

"I see," Rose said. "Jimsonweed. As I recall, that may

be used to prevent the loss of a baby.'' *Among other less benign uses,* she thought.

Rose had a lot to think about as she made her way to the Medicinal Herb Shop to tell Patience that Gennie Malone would be arriving that afternoon to help her with her work. Secrets were surfacing about the small band of newcomers to North Homage. Struggling to pinpoint any connections between these secrets and the children's misfortune, she began a mental list. Thomas Dengler, while in the world, had made and sold herbal curatives of doubtful composition. Moreover, he had a history of drinking and violence. Rose considered it possible, of course, that he had undergone a thorough conversion experience, but his wife did not seem completely convinced of it.

Irene Dengler expressed no special interest in herbal medicine, but she had lived with Thomas and might have picked up some knowledge. With her open personality, Rose found it difficult to imagine Irene involved in the creation of dangerous concoctions. Surely, if she had had a part in hurting children, she would be miserable with guilt now, not delighting in her work.

Benjamin Fulton and Andrew himself were both knowledgeable and ambitious, each in his own way. Andrew was a puzzle, which in Rose's experience usually indicated personal secrets. Benjamin, she feared, was close to breaking his vows over Irene. Those two would bear watching, though Irene seemed unaware of Benjamin's fervor. Or Irene might be a consummate actress.

Or I could be inventing melodramas where none exist, Rose thought, sighing at herself. The girls might simply have stumbled into an attractive but poisonous weed or cleaning compound and been foolish.

Nevertheless, Rose's instincts told her that something odd was going on in the Medicinal Herb Shop. Determined to find out whatever might be hidden, Rose pushed through the shop door, unannounced. Given the suspicious state of mind she'd gotten herself into, she almost expected to see the shop's inhabitants reciting incantations over a steaming cauldron. Instead, they stood at their assigned spots, absorbed in mixing and packaging and making quick notations in journals. They all glanced up at her as she entered, then went immediately back to their tasks, except Andrew, who gave her a friendly smile and beckoned her over.

"Have you brought news of the little ones?" Andrew asked.

Rose noticed Patience tilt her head toward them as if listening for her answer.

"Nay, no change, I'm afraid," Rose said.

Patience returned to her work.

"So you've returned for a more thorough tour?"

Rose shook her head. "I have something to discuss with Patience, if you can spare her."

"I'm in the middle of a delicate measurement," Patience called over, without raising her head. "I could meet with you later, if you'd like."

"I'll be glad to wait until you've finished your measuring," Rose said. She lifted a tall stool from a wall peg and planted herself at Patience's table. This was not what Patience had hoped for, clearly. Her fine, dark eyebrows knitted together more closely the nearer Rose came to her. Patience added a pinch of some powdered substance to a scale, frowned at the weight, made a note in her journal, and pushed the book away from her.

"We might as well talk now," she said. Her rich alto voice held no hint of irritation, but Rose was sure it was there nonetheless. Perhaps Patience was the actress.

"Good, it needn't take long," Rose said. "But it's dreadfully hot in here; I wonder if you would walk with me outdoors for a few moments."

Patience stiffened, but she nodded and closed her journal. She followed Rose out into the fierce sunshine. They walked in silence past the rear of the Herb House and the northern boundary of the new cemetery until they came to a small clump of trees. Rose could feel rivulets of perspiration trickle down her back by the time they found a shady spot and sat on the grass.

"Patience, I like to have an understanding of who each sister is, so I can be of utmost help to all of you. Yet I know so little about you. I realized that you have never sought me out for confession, though you have been with us for several months."

Patience looked directly into her eyes. "Forgive me, Eldress, but have you called me away from my work in the middle of the day for a confession?" Patience's tone was even, without emotion.

"Nay, of course not," Rose said, surprised by her own flustered reaction.

"I am sorry if I offended," Patience said. "It's just that I take my work very seriously, and interruptions bring delays and mistakes. I'm sure you understand."

Rose was beginning to feel as if they had switched roles and she were the one in need of confession. "Of course, Patience, we all feel the connection between our work and the worship of God," she said. "But work is not the only way—nor perhaps the most important way—to live our faith. To create heaven on earth, we strive to live like the angels—as you know, of course," she added as Patience's features tightened. "The angels are, above all, loving creatures. They guide us, speak to us, watch over us. We live in community in part to care for one another, and my being concerned about you is nothing more than my own effort to imitate the angels. When I urge the sisters to speak their confessions, and when I unburden myself in confession, it is for the purification of our souls, which is surely every bit as important as work."

Patience shifted on the grass and smoothed her apron, which had become twisted. Rose studied her profile. The smooth skin, tanned to a light olive, stretched over fine bones. Only the thin gray streaks showing at the edges of her cap and the fine lines around her pinched eyes showed

Patience to be older than Rose. Perhaps she was resentful about being lectured to by a younger eldress. Rose softened her approach.

"Truly, I only want to know you better, Patience. It is both my job and my own desire to know all the sisters as fully as I can."

Patience directed those murky gray eyes at her again. "How well do you think you know all the sisters?" she asked. "You and Wilhelm both, how well do you know your Society?"

Something told Rose not to answer.

"Sister Elsa Pike, for example. How much do you know of her so-called gifts?"

Rose's spine relaxed, but only slightly. To buy time, she rearranged her legs under the loose skirt of her work dress. "Elsa's desires are well known to me," she said.

"She seems loyal to Wilhelm, yet she plays the two of you against one another; are you aware of that?"

"I believe her loyalty to be genuine," Rose said. Indeed, Elsa's ambition and loyalty to Wilhelm were all that Rose believed to be genuine, but she hesitated to reveal that to Patience.

"I'm sure you noticed that unholy attraction between Benjamin and Irene at the Union Meeting—that could not have escaped even an unworldly Shaker."

"I am not so unworldly as you seem to think," Rose blurted out. She could hear the anger in her own voice. *This will not do,* Rose told herself. *She is attacking, and I am letting her draw me into the fight.* She allowed herself several even breaths before continuing.

"I saw what there was to see," she said.

"There is more than can be seen," Patience said. "There is much to be known about all of them. Gossip sickens me, but I am disturbed by what is tolerated in this village. At least in Mount Lebanon, Believers were under closer watch. Here their worst, most sinful natures are rising to the surface, and you and Wilhelm do nothing. Wilhelm only dreams backwards and doesn't know a true gift from a false one. You do not even see what is in front of you." Patience's eyes glittered like flames licking smoke. Rose resisted the urge to edge away from her.

"I see what you do not," Patience said. "But then, I have help that you do not. The angels speak to me, all day and night. I see the evil that infects this village."

"And what have the angels told you to do about this evil?" Rose asked, careful to speak without a hint of mockery. She could not know if Patience was mad or inspired or something else altogether, and she wanted to find out whatever she could from the sister.

Patience's smile hinted at inner knowing. "Nothing. Yet. They—and I—hope that it will not be necessary, that you will finally see the truth and root out the evil yourself."

"It would help greatly if you would tell me what you see that I do not."

"I'm sure it would," Patience said. She pulled herself to her feet and brushed the grass from her skirt. "I have received no instructions to help you. But perhaps, at the right time, I could try to point you in the right direction. And if you are wondering about my gifts, whether they are true or false, I suggest you ask Agatha. She is the only true holy one among you. Now, if you don't mind, I am falling behind in my work."

Rose watched her tall, strong body stride toward the Medicinal Herb Shop. Patience might be deranged, deluded, or simply arrogant, but she had confirmed Rose's vague sense that all was not right with the new group of Believers.

"How long has Patience been fasting?" Rose asked. She'd sent all the kitchen sisters but Gertrude to their retiring rooms for an afternoon rest. The heat was especially hard on sisters whose rotation kept them trapped in close quarters.

"Oh goodness, forever," said the Kitchen Deaconess. "Or it seems that way. She ate normally when she first arrived, but it wasn't more than maybe a month before I started noticing she was skipping meals and only pretending to eat when she did show up.'' Gertrude hooked the handle of a frying pan on a wall peg, then adjusted it slightly so its newly shined surface caught the sunlight.

"I do enjoy a sparkling pan, don't you?''

"One of life's little pleasures,'' Rose said. "We were talking about Patience. Could she really have been fasting for two months?'' Rose leaned over the large worktable to wipe bread crumbs from its nicked surface.

"Nay, of course not,'' Gertrude said, as she splashed around in the dishwater, looking for items to scrub. "Goodness, after two months, she should be dead!'' She stopped splashing. "Oh dear, I didn't mean . . . I only meant that I know for a fact she hasn't fasted the whole time. Sometimes she'd go a whole week eating regular, then she'd stop again.'' Gertrude wiped her hands on her damp apron and began to dry the last few dishes. "It's almost like she was practicing or something, to see what it felt like. Really, it's only the last couple of weeks or so she's gotten steadier about the fasting.''

"So it's been since before Nora and Betsy became ill?''

"Yea, I'm sure of that. In fact, now that you mention it, that was right about the time I noticed something different about Patience. I wondered if she might be ill because she'd started to look a little wild—you know, like when someone has a high fever, and they—''

The swinging door that led to the dining room squeaked, and Brother Hugo shambled in. "I see I've been caught,'' he said, "stalking the bread and jam.''

Normally a kitchen sister would have scolded any Believer too fond of between-meal snacks, but for Hugo to show any appetite lately was cause for rejoicing. Over the past month, illness had reduced his once impressive girth to folds of loose skin. He had insisted on staying in his own retiring room, rather than move to the Infirmary, but he rarely came to meals anymore. The kitchen sisters

brought trays up to him, many of which returned un-
touched.

"You sit right down," Gertrude ordered, "and I'll hunt
up that bread and jam for you. Could you chew on a bit of
cheese? Are you sure? I suppose it is hard on the stomach.
Never mind, here's some lovely brown bread, and I'll just
get you a fresh jam." She disappeared inside the pantry,
then reappeared holding a glass canning jar.

"I know the peach is your favorite," she said, "but I'm
afraid we used the last of it just this morning. However, I
have a treat for you!" She held up the jar and grinned.
Hugo, whose eyes were failing him, blinked and smiled
politely.

"Is that one of your experimental herb jellies?" Rose
asked.

"Peppermint! Isn't it lovely? And it'll soothe your stomach, too, Hugo, I'm sure of it." She placed the jar on the
table within his reach, and Hugo picked it up and turned it
in his hand. He did not look eager.

"You're certain the peach is all gone?"

Gertrude nodded.

"And the apple butter?"

"I'm afraid so, this time of year. But, Hugo, I promise
you'll love this. It'll be just like eating candy! Try it. Here,
let me."

Gertrude cut two thick slices of bread and slathered jelly
on both of them. To Rose, the pale greenish-brown substance looked unappetizing, and the thought of sugary peppermint on her morning bread made her consider the
positive points of fasting, but Hugo liked his sweets. Maybe
it would be just the right treat for him.

Hugo sniffed the bread, then took a bite and chewed
slowly. He swallowed, nodded. Rose and Gertrude waited.

"Not at all bad," he said. "In fact, surprisingly good."
He took another bite.

As Gertrude, humming happily, turned back to the
dishes, Rose pulled a chair to the end of the table.

"As long as you're here, Hugo, could I borrow your memory for a few minutes?"

"What there is left of it, Rose. I'm afraid the last month is nothing but a blur." He finished one slice of bread and licked his fingers.

"I just wondered about a young hired hand who is working in the Medicinal Herb Shop, Willy Robinson. Andrew said you'd spent some time talking with him. What was your impression of him?"

"Ah, young Willy. In fact, he sought me out, and we had several chats. Seems a nice young man, full of questions." Hugo frowned at his second slice of bread. "Willy is not so simple as he appears."

"Why do you say that?"

"Well, his knowledge of traditional herbal cures, for one. But it's more than that. It's the way he approached me." Hugo pulled off a crusty corner and nibbled it. Rose waited, torn between wanting him to eat and impatience to hear about Willy.

"He talked about all sorts of topics before he asked what he really wanted. He really wanted to know about his parents."

"His *parents*? Somehow I thought they were dead."

"They are now. But first they left him with his grandmother and came to North Homage to become Believers. That was in 1916 or so—I know because I looked up their names on the covenant for him. They signed with Xs in the fall of 1917, and they'd have spent about a year in the gathering order beforehand."

"How old was Willy when they left him?"

"Must have been about five years old, maybe six. He remembers them, but some of the memories sound like they were fed to him by the grandmother. He says they were good, honest people, wouldn't hurt a fly. Said that several times in the exact same words, as though he'd memorized them. Apparently the neighbors in his hollow spread it around that they had been shiftless, dishonest, and violent.

In Willy's hearing, they'd say that the acorn wouldn't have fallen far from the tree.''

"Did Willy tell you why he had to leave home?"

Hugo nodded. "That's why he was so curious about his parents, you see. He hoped to clear their name, and his own in the process."

As Hugo swallowed the last of his snack, his eyes half closed. Rose thought he was falling asleep. "You know, it's odd," Hugo said, as Rose reached for his empty plate. "It's odd that I never knew Willy existed."

"I don't understand."

"I knew both of them, after all—Willy's parents. They never mentioned a child."

"If they'd abandoned him, perhaps they didn't want to admit it," Rose said.

"But why even abandon him? We'd have raised him. If they truly wanted to become Believers, why not bring the child along? It makes me suspect the rumors were true. At the time they arrived, some Believers suspected they were just winter Shakers, wanting hot meals and a roof over their heads until spring. When they signed the covenant, the rumor was that Willy's father was just trying to get out of serving in the war.

"Ah, but who's to say what they would have done in the long haul. They both died in the influenza epidemic of 1918, the only ones we lost. My guess is, they hadn't lived with us long enough to recover from lifetimes of poor eating, so they were weaker than the rest of us." Hugo laid a hand on his greatly reduced stomach. "And speaking of weak," he said, "my digestion isn't what it once was. I'd better put myself to bed for a nap."

"Shall I call in one of the brethren to help you?"

"Nay, I'll be fine." Hugo eased to his feet and steadied himself on the table. Rose reached toward him, but Hugo shook his head and managed a weak smile. "I'll be all right, Rose. Just need to let my stomach settle."

Rose blinked back tears as she watched him shuffle toward the door. She didn't want him to hear her grief; it would only sadden him, and he needed his strength. Her resolve cracked, though, when she turned and saw Gertrude's streams of silent tears.

"Does Patience truly have the power to heal, do you think?" Gertrude asked.

"I don't know."

"I was wondering . . ." Gertrude sniffled, then wiped her wet cheeks with the corner of her apron. "I was just thinking maybe we could ask her to try with Hugo."

"Perhaps," Rose said, wishing she believed it would do any good.

NINE

By late afternoon, Rose made sure she'd returned to the Ministry House library to await Gennie Malone's arrival. Even with the curtains closed and the lights out, the room glowed with sunshine. A copy of Mother Ann's sayings lay facedown on her lap as she sat caught up in her own thoughts. The interview with Patience still disturbed her. She had some clues to act upon, true, but she had learned nothing about Patience herself. Except that she was a clever, intense woman.

The outside door clicked open and shut.

"Gennie? I'm in here," Rose called through the open door of the library. Too late, she realized the steps were too heavy for a petite young woman. Wilhelm filled the doorframe.

"I am glad that thy work is so light as to allow thee time to relax and visit with old friends," he said.

Rather than be drawn into a battle, Rose stood and returned her book to its place. She hung her chair from a peg and began to straighten the room, hoping Wilhelm would leave without demanding further explanation—and before Gennie arrived. Instead, Wilhelm entered the room and pulled a book from the shelf, almost as if he knew all her hopes and was determined to dash them.

"I'm astonished at thy calmness," Wilhelm said. "After

what has just happened. But then, I suppose the brethren are of no concern to thee.''

"What do you mean?"

"Hugo, of course," Wilhelm said. "He just became very ill and slipped into a coma. He managed to get to the phone in the hallway and call for help. Some of the brethren came in from their work and carried him to the Infirmary. I'm surprised Josie did not call thee."

"I am saddened to hear this," Rose said. Unwilling to expose her heart to Wilhelm, she fought back quick tears. Despite a prick of guilt, she did not mention that she had exhausted Hugo by keeping him talking. Wilhelm was not above shifting the blame for Hugo's collapse in her direction. She said only, "I'll consult with Josie later."

"If it fits in thy busy schedule, by all means. Are thy preparations for the sweeping gift completed?" he asked, before Rose could react to his barb. Wilhelm scanned a page in the book instead of her face.

"Yea," Rose said, "I'll speak with all the sisters this evening about the ritual. But I still don't understand why, now of all times, we should—''

"Call it an inspiration," Wilhelm said, smiling into his book.

Rose thought it wise to withdraw and wait for Gennie upstairs. She chose a book to take to her retiring room for evening study.

"By the way," Wilhelm said, just as she reached the door, "I've spoken briefly with Elsa and Patience about following behind thee in the sweeping. Then, if thy energy flags—or perhaps a desire to stop and chat comes upon thee—they can take over leading the ceremony. They were agreeable."

"No doubt," Rose said.

Hearing the ice in her voice, Wilhelm glanced up at her. "These ceremonies are deeply important to our strength, our common understanding as a Society. I want the sweeping to be conducted with the utmost devotion, by Believers who do not waver in their commitment to—"

"My devotion is passionate, which God can see, even if you cannot. Furthermore, I will not have you interfering with the sisters anymore. They are *my* responsibility. I know your motives in this, and they are far from pure."

Wilhelm slammed his book shut.

"I will arrange the sisters' parts in the sweeping," Rose said quickly, as Wilhelm sucked in air to blast her. "In case you have forgotten, we are all equals in the eyes of our Mother and Father, and I will not allow two sisters to be pitted against one another just so you can feel that Mother Ann's Work is with us again."

Wilhelm's fingers kneaded his book, and his half-closed eyes skewered the wall above Rose's head. He said nothing. But it was his faint smile that nipped Rose's fury. She knew that smile.

"We will not discuss this any further," she said. "I will do as I think best." She spun out the door and slammed into Gennie Malone. Gennie leaped back and questioned her with wide brown eyes. In silent agreement, they hurried upstairs to Rose's retiring room and closed the door behind them.

Rose sank into her desk chair, while Gennie threw herself onto a nearby rocker and giggled. "It's so comforting to know," Gennie said, "that mountains may wear down, but Wilhelm will never change."

"Comforting from a distance, perhaps," Rose said. She reached over for Gennie's hand and squeezed it. Gennie had a way of calming Rose's temper as no one else could—except Agatha, of course.

"Any changes in Nora and Betsy?" Gennie asked.

"Yea, Josie says they have both come around, thank God, but neither seems to remember what happened." Rose did not mention Hugo's apparent collapse. She never knew if Wilhelm's announcements were to be taken at face value, and she preferred to assess Hugo's condition for herself before alarming others.

"I'm sorry to drag you into the middle of this mess," Rose said.

"I'm not. Life was getting just a bit dull in the flower shop. Not enough herbs, I guess."

"Well, you will have your fill of herbs here." Rose worked her shoulders to loosen them. "You may find your time here more irritating than exciting, I'm afraid. My fears might be completely without foundation. We might find that all we have here is a group of secretive Believers who value their personal success more than their vows."

"Something tells me Elsa is involved," Gennie said.

"Yea, but Elsa is the least of my worries. I know Elsa; by now, I can almost predict how she will behave. But the others . . ."

"The Believers from Mount Lebanon, you mean?"

Rose nodded. "Most of them work together in the Medicinal Herb Shop, where I am placing you as a 'hired hand.' I've told them that you lost your job and will be staying with us, sleeping in the Center Family Dwelling House. The room next to Patience's has been prepared for you. She is a puzzle to me, almost alarming and . . . well, I'll be intrigued to hear how you respond to her. On the surface, she seems much like Elsa, but I sense there is more, much more. She seems to know a great deal about all of us; she hints at her knowledge but keeps most of it to herself. She displays the gifts of the spirit, and I am inclined to believe they are real."

"Rose, you know I have my doubts about the gifts," Gennie said.

"I know, and that's one reason I want you to observe her for yourself. And the others in the Medicinal Herb Shop, as far as that is possible." Rose leaned back and smiled at Gennie. "And now I want to hear more about you," she said.

"Wilhelm would judge you harshly if he knew you were chatting," Gennie said, arching an auburn eyebrow.

"All the more reason to do so," Rose said.

Gennie grinned. "I am well and happy—and, as I said, somewhat bored. I love the flower shop, and I love Grady, but I've seen so little of the world still. Or maybe that isn't fair; in some ways, I've seen more of the world in this village than I have being a part of the world. We were all so close and knew each other so well. Aside from Grady and Emily, I don't get a chance to talk much with other people—not enough to see inside them, the way I could here. I'm really excited about helping you."

"I wish I could hear a call to come back to us in what you just said," Rose said.

Gennie ran a hand through her short curls. "I think we both know that I belong in the world. I just wish it were as cozy as here."

"Cozy?!"

Gennie's laughter rang like a joyous carillon. "Well, you know what I mean. With everybody knowing everybody and at least trying to be friends."

"I know what you mean," Rose said. "I miss you very much, my young friend, but if you belong in the world, that is where you should be. Perhaps it is your calling to bring some Shaker friendship to the world's people." Rose pushed herself out of her chair and stuffed a few damp red curls back under her cap. "But for now you are here, and the sooner we get you settled in the Medicinal Herb Shop, the sooner we can determine what, if anything, is going on there."

Gennie sprang from her chair, seemingly unaffected by the heat. "Lots of herbs and a chance for excitement—I couldn't ask for more."

As they approached the open door of the Medicinal Herb Shop, Rose lowered her voice and finished telling Gennie what she had observed so far. She had already discussed Benjamin's ambitions and obvious feelings for Irene, Thomas's failings as a husband and father, Andrew's sometimes odd and secretive ways, and Willy Robinson's background.

"Lately I've noticed," Rose said, "that Patience doesn't show up for meals. And when she does, she eats little. I don't know what to make of that. I took her to task for it, but she insisted that she had important experiments to watch over and she required very little food. I find that hard to believe. She is nearly as tall as I am, and I require a great deal of food! Look to see, if you can, whether she eats at all."

"I hope I don't have to follow her if she doesn't attend meals," Gennie whispered. "I'd hate to miss too much of that lovely Shaker food."

By the time Rose had introduced Gennie to the inhabitants of the Medicinal Herb Shop, only an hour remained before evening meal. Rose left her young friend under Andrew's direction, then cut through the kitchen garden to the Center Family Dwelling House. She resisted entering through the kitchen; the kitchen sisters were often shorthanded, and she always seemed to end up helping them. And right now she wanted to talk to Agatha.

She rounded the corner of the dwelling house and entered through the sisters' door. Since the inhabitants were still at their assigned tasks, Rose encountered no one as she scooted through the hallway to one of the few ground-floor retiring rooms, reserved for the ill and elderly, who had difficulty climbing stairs. She knocked softly, and a quavering voice bade her enter.

"Rose, my dear, how lovely." Agatha Vandenberg held out her left hand. Her right was still weak but no longer useless, and her smile was less lopsided. She had come far since her third and near-fatal stroke. Rose took her hand in both her own.

Agatha sat in her tiny rocking chair, made for her diminutive body. A *Life* magazine lay open on her lap, and a small radio quietly announced the news of the world from her plain pine bedside table. To be caught reading a magazine from the world and listening to a radio would be humiliating for anyone else, but Rose was delighted to see Agatha doing so. The former eldress could no longer read small print or do embroidery, after all. Furthermore, the few other Shaker villages still alive, all in the East, were known to have loosened their strict separation from worldly influences. Still, Rose thought she wouldn't mention the magazine and radio to Wilhelm.

"Pull a chair over here, close to me," Agatha said. "I've just been listening for more news about that poor, brave girl flyer who disappeared over the Pacific. I am praying for her safe return—and for her soul, if she cannot return."

Rose blinked in confusion. Her contact with daily happenings in the world had shrunk considerably since her shift to eldress, and she had heard nothing about a girl who flew airplanes across oceans. The idea pleased her, but it sounded as if this time it hadn't worked out so well. However, she curbed her curiosity. She had questions to ask before evening meal.

"Agatha, have you had a chance to get to know our new group of brothers and sisters?"

"The ones from Mount Lebanon?" Agatha asked.

"Yea. I'm thinking especially of Patience McCormick."

"Ah. You are wondering about her gifts, if they are true or false." Agatha closed her magazine and placed it on the small table next to her. "It is natural that you would be highly suspicious, Rose. Your experiences with the gifts have been few and unfortunate. Elsa . . . well, there is no need to discuss that incident; it is over and done. But when I was a child, it was quite different." Agatha's cloudy blue eyes looked back through eight decades with clarity. "Mother Ann's Work was just ending when I was brought to the Shakers as a tiny child. In reality, it still took hold of Believers from time to time, though I suspect the power of it had made the Ministry nervous, and they were tamping it down as best they could. But I remember it as glorious—about that, Wilhelm is quite right."

Agatha grew silent, and Rose would have thought her asleep except that her eyes darted around as if watching a performance. "I remember one sister," she said, "who went into a trance during dancing worship, and she didn't come out of it for eight hours! She spoke in tongues, took messages from Mother Ann and Mother Lucy, trembled and twirled and beat her breast, all without pause, without taking nourishment. After eight hours, she crumpled in a heap and the other sisters had to carry her to her retiring room. She had given us six lovely new songs and two new dances. It was true and real; one could not doubt."

"And you think that Patience is like this sister you remember? You believe in her gifts?" Rose asked.

Agatha let out a long sigh. "I don't know. Yea, I sense that they are real, yet . . . Patience is mystifying. Now that I can no longer dance, I watch the worship service with great interest. When I watch Patience dance, I sense something powerful in her. Yet somehow the feeling it gives me is different from what I felt as a youngster, watching the manifestations of Mother Ann. Perhaps it is my age, making me brittle in spirit, but I cannot tell if Patience's gifts are truly born of goodness"—Agatha rested her head against the back of her rocker—"or of something darker."

৵৵৵

TEN

GENNIE'S EYES OPENED TO BLACKNESS, AN ANGUISHED CRY still sounding in her ears. A faint rectangle of light traced the outline of what must be a closed door. It wasn't in the right place. Her mind wavered between waking and sleeping, but her heart knew to be afraid. As her eyes accustomed to the darkness, they picked out shapes that confused her: a stovepipe; two other beds, both apparently empty; a small dresser with no mirror glow above it.

Then, as she came fully awake, she remembered. She was not sleeping in her boardinghouse room. She was in a retiring room in the Center Family Dwelling House in North Homage. And someone had screamed. But was it someone else's scream or her own? She held her breath for several seconds, listening, but she could hear nothing.

While she waited for the silence to reason with her fear, she thought back over the afternoon and evening. She had spent an hour in the Medicinal Herb Shop, watching the tense inhabitants and trying to convince Sister Patience McCormick to tell her about some experiments. Then she had watched Patience pretend to eat her evening meal. Afterward, she had listened while Rose told the sisters all about that strange sweeping ritual, during which Believers would receive invisible brooms with which to mime the cleaning of the village and drive out evil. Finally, Gennie had settled in to sleep in the room next to Patience.

83

Gennie's heart slowed to normal, probably bored back to sleepiness by the recitation of her day. The cry must have been part of a dream. Or perhaps the clammy air, barely cooler with the night, had disturbed her sleep. She yawned and pushed away her light sheet so a slight breeze could skim over her body.

This time she bolted upright, instantly awake, as a low moan crescendoed, then resolved into a babbling sound. She couldn't remember where the lamp was, so she slid out of bed and fumbled in the dark toward the pale glow around the door. She stopped with her hand on the knob, suddenly fearful. What if the moan had come from just outside her door? What should she do? The only phone was outside in the hall, so she couldn't call for help unless she went out there.

She made her way back to her bed, where she could now make out the shape of a lamp on her bedside table. She switched it on. As she did so, she heard the moan again, spiraling up the scale and back down. She turned her head toward the sound; it seemed to come from Patience's room.

Gennie knew she had to investigate. She had brought her own blue silk robe, an eighteenth birthday gift from Emily O'Neal. She tied it around her and tiptoed barefoot out of her room, taking care to turn off her light and to latch her door soundlessly. Patience's door was closed. She leaned close to listen. North Homage's doors did not have key-holes, since locked doors were almost unheard-of, so she had to settle for the slight crack between the door and the jamb.

The sounds were soft but distinct, and Gennie wondered why no one else on the floor seemed disturbed by them. Perhaps their own closed doors and their long days of phys-ical labor were enough to keep them asleep. Patience's low, melodic voice moved incessantly through babbling tongues, prayers, snippets of song, and occasional moans. She must be in a trance. There was no other explanation. And it had to be real—there was no one here to impress.

Gennie hesitated. Should she let Patience have her trance and go back to bed? Call Rose at the Ministry House and risk alerting Wilhelm? She was loath to intervene herself, since she had no idea what should be done for someone in the grip of a trance. Her confusion ended abruptly when she heard a clear thump from inside the room. It sounded very much like a body hitting the floor, hard.

She knocked quietly. There was no answer, not even a moan or a cry for help. She turned the knob and pushed open the door. Night lamps from the hall spread light inside the unlit room and marked Patience's body, curled in a heap next to her bed, her knees pulled nearly up to her chin. She still wore her brown work dress, but her long black hair spread out around her head, its silver streaks gleaming in the dim light.

Gennie ran to her. Kneeling beside her, she took Patience's hand and felt her wrist for a pulse, as she'd seen Josie do. It was there, though weak.

"Patience, can you hear me?" Gennie asked, not sure what else to do. Patience twitched in response to her name, then went limp again. Gennie glanced around the room and saw a white basin on a dresser. Patience would probably keep it filled with water to splash on her face in the morning. Gennie could flick a few drops in her face now; maybe that would help bring her to consciousness. Failing that, she'd call Josie.

As Gennie rocked back on her heels to stand, Patience's head lifted off the floor and her eyes snapped open. She stared at Gennie. Was it a trick of the dimness, or had Patience's gray eyes turned a disturbing black? Gennie fell backward and plopped to a sitting position.

"Are you all right, Patience?"

No answer, just that black stare. *She doesn't see me.*

Patience's head fell back to the floor, and her eyelids closed. Gennie jumped to her feet and ran to the hall phone to call Josie at the Infirmary. Josie's health was superb for an eighty-year-old, but her hearing wasn't as sharp as it once had been, and it took many rings for her to answer the phone. Gennie fidgeted, wishing she had thought to knock on a few doors before making the call. But finally Josie responded and agreed to come right over. Gennie's near shouting into the phone had roused Sister Gertrude, whose room was closest. She peeked out her door.

"Gertrude, come quick," Gennie said, reaching in and grabbing her by the arm. Gertrude stumbled into the hall, tripping over her cotton nightgown. Her knees buckled, and she fell against Gennie, knocking them both into the wall. Gennie's head snapped backward, against the edge of the wall phone.

"Oh, I'm so sorry, Gennie. Are you hurt? You've banged your head. Let me see." Gertrude's gray hair hung in strings around her face, which Gennie suddenly found amusing, and she giggled. "Oh dear, you're bleeding," Gertrude said, propping her up against the wall with both hands. The room wouldn't hold still for Gennie, but she had to remain alert, though she couldn't remember why.

Two nearby doors opened and more white-nightgowned sisters gathered around Gennie. Josie's face joined them. With gentle fingers, Josie probed the back of her head.

"Quite a bump you've got yourself," she said. "But you'll be fine. Is your head clearing?"

"Yea," Gennie said. She was feeling much more steady, in fact. *Patience!* "Josie, forget about me, I'm fine. Go take care of Patience."

"Seeing as how you were being well cared for by the sisters, I looked in on Patience quickly first. There's nothing for me to do."

"Oh, dear God," Gennie said. "Are you saying that she is . . ."

Josie nodded. "Yea, indeed. Sound asleep in her bed. Oh dear, Gertrude, catch her, would you? Goodness, Gennie, you aren't as strong as I thought you were. We'll just carry you to bed, and I want you to stay there tomorrow."

Gennie wriggled away from the arms that reached for

her. "Patience was unconscious on the floor. How could she be asleep in her bed?" Unsteadily Gennie made for Patience's door, four sisters behind her, making soft clucking sounds. She opened the door wide and stared at Patience's bed, where a still form lay covered up to her neck by a white sheet.

"You see?" Josie whispered behind her. "Sound asleep."

"Did you check to make sure she was breathing?"

"My goodness . . . I didn't have to; she turned in her sleep, and I could hear her breathing. She does sound wheezy, probably coming down with something. I'll bring her a tonic in the morning. But she is certainly breathing. Now, I want to see you fast asleep in your own bed, young lady, for the next twenty-four hours." Josie pulled Gennie into the hallway and closed Patience's door. "You've surely been having nightmares, and I'm not surprised, with you out there on your own in the world, exposed to all sorts of horrors. I'll be bringing you a tonic in the morning, too, and I expect you to drink it up completely. Come along now."

Her head ached, and her body barely moved on its own, so Gennie gave in. Josie tucked her in, just as she used to when Gennie was a child, staying overnight in the Infirmary to nurse the mumps or measles. She was drifting already as the group of sisters let themselves out of her room. Her last conscious thought was a question. She knew it was an important question, too, but sleep had too strong a grip on her. She had time and energy only to hear the words: What was Patience wearing under that sheet?

Except for a dull headache, Gennie felt like herself again the next morning. And deeply curious. She'd drunk Josie's tonic and climbed back into bed with a docility that should have made the Infirmary nurse suspicious. Fortunately, it didn't. As soon as Josie left for the Infirmary, Gennie slipped into her borrowed work dress, snatched a leftover muffin from the kitchen, and hurried to her post, the Medicinal Herb Shop.

Patience glanced up sharply as Gennie entered the shop, then ignored her. Feeling awkward, Gennie stood at the end of the table and looked around. The three brethren conferred over an open journal, on their side of the shop, while the hired hand, Willy, swept a growing pile of herb detritus out the front door. Clusters of herbs and flowers hung upside down on pegs circling the room. Several of the plants looked unfamiliar to Gennie, who prided herself on her knowledge of herbs. Others reminded her of drawings she'd seen in old Shaker journals, from the days when Believers conducted a thriving medicinal herb industry. The Mount Lebanon Believers must have brought some with them from New York; there wouldn't have been time to grow them here.

"Josie said you'd be staying in bed today after being injured last night," Patience said. Gennie whipped her head around so fast that her bruised brain felt as if it bounced against her skull. Patience seemed intent on her task. She held a small bag of brown-green dried leaves, with lavender and pink flowers mixed in. From the mildly minty aroma, Gennie guessed they were wild bergamot leaves. Patience began to drop crumbled bits of the leaves onto a weight measure.

"She said something similar about you," Gennie replied.

Patience hesitated, her hand still holding the bag of leaves above the weight. Her eyes narrowed. "Josie brought me a tonic and insisted I drink it. I have no idea why, though it sounds as if you do. What have you been telling her?"

Gennie was startled into silence, which seemed to irritate Patience even more. "Why are you here?"

"Well, I only bumped my head. I'm not really ill, so I thought I'd come—"

"Nay, why are you here in North Homage, working in this shop?"

Gennie prodded her aching brain to think quickly. She hadn't expected Patience to be so suspicious, and obviously, neither had Rose. "As Rose explained yesterday, I've worked a lot with herbs, and I lost my job, so—"

"I know what Rose explained."

"Patience? Is there a problem with that headache curative?" Andrew had crossed from the men's side of the shop. He glanced from Patience to Gennie and back again, his expression concerned.

"None at all, Andrew," Patience said. "In fact, I was about to ask Gennie to test it out, since she has a headache this morning."

"Ah. Very good."

With misgivings, Gennie watched Andrew return to the men. "I'd love to help out," she said, "but, really, my headache is nearly gone, so it wouldn't be much of a test."

Patience's mouth curved upward into the faintest of smiles. "Too bad," she said. She made a notation in her journal and poured her concoction into a tin wrapped in a handwritten label.

This is ridiculous, Gennie thought. *Rose sent me here for a reason, and I'm not getting anywhere. I won't let this woman scare me.* She studied Patience closely. The sister must be well into her forties, but she carried her years lightly. She was tall and well built, as far as Gennie could judge, since her roomy Shaker dress hid the curves of her body. The skin stretched tightly across her high cheekbones, as if she had recently lost weight. Deep circles marred the area under her eyes. Lack of food and sleep were taking their toll. Why did she want to hide her fasting and her trances? Surely most Believers would not do so. Or did she truly not remember what had happened to her the night before? Gennie could be quite determined, and this was one of those times—she wanted answers to all of her questions about Patience. She wouldn't be chased away.

"Patience, I realize I know little about medicinal herbs, so I may not be of much help immediately," Gennie said,

settling herself on a high stool, "but I learn quickly, and
I've always been fascinated by herbs."

"I have no calling to teach."

"Then I will simply watch." Gennie's stubbornness was
seeping into her voice. "I can learn by watching. You don't
have to go out of your way to teach me."

"Just don't get in my way," Patience said. "And move
that stool back. You are distracting me."

Gennie remounted her stool, feeling out of place. Patience wouldn't let her near, so she couldn't make good her
boast that she could learn from watching. She slid to the
floor and began to circle the room, fingering each herb
bunch that hung from wall pegs. Some were crispy, as if
they'd been dry for months. Others were freshly picked.
She played a favorite game from her days in the Herb
House—guessing the herb by its shape, fragrance, or flowers. She quickly discovered that the fresh herbs were all
ones she was familiar with, such as oregano, peppermint,
calendula, and thimbleweed. The dried herbs, however,
proved impossible to identify. Most of the leaves were
brownish-green and broken, indicating they had been dried
for many months. She decided to do a little research on her
own as soon as she could. Maybe later she could break off
a few bits and take them to Rose. Together they might be
able to recognize a fragrance or a shape.

"Be careful where you stick those elbows," said an annoyed male voice behind Gennie. She spun around to find
Brother Benjamin scowling at her. She'd wandered around
to the men's side of the workroom and was in danger of
knocking some infusing equipment off the end of a large
table. Gennie smiled at him, and his scowl deepened. It
struck her that, while he would be nervous with a woman
so close by, she was no longer under the Shakers' care. Her
usefulness to Rose was all the greater because she was now
truly an outsider; she could converse with the men—from
a respectful distance, of course.

"I'm fascinated by herbal remedies," she said. "It must

be very difficult to figure out what really works. I'd love to hear what sort of curative you're working on now." She was being truthful, if perhaps overenthusiastic. To her surprise—and relief—Benjamin's expression mellowed.

"Yea, it is indeed extremely difficult to know what works. We must be precise in our calculations and thoroughly versed in the effects of our ingredients."

Gennie kept her eyes wide and interested, to encourage him and so she wouldn't smile at his pomposity. She needn't have bothered. Engrossed in his topic, Benjamin had pushed his work closer to her. She had ceased to be an interloping female; she was now his audience.

"What I am working on here," he said airily, "is a refined curative for various stomach ailments."

"Do these plants grow around here?" Gennie asked, though she already knew, from their names, that North Homage had never grown them.

Benjamin lightly touched an unmarked apothecary jar half full of beige powder. "Nay, I knew this place would never have the variety I needed to conduct my experiments, so I brought these along, already dried."

"So these unusual herbs hanging around the room are all yours?"

"The interesting ones are," Benjamin said, glancing at some pegs near his table.

"What will you do when you run out?"

"Send for more, I suppose," Benjamin said, frowning at his recipe journal. Clearly he was growing bored with the way the lecture was going. Gennie decided to save the rest of her questions.

After a few moments of silence, Benjamin's enthusiasm reemerged. He held up a vial containing a clear liquid. "This has the power to cure or kill," he said. "If someone were to mix the ingredients incorrectly, one swallow would fell a man in minutes." His smirk implied that the "someone" could be anyone else but him. "Even my formula, administered by incompetent hands, could easily prove fatal.''

"But how can you bear to let it out of your sight, then—to sell to the world, that is?'' Gennie asked, then held her breath. But Benjamin missed the irony in her voice.

"One can only pray that God will be watching,'' he said.

Gennie stifled her immediate response. Before she could formulate a more moderate one, Brother Thomas Dengler appeared at her elbow.

"Benjamin tends to exaggerate a bit,'' Thomas said. "We rarely use poisonous herbs anymore.'' With a beefy hand, he pushed straight blond hair off his broad forehead. "We're not in the world anymore, Benjamin. No need to impress the girls.''

The hollows in Benjamin's cheeks darkened a shade, but otherwise he ignored Thomas.

"I thought you were supposed to help Patience,'' Thomas said to Gennie. "You should not be on this side of the room, tempting a weak brother.''

Benjamin skidded his stool across the floor as he slid off. His narrow-shouldered, delicate body assumed a menacing tilt in Thomas's direction. Thomas, bigger and tougher, could threaten without even trying. Gennie felt small and trapped between them.

"She is not a sister,'' Benjamin said. "She can do as she pleases.''

"But you cannot. You should not be talking to a woman.''

Yet another male figure joined the group surrounding Gennie as Andrew arrived. "Is there a problem with your work?'' he asked. He looked from Benjamin to Thomas, then smiled as his gaze dropped to Gennie, more than a head shorter than all of them.

"Ah, Gennie Malone, isn't it? I'm sorry I didn't greet you at first; I was distracted. We're most grateful to Rose for finding us extra hands for our workload. She said, too, that you are quite experienced with herbs.''

Despite her worldly status, Gennie's discomfort urged her to step sideways, out of the masculine circle. "Only with the culinary herbs, I'm afraid," she said. "But Rose knows how much I love to learn about herbs, so she thought we might help each other."

"Ah. I see. And are you learning?"

There was nothing harsh in his tone, yet Gennie felt chastised. "A great deal," she said, a shade too quickly. "Brother Benjamin was just—"

"She shouldn't be talking to the brethren," Thomas said. He and Benjamin glared at each other.

"I'm sure she meant no harm," Andrew said. "And she'll be more circumspect in the future." Again he flashed a brief smile at Gennie, which did not comfort her, and he turned toward his own desk before she had a chance to respond. Leaving Thomas and Benjamin to wage their own private battle, she slipped back toward the women's worktable. In the middle of the room, she stumbled to a halt as she faced Patience, whose dark eyes watched Gennie. Somehow Gennie knew that Patience had been observing her every move since she'd left her stool.

ELEVEN

"Elder said I'd be right behind thee, helpin' lead, like I should," Elsa said. "Why should I be in the back and her in front? That ain't fair." She crossed her arms over her crisp new work dress, made a size bigger to accommodate her expanding figure. All the other sisters, gathered together in the family meeting room of the Center Family Dwelling House for the cleansing ritual, looked from Elsa to Rose and waited.

A whining middle-aged woman was a stern challenge for Rose's temper. She sped through three silent prayers for patience. Then she changed her plans.

"All right," she told Elsa and Patience, "we have too many buildings to cover anyway. I'm going to divide the sisters into two groups. Patience, you will lead the group in sweeping the buildings north of the central path, and, Elsa, you'll take the south."

Elsa's pout melted into triumph. Patience looked unconcerned. *The question is,* Rose thought, *who needs watching more, Elsa or Patience?* She'd have Gennie's help. Everyone was used to Elsa's ways by now. Separated from Patience, she probably couldn't do any real harm. Gennie could accompany her group and alert Rose if trouble erupted. Rose could then focus on keeping Patience in line. Patience had missed the noon meal, as well as breakfast. Clearly she was fasting. For most, such persistent fasting would cause weakness, but Patience seemed to have a high tolerance. It was likely her self-denial only fostered increasingly frenzied trances.

"Gennie," Rose called to the girl standing off to the side. "Gennie, why don't you go along with Elsa and her group of sisters. You'll be purifying the south side of the village, except for the brethren's shops, of course." She fixed Gennie with as meaningful a stare as she could manage. Gennie opened her mouth to protest, then snapped it shut.

"Certainly," she said, with a compliance Rose had never before seen in her.

Rose dared not say, "Bless you" outloud, so she gave Gennie a light pat on the shoulder.

"Patience, you will follow behind me."

Now Elsa glowed, obviously thrilled to the marrow. She would lead alone, while Patience must follow Rose. The plan would probably encourage Elsa to perform, but Rose decided it was worth the risk. Patience was the unknown factor. Rose was reasonably certain that Patience would be the chosen instrument of the angels during the gift, but she could not know how Patience would manifest the messages she received. It was worrisome.

Elsa led her band of sisters out of the dwelling house. Gennie, bringing up the rear, turned and glanced back at Rose, a combination of understanding and discomfort in her brown eyes. Rose made a wry face to convey her gratitude and apology. Taking a deep breath, she prepared herself for whatever the cleansing ritual might bring.

With Patience, silent and intense, beside her, Rose led her group out the women's door of the building. She had decided that they should start at the west end, with the kitchen in the Trustees' Office. Since Andrew was now trustee, the rest of the building would be cleansed by the brethren.

They followed the walkway single file to the central path and turned right. Rose heard Patience hum softly behind

her and remembered that she had chosen marching songs
for them to sing as they went from building to building.
Her own alto was strong but too low for most of the sisters,
so she had asked Sister Irene to begin the songs. She raised
her arm to give the signal, and Irene's sweet soprano responded.

"Living souls let's be marching on our journey to heaven
With our lamps trimmed and burning with the oil of
    truth.
Let us join the heav'nly chorus and unite with our
    parents.
They will lead us on to heaven in the path of
    righteousness."

They repeated the lyrics six times as they marched down
the central path, then turned right again and mounted the
steps of the Trustees' Office. The front doors were open,
and from inside they could hear deep voices chanting a
different tune. Rose led the sisters inside and straight past
the office, suppressing an instant of sadness that it was no
longer hers to purify. The brethren were in the room, wielding imaginary brooms as if they had been waiting all their
lives for the chance to do the sisters' tasks.

Andrew sang with zest, attacking presumably dusty corners with invisible broom straw. Rose was so startled by
this display that she stumbled and had to hop to get back
in step. She had never seen Andrew show such joy, even
when he rhapsodized about medicinal herbs. His face
looked fuller and younger, and his brown hair fell in waves
across his forehead.

Rose had begun to march down the hallway to the
kitchen when something told her to turn her head and look
behind her. No one had followed her. The sisters were jum-
bled in front of the office door, with Patience at their center.

"A thousand angels have arrived," Patience said, raising

her arms to the ceiling. "They are with us in this place, and they have designated me their instrument." The boisterous singing in the office stopped. Rose hurried to join the circle of sisters. She could see the brethren in the office, keeping their distance but all watching the scene unfold in the hallway.

"Mother has sent us all brooms to make this place clean," Patience said. "She has sent the angels to deliver the fire of righteousness to light the corners and purify this ungodly place. Some of us must carry the fire—there, take some, be careful now," she said, as she scooped a handful of invisible flames from the air and handed it to a nearby sister. The sister took it, careful to cup her hands together tightly so as not to spill the sacred gift. She stepped away and another sister received a portion of the fire. Patience handed each sister either a broom or some cleansing fire, and each responded in mime, until only Rose remained empty-handed.

Patience tilted her head as if cocking an ear to hear a hushed voice. Her features hardened and she turned slowly. "You!" she said, raising her arm and pointing her finger at Rose. "Mother has sent a warning angel to tell us that you are unworthy. Her heart is so broken she could not come herself, for fear her tears would drown her beloved children. You have betrayed her." Her eyes were angry slits that widened to black omens of vengeance.

Rose felt her body turn to limestone, and her mind to molasses. She had no idea what to do or say to stop this horror. The other sisters murmured and pulled away from her, and the men stared at her from inside the office. Andrew stood nearest the door, and behind him, Wilhelm. Was it a trick of the shadow, or did Andrew look sad? And was Wilhelm smiling?

Patience closed her eyes and raised her face toward the ceiling. She stretched out her arms and turned, slowly at first, then faster into a twirl. She halted so suddenly that her billowing dress kept swirling back and forth around her.

Her outstretched arm now pointed toward the brethren, apparently singling out Andrew and Wilhelm.

"And you!" Patience said, her voice deepening as if speaking now for a male angel. "You have sinned in deed, and you have blasphemed in your heart, which God can see clear through."

All eyes turned to Wilhelm and Andrew. Slowly Wilhelm eased backward, into the shadows. Patience's accusatory finger did not move. Now it pointed directly at Andrew, whose long, lean body stood rigid, his hands still clutching his invisible broom. His face was pinched, and his eyes, haunted. It lasted only a moment. Patience's arms dropped to her sides and hung limply. Her head slumped toward her chest as if a puppeteer had dropped the strings. When Rose glanced back at Andrew, his face was composed again.

Everyone began to chatter at once. Rose edged through the sisters surrounding Patience, who had regained her strength but remained silent, unmoving, staring at nothing. Rose held Patience's shoulders, resisting the impulse to shake her.

"Patience, are you ill?" she asked. "Do you need help?" Patience shifted her gaze to Rose's face. Her eyes were dark as loam. She wriggled out of Rose's grasp and stepped away from her.

"Mother's angels would never harm me," she said. "They know my strength. And they will use me to tell the truth."

No angels had appeared for two hours, and Rose dared to hope that the worst was over. They had sung and swept and marched their way in a circle around the north end of the village, covering the Center Family Dwelling House, the Herb House, and the Laundry. From the ironing room, they had heard the Brethren cleansing the barn and counted their blessings. The nearness of the brethren did not seem to trigger another angelic visitation. Now they had only the Infirmary to cleanse.

Rose allowed the sisters to sing as they approached the Infirmary. Aside from Hugo, whose door was kept closed, the only other patients were Nora and Betsy. They were much improved, so Rose thought they would enjoy the ritual. The girls still claimed to remember nothing of their adventure before awakening in their cradle beds. Perhaps the excitement would help pull them out of their lingering stupor.

Josie ushered the group into the patients' waiting room, where she kept a large desk, usually cluttered with apothecary jars and tins filled with herbal infusions, powdered barks, and crumbled dried herbs. For her part in the ceremony, Josie had tidied the desk and dusted off all the little bits of leaves and bark that seemed to bury themselves in the wood grain.

"Make this place clean," Rose announced, as she had at the entrance to each building. The sisters got to work. With their transparent brooms and dustcloths, they swept and cleansed. The carriers of the gospel fire marched after them, purifying the newly swept corners and offering each area for Mother Ann's approval and blessing.

The sisters seemed to stay closer now to Patience, taking their cues from her rather than from their eldress. Rose had noted this in each building but kept hoping it was only her imagination. In these tight quarters, it was clear. The sisters avoided Rose. They followed after Patience, sometimes even copying her movements.

"Has it been a good cleansing?" Josie whispered to Rose.

"You can't imagine," Rose said. For the moment, she gave up trying to lead and stood in a corner with Josie. Irene Dengler looked up from her sweeping and gave Rose a slight smile. She was the only sister who had so much as glanced in Rose's direction since Patience had singled her out as unworthy. Rose nodded in gratitude.

As eldress, of course, she should be guiding the ceremony. In the days of Mother Ann's Work, the eldress would be at least one of the instruments chosen to receive messages from the holy angel. Rose would be untruthful if she did not admit to some relief—much as she loved the Society, her talents had always been more practical than supernatural. She had fit well into the trustee's position, but she sometimes felt herself lacking as eldress. She resolved to redouble her efforts toward spiritual understanding. But she doubted she would ever become more than an indirect instrument of Holy Mother Wisdom. It simply wasn't in her nature.

Following Patience, the sisters wove out of the waiting room and headed for the sickrooms. Rose and Josie brought up the rear. They marched into Nora and Betsy's room, singing a rousing tune. The girls were sitting up in their cradle beds, their eyes wide and their cheeks spotted pink with excitement. The sisters swirled around the girls, sweeping carefully underneath their beds and over their heads, as if chasing away evil spirits. Irene paused in her sweeping to pat Betsy's head.

"Isn't it lovely, Rose?" Josie's plump face beamed. "I can just feel Mother Ann watching on with pleasure, can't you?"

Rose drew in a breath to answer, but her response froze on her lips. Patience had stopped marching. She turned around to face the line of sisters behind her. They halted so suddenly that they ran into each other. Patience stretched her arms straight up in the air with her hands cupped as if holding a bowl. She squeezed her eyes shut and clenched her jaw.

Her scream began as a low rumble in her throat, like the growl of a wild beast. The sound grew in power and swelled into a human cry of anguish.

"Nay!" Patience shouted. "Nay, sweet Mother, the feel of it is too terrible for me. Let me be free of it." Her grimace of pain melted into a peaceful expression, as if her prayer had been answered. Slowly she turned in a circle, keeping her hands cupped and steady so as not to spill their contents. Her speed picked up. Twirling now, faster and faster, she moved her lips in silent prayer until, with a grunt, she flung her invisible burden toward the group of sisters gathered around Nora's and Betsy's beds. She lowered her arms and stood still, panting.

When she spoke, her voice was low and menacing. "You are fools," she said. "There are no secrets from Mother, and what Mother knows, I now know. In this village there are sins the angels blushed to tell me. Even the children are sinners here." She looked from Nora to Betsy, who clutched the sides of the cradle beds. "The sacred fire cannot cleanse the hearts in this room, in this village. The holy angel gave me all he could, and it wasn't enough."

Irene put a hand on Nora's shoulder, and Patience flashed a dark look at her. "The sinner comforts the sinner," she said. "If you have not given up all worldly ties, you are not a Believer!"

Patience's fierce gaze scanned the group, then traveled over their shoulders. Rose looked behind her to find the brethren gathered just outside the sickroom door. Benjamin and Thomas stood in front, both returning Patience's stare with simmering anger. Patience's lips curved in what might have been a smile, if any warmth had reached her eyes. She took two steps toward the door, and the sisters parted to allow her to speak to the brethren. She pointed to Benjamin.

"Your sins are too many to recount. Mother knows them all, and she weeps for you. The sin of pride is only one, and perhaps the least. There are others . . . Mother warns me not to defile the air with them. They are too horrible. You must confess them all to the Society, or she will be forced to reveal them for you."

Patience turned her attention to Thomas. "Your sins are recorded," she said. "On earth as in heaven."

Thomas blanched. He took a menacing step into the

room, but a strong hand grabbed his arm from behind. Rose recognized Wilhelm's corded forearm.

Patience closed her eyes and released a sigh that seemed to deflate her whole body. "The angel is gone," she said. "Mother has left, and she has taken back her brooms and her holy fire. The cleansing gift is closed."

Wilhelm pushed Thomas aside and stepped into the room. "Is Mother angry with us?" he asked.

Patience opened her eyes and studied him in silence for a few moments. "Mother was disappointed," she said, "but there is hope."

Wilhelm took another step into the sickroom and reached out his arms, palms upward, in supplication. "What must we do?"

"There must be a purging," Patience said. "We must rid ourselves of the evil that has been allowed to thrive in this Society. All sins must be dredged out, confessed, atoned for—not just sins of deed, but sins of the heart and mind, as well. We must do this, or Mother, who loves us beyond human comprehension, will do it for us."

❧

TWELVE

A LIGHT, LATE SUPPER FOLLOWED THE CLOSING OF THE sweeping gift, but it did not end Rose's misgivings. She had decided to dine in the Center Family house, preferring to face suspicious sisters and brethren than Wilhelm. She still had no idea why Patience had relayed an angelic message that she was unworthy, so she had no way to defend herself.

Gennie's report of Elsa's behavior during the cleansing was now known throughout the community. Elsa had enjoyed herself, but her only interesting accusation was that Patience was a witch, a follower of false spirits.

With Elsa accusing Patience of witchcraft, and Patience accusing numerous others of a host of sins, the dining room air was tight with foreboding. Rose found herself in the unaccustomed position of being grateful to Elsa for casting some doubt on Patience's credibility. Some of the sisters seemed less wary around Rose now, while others still doubted her. Gennie, of course, was defiantly loyal, even to the point of speaking to Rose during the meal. Rose did not rebuke her. She knew Gennie had chosen the most public arena to show her support.

Patience was once again absent from the meal. Rose searched her memory and realized that, unless she had another source of food, Patience had not eaten in two days. And before that, she had eaten only a few bites of her meals. Rose looked at her own full plate. She wasn't eating well herself just now, and waste was sinful. Unless she was ill, she was honor-bound to clean her plate. For a tiny second she considered pleading illness so she could retire to her room, but instead she swallowed a large bite of corn pudding. Once she started dissembling to avoid difficulty, it would be time to withdraw as eldress. Nay, she would not run away. After supper, she would find Patience, and they would have a good, long talk.

"If that woman thinks she can get away with this," Gennie hissed under her breath, "then she needs her thinking corrected." Gennie had remained calm through the evening meal, for Rose's sake, but once she was alone in her own retiring room, her temper erupted. She paced the room, flung the top sheet to the foot of her bed, threw herself on the mattress, then jumped up to pace again. Patience's door had been open and her room empty when Gennie had arrived, so she didn't care how much noise she made.

"She has got to be stopped," Gennie announced to one of the other two beds, as if someone were in it. "Rose may believe in this holy-angel nonsense, but I don't. That woman is no better than Elsa. She's faking, she's got to be. But why? What's her purpose? Well, I'll just have to find out."

She was supposed to go to bed and stay out of it; Rose was planning to talk with Patience. But Gennie couldn't do nothing. As if on cue, she heard Patience's door close. At least she could listen in on Patience, maybe find out if she had some secret source of food no one knew about.

Gennie heard familiar noises in the room next door. Drawers opened and closed. A light sound like the splash of water. Patience must be preparing for bed. Then the retiring room door opened and closed. The clicking sounds were quieter this time, but Gennie was sure she'd just heard Patience leave. Of course, she could just be visiting the bathroom. That would make sense. But usually the sisters left their retiring room doors open except when they were in them, dressing or sleeping. Patience's door had been open before she returned. Why would she close it now? Of course. Patience wanted everyone to think she was in her room, asleep.

Gennie raced for her own door. She was so glad that she hadn't undressed—and that she no longer had to worry about hiding her curls under a white cap. She closed her own door, too, just in case someone decided to come looking for her. Quickly she checked the bathroom and found it empty, as she'd suspected. She wasted no more time being quiet. She wished she'd insisted on wearing her own worldly clothes as she gathered up her ankle-length work dress to avoid tripping as she ran down the stairs.

When she reached the front door of the dwelling house, she quieted down. She really didn't know if Patience had left the building. What if she were making secret visits to the kitchen? She eased open the swinging door between the dining room and the kitchen and peeked through the crack. The room was dark. She held her breath and listened, but not a sound reached her. Gently she slid through the door into the kitchen. If Patience was there, she was either dead or hiding in the pantry.

Gennie turned to leave, then stopped herself. She was being a coward, and she knew it. She had to make absolutely certain that Patience wasn't ill or hidden, even if it led to an embarrassing situation. Gennie avoided thinking about possible danger. Patience was odd, but surely she wasn't dangerous. Was she?

This is silly, she told herself sternly. She flipped on the light and called out, "Hello, is anyone in here?" She walked toward the pantry at the far end of the room. "I thought I heard a noise, so I . . ." She had nearly reached the pantry, and fear tightened her throat. She breathed in deeply and focused on keeping her voice steady. "I was feeling a little hungry," she said, hoping there was no one nearby to notice the change in her story. "I thought there might be some of that apple cobbler left. Or, that is, maybe just some spiced apples,'' she finished, realizing that apple cobbler would not be kept in the pantry. *I certainly hope my life doesn't depend on this performance,* she thought.

She reached for the pantry door. Her sweaty palm slid on the handle. She wiped it on her dress and tried again. Feeling as if she might faint before she could see inside the pantry, she yanked the door open. The pantry was dark, but light from the kitchen spread a few feet inside. The shelves were filled with neatly stacked jars and sacks, all resting motionless, as they should. Thank God the Shakers were so fastidious, Gennie thought. If so much as a mouse had moved in that pantry, her heart would surely have frozen. They'd have found her in the morning, still clutching that doorknob.

Patience was not in the kitchen. And Gennie wasn't sure where to search next. There were other kitchens in other buildings. She could be raiding those. But maybe she was going at this all wrong, Gennie thought. Maybe Patience really was fasting. Maybe fasting was part of her gift. Surely that would be how a Believer would think. And if that was the case, what other reason would Patience have for slipping out at night? She was so secretive about her precious experiments with medicinal herbs. Could they be connected somehow with her behavior? If so, she might have gone to the Medicinal Herb Shop.

No sooner had she thought the words than Gennie sped out the dwelling house into the darkness. It seemed cooler, but perhaps that was because Gennie was creating her own breeze. Eager again, she ran around the corner of the dwelling house and cut through the kitchen garden to reach the Medicinal Herb Shop. The moon had yet to appear, and she trod on at least two plants in her haste. They would be noticed, but with any luck, the kitchen sisters would assume that some clumsy but hungry neighbors had helped themselves to some food.

She knew her worldly status would not be enough to

excuse her presence at the shop after dark, so she stole around the side of the building until she reached a small window. Gennie was barely five feet tall, so even on tiptoe she could not see inside. She looked around for something to stand on. The Shakers were so tidy, though, that nothing was ever left lying around. At least she could tell that the window was dark, so it was possible that Patience had gone elsewhere. She decided to take a chance. Bending her knees, she bunched her muscles and leaped into the air as high as she could, which was just enough to give her a split-second view inside the shop. She couldn't be sure, of course, but it looked empty. She saw no movement, no pinpoint of light to indicate someone working. Just to be sure, she crouched for another jump. Again she could find no sign of anyone inside.

Gennie was panting, sticky with sweat, and feeling shaky. Since leaving North Homage, she'd done much less physical labor, and she wasn't as strong as she'd been. It had been a while, too, since she had been so nervous—or so excited. She peered around her to make sure no one had decided to roam about after dark—a frowned-upon activity in the Society—then slid around to the back door. Her plan had been to follow Patience, but something told her that secrets resided in the Medicinal Herb Shop. She wanted a look at some of those journals the workers were always scribbling in.

She hesitated with her hand on the back doorknob. Now she was really stepping over the line. If she was caught, she'd never be allowed to stay or even return, and her behavior would reflect on Rose, perhaps throw suspicion on her. Yet Rose truly needed her help. If she could find out what these people were up to, it might help erase Patience's smear on Rose's good name, and possibly explain what happened to Nora and Betsy. It was worth the risk.

The door would not be locked, Gennie knew. As deputy sheriff of Languor County, Grady had warned the Shakers repeatedly to install locks, but so far they had refused. And with any luck, the brethren would be efficient as always, so the door would open smoothly and quietly. She turned the knob and eased the door open a crack. She peered inside and saw nothing to alarm her. She had a full view of Patience's end of the room, and it was empty. She edged the door open another inch to see into the rest of the room. It, too, looked unoccupied.

She heard something in the distance—it sounded like the wail of a wild animal. Was that a branch cracking underfoot behind her? She dove through the door, pulled it shut behind her, and leaned her shoulder against it. Alternately gasping and holding her breath, she listened for sounds outside. Nothing. It was her guilty imagination, administering punishment. Grady would probably put a protective arm around her shoulders and tell her to leave the detecting to him, if she told him about this episode. She decided she wouldn't tell him.

Gennie turned and took in the room. A marbled moon had risen and sent pale streaks through the high windows and across the worktables. It was enough light, she decided. Better not risk turning on a lamp. Both tables had been tidied, so nothing was left in midexperiment. Gennie located the journals—one set precisely in the corner of Patience's table, two more in a neat stack on the brethren's table, and a fourth, still open, on Andrew's small desk.

She went first to Andrew's. Flipping back page after page, she found herself getting bored. It contained nothing but lists of herbs produced and packaged, comments about the crops, ideas for increasing or improving yields, new ideas for businesses, and an occasional comment about the weather, all written in a sprawling hand. Didn't Andrew participate in the experimenting? Rose had seemed to remember him saying that he did. So where were his ideas for various concoctions?

She moved on to the brethren's table and lifted off the top journal. It contained precise columns of names and numbers—customers, orders, amount of product delivered, remuneration received, and profit for the Society. The profits were solid, if not stunning. The journal contained no personal comments or observations. Surely it belonged to Thomas Dengler.

As she reached for the next journal, probably Benjamin's, a shadow crossed her hand. It had no shape and was gone so quickly she wondered if she'd imagined it, but her heart gave a lurch and she froze. She forced herself to look toward the window. Unbroken moonlight filled the small square. Must have been a bird; it was too quick for a cloud.

Gennie exhaled and pulled the journal toward her. Benjamin's handwriting was virtually illegible. Pages were filled with what looked like calculations, some crossed out, some with exclamation marks next to them. Short comments filled the margins, but Gennie could make out none of them in the dim light. At least this was more what she'd expected to see, but she'd never be able to interpret this scribbling. She flipped through all the pages. Most showed the same pattern, but a few contained paragraphs of writing. Gennie squinted with all her might and could make out only a few words—''shade'' and ''sun'' seemed scattered through the pages, along with the names of various months. He must have been recording observations about growing conditions and patterns.

About halfway through, the writing stopped. Growing impatient, Gennie held the journal above the table and shook it, in the dim hope that she had missed something, maybe a loose note that she could sneak away with her. Nothing fell out, but as she waved the pages back and forth, she noticed some writing on the end pages. She put the book down and opened the back cover. The last two pages, laid flat, held some sort of design. The area was divided into equal squares, some with various-sized dots or circles inside. It reminded Gennie of something, but she couldn't think what. She held it up and back a ways, which made it harder to see but showed the pattern more clearly. Now she recognized it. The design looked like a diagram for a garden.

She laughed out loud, then glanced around nervously. Who would have thought that arrogant, earnest Benjamin would be given to flights of gardening fancy? No wonder he hid his doodling on the back pages. She held the book closer and noticed tiny letters in or near the circles. His dreaming must extend to identifying plants and where they should go. Like the rest of his writing, the abbreviations were unreadable. Too bad, Gennie thought, grinning. She'd love to know if he had any flowers planned for his garden—especially those with no useful purpose.

Aware of the passing time, Gennie replaced the two journals as she had found them, then hurried to Patience's table. Her journal was much like Benjamin's, only neater. Gennie could read the writing, for all the good it did her. She realized how little she knew about medicinal herbs, beyond the little she had picked up from Josie, who used fairly well known remedies. Many of the ingredients were unfamiliar to her, and to make matters more difficult, Patience seemed to have her own naming scheme. She switched from common names to Latin names, then back to a different common name. Gennie recognized the name "yellow coneflower," a daisylike flower that Josie sometimes used as a diuretic. On other pages Gennie saw instead the plant's Latin name, *Rudbeckia laciniata,* and again later, "thimbleweed." Was Patience scatterbrained, or was this an attempt to keep her recipes confusing to the casual reader? Could some of the names Gennie didn't recognize actually be invented, or could they perhaps be plants that grew in the East?

As she had done with the others, Gennie skimmed through the book until she came to blank pages. On a whim, she flipped to the last two pages. It took a moment for her to comprehend what she was seeing. There it was, the very same design she'd just seen in Benjamin's journal. She held the book up so that it caught the moonlight. The same division into squares, with dots and circles marking plantings. Only the handwriting was different. Here the notations next to the circles were in tiny, neat printing. Even so, she couldn't understand what she was reading. It must be some sort of abbreviation system or code. She couldn't be sure without more light, but some of the letters looked more like symbols or tiny drawings.

She sighed and closed the journal. But her curiosity wouldn't leave her alone. More than anything, she wanted to know what those letters and symbols looked like, and she needed light to find out. It was worth the risk. Besides, Shakers worked from before sunrise to after sundown— surely no one would be awake to see a small light in the Medicinal Herb Shop.

Grabbing the book, she wove through the shadowy room to Andrew's desk and switched on the small lamp. She slid onto Andrew's chair, sitting on the edge because her feet did not touch the ground. Some instinct told her to be ready to move quickly. She leaned over the book, trying to keep her head out of the small circle of light, and puzzled over the last two pages. She'd been right in her guess—tiny letters were interspersed with equally minuscule drawings. One looked like a bell; another resembled a musical instrument, a horn of some sort. The letters meant nothing to Gennie. They didn't seem to represent any herbs, or any other plants, whose names were familiar to her. Could she have been mistaken in her first impression? Might this be more than a garden design? Maybe it was a map of some sort.

She didn't have time to let her imagination wander unfettered. It must be past midnight. If she wanted to be up and ready to work at 4:30, she'd better work fast. She rummaged through the storage area under the flap that served as a writing surface. It was surprisingly messy for a Believer's desk. Finally she found a scrap of plain paper and a pencil. As faithfully as she could, she began to copy Patience's drawing onto the much smaller paper.

She clicked her tongue with frustration, and the sound startled her. All these little details . . . This would take her all night. Maybe she could find a larger piece of paper, thin enough for tracing. She ripped up her partial drawing and tossed it in a wastebasket.

Finding nothing in Andrew's desk, she began a quick search of the room, taking the journal with her. Just to be safe, she turned off the lamp. It didn't light anything beyond the desk anyway.

Against the wall, behind Patience's table, Gennie found a narrow door. She hadn't noticed it before. Must be a storage closet. Tossing the journal back on the worktable, she opened the door and peered inside. The room beyond really was no deeper than the cupboards and drawers built into the walls in other Shaker buildings. It must have been used to store tall, narrow objects—perhaps broom handles—used by the broom makers who had originally used the shop.

Gennie stepped inside. She just fit between the door and the wall. The room had a musty smell. Before the door swung shut behind her, a quick scan revealed nothing resembling forgotten stores of paper. Gennie turned to leave. She grasped the inside knob and began to push when she heard a sound she could not mistake—the faint whoosh of a well-oiled door opening to the drone of crickets, followed by the shuffle of footsteps. Gennie followed her instincts. She kept the closet door shut, with her inside.

Through the thin door Gennie could hear someone walking around the shop, coming closer to her, then apparently stopping at or near Patience's table. Was it Patience herself? Where had she been until now? Her heart fairly bouncing in her chest, Gennie tried to remember where she had left Patience's journal. Was it close enough to where she'd found it that Patience wouldn't suspect that someone had been looking at it?

The air in the closet was laden with ancient wood dust and mildew. Gennie's nose tickled. She held her breath and pinched her nose until she saw spots before her eyes. The footsteps stopped right in front of her door, and Gennie leaned against the back wall, praying to God, Holy Mother Wisdom, Jesus, Mother Ann, Mother Lucy, and a couple of long-dead elders, just for good measure. The footsteps tapped away.

A long period of anxious confusion followed. Gennie pressed her ear against the door, hoping to hear the sounds of someone leaving the building. Her legs were beginning to ache, and every few minutes she had to stifle a sneeze. In the close quarters, the air grew increasingly stuffy as her body heat combined with the hot air left over from the day. The cotton of her work dress stuck to her back and chest. She considered trying to strip it off, but she envisioned an elbow hitting the wall and the door flying open to reveal her in her underclothes.

The minutes dragged, and the oppressive atmosphere was making her sleepy. She began to drift, not sure if she was fully awake at all times. The silence lasted so long that she thought she must have fallen asleep and missed the sound of a door opening and closing. Then the footsteps jolted her again, though they seemed farther away now. Was the visitor over on the brethren's side of the room?

Gennie's legs were shaking, and she was afraid she would fall, so she leaned against one of the narrow walls that formed the side of the closet and let herself slide down until she sat on the floor, her body parallel with the door. She could not fully stretch out her legs, so she wedged her toes against the opposite side wall and leaned her head back. She could stay awake no longer. Again she worked through her list of prayer recipients. After all, they had been good to her before; perhaps they would listen to her one more time. *Please,* she prayed to each by name, *whatever you do, please don't let me snore.* By the time the front door finally opened and closed again, Gennie was fast asleep.

THIRTEEN

ROSE SPED ACROSS THE DEW-SOAKED GRASS IN THE DARK. She cut around the back of the Infirmary, through the medic garden, to avoid curious, sleepless eyes that might be watching the central path from their retiring rooms. The humid night air weighed on her, but not as heavily as the memory of the evening she had just endured.

Rose had been in demand since the evening meal, and it had been far from pleasant. Moreover, she'd been frustrated in her plan to corner Patience for a pointed talk. She'd had to wait until now, well after bedtime, and not far enough from tomorrow's wake-up bell.

Wilhelm's harangue had been the low point of the evening. They'd spent nearly two hours in the library of the Ministry House, following evening worship, rehashing the sweeping gift until Rose regretted her vow of nonviolence. All Wilhelm really wanted to know was precisely how Rose was unworthy, as Patience had declared her to be, and it was the one question that Rose could not answer.

Many others had avoided her, doubt in their faces— except for her friends, of course, who drove her frantic with their solicitousness, thereby showing that they weren't sure of her, either. Only Gennie and Agatha seemed to understand that she needed to be left alone to track down the details of Patience's accusation. Gennie had sat, polite and silent, through the brief evening worship service, then yawned and gone straight to bed, pausing only to hug Rose in front of the entire village. Frail Agatha, who often stayed in her room during evening activities, made her way to the family room and sat next to Rose for the service, reaching over to squeeze her hand during prayers.

Rose had no idea what time it was, and she didn't care. Nor did she care that Patience would undoubtedly be asleep. She had no intention of waiting for morning to confront her accuser. Rose believed in her heart that Mother Ann sent angels to speak to Believers through her chosen instruments, but nothing could convince her that Mother would have chosen Patience, or anyone, for such a vicious mission. Agatha was right, Patience's gifts seemed authentic. Rose was prepared to concede that someone—or something—spoke through her. But she doubted it was a holy angel. She did not intend to waste any more minutes allowing possible wickedness to fester in her Society.

The Center Family Dwelling House was dark and silent as Rose slipped in the front door. She climbed the sisters' staircase as quietly as she could, given her simmering temper, and went straight to Patience's retiring room door. As she raised her hand to knock, she was glad to note that Gennie's door was closed, so the sound probably would not awaken her. Apparently Patience slept through the knock, as well. Rose tried again, this time a shade louder. Still no response. Fearing Patience might be in another trance, or worse, Rose cracked open the door.

The room had three narrow beds, left over from the days when Believers filled the dwelling houses. Now each Believer had a private room, unless he or she preferred company. Even in the dim room, she could see that all the beds were empty. Closing the door behind her, she flipped on a lamp. None of the beds had been turned down, but the sheet on one showed an indentation, as if someone had sat on it.

The rest of the room was spartan, even for a Shaker retiring room. In addition to the beds, it contained a small table with a ladder-back chair, a rocking chair, and several drawers. A small, square storage area was built into the wall. The wall pegs circling the entire room were mostly empty. Hangers hung from two of them—one holding a light blue, striped Sabbathday dress, the other, a second brown work dress. Rose saw no sign of a journal, which most North Homage Believers kept on their desks or tables, even if they wrote only occasionally.

Despite her eagerness to find Patience, Rose couldn't miss the opportunity to look around the room. She told herself it wasn't really snooping; she truly needed to find out more about this strange and perhaps dangerous woman. She began with the drawers, which were less than half full. Patience had the usual supply of underclothing, stockings, kerchiefs, and caps. A quick perusal revealed nothing suspicious or threatening. No pact with the devil, Rose thought, tempted to laugh at herself.

She opened a small, square door at about shoulder level, revealing a recessed storage area, similar to the one in Rose's own retiring room. In hers she might keep a few small books, or papers, or the few letters she received from the world. Patience kept nothing in hers. Rose gazed around her in puzzlement. She'd found not a single book or journal or scrap of paper in the entire room. Nothing at all to mark Patience as an individual.

Her search had raised more questions than it answered, and Rose was all the more determined to find Patience at once. The Medicinal Herb Shop seemed the obvious place to start looking. Forgetting any need to be quiet, she flung open the retiring room door and found herself staring into an ear. The ear became a face—a scarlet face with wide eyes. A disheveled Sister Gertrude, in her summer nightgown, stood frozen in the doorway.

"I . . . Rose, I . . ." Gertrude stammered as she backed into the hallway.

Rose felt laughter bubble up in her throat, as much from relief as from amusement. She grinned, which didn't alleviate Gertrude's embarrassment, but it seemed to calm her.

"I'm sorry, Rose, truly," Gertrude whispered. "This isn't what it seems." She grabbed her long gray hair and began twisting it into an awkward braid.

Rose beckoned her into Patience's room and closed the door. "Patience could return at any moment, so we must be quick," she said.

Gertrude gave a hesitant nod. "It was the heat, you see. I couldn't fall asleep, and then I heard so many doors opening and closing, and footsteps on the stairs, followed by more footsteps. It just didn't seem a normal night at all. So I decided to get up for a while. I pulled my rocking chair over to the window and started to catch up on my journal. I've been so tired lately, you know, running the kitchen in this dreadful heat, that I haven't had time to record how many jars of the new herbal jams and jellies and so forth we've finished canning, and—"

Rose arched her eyebrow a fraction to quell the flood of time-wasting details.

"Well, anyway," Gertrude continued, "I glanced out the window now and then, and I saw her, clear as clear, in the moonlight."

"Patience?"

"Had to be. Tall woman in a Shaker work dress and white cap, stumbling along like she was—well, I hate to say this, but it looked like she was drunk."

Rose was puzzled. "What direction does your room face?"

"West."

"So she couldn't have been heading for the Medicinal Herb Shop," Rose mused. "But where . . ." A dreadful thought occurred to her. "Gertrude, she surely wasn't going to the Trustees' Office, was she?" Only brethren lived in the Trustees' Office now, including Andrew.

"Nay, she went right past it, far as I could tell." Her brow furrowed as she remembered the scene. "It seemed as if she might be heading out toward Languor."

"Good heavens! On foot? That's eight miles. And at

night! Why would she cut through the grass? Why not take the road? She'd be seen leaving the village just as easily either way." Rose sighed. "I can see I won't be getting any sleep tonight. But you get back to bed, Gertrude."

"I'm not sleepy at all," Gertrude assured her. "I can be dressed in a minute, and I could help you look for her. I don't believe a word that woman said about you."

"I'm grateful for that," Rose said, as she transformed a pat on Gertrude's shoulder into a firm grip on her elbow, "but you can do the most good by getting some rest so you can run the kitchen tomorrow. We need you." She guided Gertrude back into the hall and gave her a gentle shove toward her own retiring room. Gertrude's face reflected her disappointment, but to Rose's relief, she returned to her room without further objections. Rose had no intention of providing even more fodder for the morning's kitchen gossip, if she could help it.

As she headed for the women's staircase, Rose's mind sifted through her alternatives. She noticed that Gennie's door had remained closed, so all the ruckus must not have awakened her. Good, she'd leave her to sleep. Now, how to locate Patience? Rose certainly wasn't going to walk to Languor, if that was where Patience had gone. However, it wouldn't be a good idea to drive right now, either. The Society's black Plymouth was kept next to the Trustees' Office, and Andrew would surely hear if she tried to start it up. In fact, much of North Homage might hear. She decided to walk in the direction Patience had taken, at least to the edge of the village. She might be wasting her time, but it was all she could think of at the moment. If she found no hints to Patience's whereabouts, she'd consider awakening Andrew to discuss the next step. She'd best call him from another building, though, in case someone saw her enter, at night, a building inhabited entirely by brethren.

By the time she'd formulated her plan, she was already out the women's entrance to the Center Family Dwelling House and walking past the back of the Trustees' Office.

Though she refused to turn around, she imagined she could feel Gertrude's eyes on her back.

The moon bathed the Trustees' Office in milky light, and the damp Kentucky bluegrass swished faintly under her feet. Going west, there was nothing beyond the Office except the road to Languor. To her right were acres and acres of herb fields. The straight rows of mounded plants looked like hills of snow as the moonlight reflected off the heavy dew. Just west of the fields was the old cemetery, unused since 1882, with some woods to the north. In front of her was a hilly, wooded area, unsuitable for cultivation. Rose guessed that if Patience had not gone to Languor, she might have gone to the cemetery or the woods, either of which would provide her with privacy, if that was what she sought.

Rose veered off to her right, toward the cemetery. As she did so, she heard a wail coming from somewhere in the hills to her left. She stopped and listened. Wild dogs sometimes roamed the area, looking for food they could no longer get from equally hungry humans. Perhaps one was ill or injured.

Rose waited for several minutes, but the cry was not repeated. She began walking again, but she'd gone no more than a few steps when she heard sounds that were distinctly more human. At least, she had never heard a dog call out to the angels by name. She hurried toward the voice, though some instinct told her to approach quietly.

The hilly area had been allowed to grow wild. Misshapen trees, some many decades old, ringed the land in a scraggly circle. By this time of year, the undergrowth was knee-high. Since the land was unusable, no one had beaten down any paths, so Rose picked her way through the weeds and brambles as best she could. She tried not to think about what she might step on.

Rose followed the bursts of talking and came to a small stand of trees at the foot of a steep slope. The voice was close. She edged as close to the hill as she could, knowing the trees kept her hidden in deep shadow.

At the top of the hill, silhouetted in moonlight, stood Sister Patience. At first Rose thought she must be in another trance, but her gestures were tame, everyday. She seemed to be conversing with someone Rose couldn't see. She reached out with one hand, as if imploring, then sank to her knees and her mouth moved in prayer, though Rose could hear no words. The weight of her prayers seemed to push her toward the ground until she lay facedown, her arms stretched out in front of her.

Perhaps this is a trance, after all, Rose thought. She watched and waited. If Patience didn't move soon, she should intercede. Just as she was about to move out of her hiding place, Patience drew herself slowly up to her knees, then leaned back on her feet and pushed to a standing position. Again she conversed with the wind, but this time, it seemed, with pleasure rather than in supplication. Rose had never seen Patience's face lit with joy before; the emotion transformed her stern features into dark beauty.

Patience reached out with both hands this time, then drew them back, cupped as if something had been poured into them. The gesture was similar to her movement in the sweeping gift when she had taken the symbolic fire. However, instead of sprinkling invisible fire, she placed the object on the ground and sat in front of it. She leaned over it and broke off a piece, then put it in her mouth and chewed with ecstasy. In six more bites, she had consumed the invisible food.

The movements struck a chord in Rose's memory, but she couldn't identify it yet. She knew she hadn't seen anything like this before, but perhaps she had read about it. Had Agatha described it? She would ask as soon as possible.

Patience began to speak, more loudly this time, so Rose could catch a word here and there. It sounded like a prayer of thanks for what Patience called "celestial food."

With a sudden twist of her body, Patience faced toward Rose and started to march down the hill, singing a lively but unfamiliar tune. In her curiosity, Rose had stepped around her protective tree. In her dark blue dress, the shadows might still hide her, but if Patience continued toward her, she would surely be exposed. Her first impulse was to jump back behind the tree, but a split second of thought told her the movement would make her more visible. She stayed where she was, rigid and still as the trees around her, trying to govern her ragged breathing as Patience marched directly toward her.

Halfway down from the crest of the hill, Patience stopped, did a marching turn, and circled the circumference two times. Rose slid back into her hiding place before Patience returned to the summit and stopped.

Again Patience prostrated herself in prayer, then stood and accepted an invisible object from invisible hands. This one she held to her lips and sipped. After placing the vessel on the ground with care, she twirled around it, her arms flung out from her sides.

The pantomime repeated, again and again, each time with a different nourishment and a unique response. The fascination had worn off, and Rose felt her knees begin to buckle. Her determination to have it out with Patience had dimmed long ago. Yet she kept watching. Patience was exerting enormous energy for someone eating only air. Rose herself was almost fainting from exhaustion, and she longed to know how Patience kept going. Perhaps she was witnessing a true gift?

Finally Rose conceded. She considered interrupting Patience's activities, but to intrude upon a gift would be considered tantamount to unbelief. As eldress, she could not afford to give such an impression, especially as she herself inched toward accepting the gift as true. She left Patience enjoying yet another celestial dish and made her weary way back to the Ministry House and a few hours of sleep.

FOURTEEN

IN HIS SEARCH FOR A RAG TO CLEAN OFF HIS WORK SPACE Sunday morning, Andrew opened the closet door in the Medicinal Herb Shop, and out tumbled Gennie. At least, she felt as if she'd tumbled out. She'd been jolted awake by the sound of someone's shoes approaching the closet, but hoisting herself to a standing position in the narrow space proved difficult for her stiff joints. By steadying herself with one elbow against the wall and the other against the door, she had achieved a crouch when the door opened, removing half her support. She tilted sideways and sat down sharply.

Andrew stared at her, his mouth slightly open but no words forming. Gennie rolled to her knees and winced as her sore neck complained. Still mute, Andrew reached down and pulled Gennie to her feet. He showed no embarrassment over having touched a woman—and a young, worldly one, at that.

"What . . . ? Are you all right?" he asked, as she brushed clouds of dust from her wrinkled work dress.

"Fine, thanks," Gennie said, aiming for a sunny grin. She searched her groggy mind but could find nothing to say that would reasonably explain her presence in the closet. So she didn't mention it. "Gosh," she said, rushing toward the front door, "it must be close to breakfast time. Rose will be wondering where I am."

125

"Now, wait a minute," Andrew said. "You can't just roll out of the closet and run off. What in heaven's name were you doing in there?"

"Really, it would take too long, and Rose will be worried if I'm not at breakfast, so perhaps we could talk later?" Gennie whirled around and reached for the doorknob just as the door opened. Benjamin and Thomas appeared. She couldn't stop in time and crashed into Thomas's beefy torso. He didn't budge as Gennie's small body bounced off him and she stumbled backward. This time Benjamin caught her before she fell. *Wonderful,* Gennie thought, *now all I need is to find that Patience has been watching and will denounce me at worship for touching three brethren, all before breakfast.*

The three men encircled Gennie, so a casual rush for the door would be awkward. Though she couldn't tell them, she feared she was late making the first of her promised twice-daily calls to Grady. If he didn't hear from her, he'd come roaring into the village, and that would be an even bigger mess than she was in now. She tried her grin again, but she could sense its feebleness. She glanced around at the brethren's faces. Thomas's features were tight with irritation, Andrew still looked befuddled, and Benjamin exuded anger and suspicion.

"What were you two doing in here alone together so early in the morning?" Benjamin asked.

"I have no idea," Andrew said. He shrugged his shoulders with such innocence that Gennie realized the implications of Benjamin's question had escaped him.

Benjamin's frown deepened. "How can you not know?"

"What I meant was, we weren't here together. I just found her here in—"

"What Andrew means is that I just came here to do a bit of cleaning up before Patience started to work again after breakfast," Gennie said with breathless speed. "After all, I am being paid to help, and there's so little I can do yet—until I learn more about medicinal herbs, which I truly want to do, and I plan to study up on them right away. In fact, I haven't heard the breakfast bell, so maybe I'll have some time to start my studies right now, if I hurry.''

As Gennie inched around Thomas, she flashed a wide-eyed, pleading glance at Andrew. For once, he seemed to comprehend, for though he had no reason to do so, he kept quiet about finding her in the broom closet. But a warning look in his eye told her she'd best explain herself soon, or his silence wouldn't last forever.

Neither Thomas nor Benjamin appeared convinced, but they stood aside and let her pass. The breakfast bell rang as Gennie lifted her skirts and sprinted through the grass toward the Ministry House. She could feel the disapproving stares of Believers following the paths to the Center Family dining room, but she couldn't afford to slow down and heed the rules. She had to get to a phone, and fast. She picked up her pace, kicking up dust as she crossed the central path.

She was too late. She knew it as soon as the Ministry House came into view, with a dirt-streaked black Buick parked crookedly on the grass beside it. Grady had already arrived. Gennie stopped abruptly and stood in front of the building, panting. The front doors of the Ministry House opened. Rose stepped through one door, Wilhelm and Grady through the other. Gennie groaned. She did not fear Wilhelm's wrath or Grady's scolding so much as she regretted letting Rose down. Her behavior reflected on Rose. She steeled herself and began to walk toward the group.

"Gennie!" Grady bolted through the grass toward her, then swept her up in his arms. "My sweet one, what happened? Where have you been?" He held her away from him and looked at her disheveled condition. "My God, has anyone—''

"Grady, I'm fine, truly. No one has done anything to me, and to be honest, I just don't think I have the energy to explain right now." The effects of her brief sleep scrunched up in a closet were catching up with her.

"Thy lack of energy is of no concern to us, young

woman. Explain thyself.'' Wilhelm folded his thick arms
over his chest and glared at her. Even Rose looked a bit
cross. Gennie ran her hand through her rumpled hair, which
only served to draw attention to her unkempt appearance.
She couldn't tell the truth; that would start an uproar. She'd
be thrown out, and Rose would be embarrassed. Yet she
couldn't lie to Rose. So she fainted. It was all she could
think of, and it was a lie, of course, but a lesser one, she
hoped. Grady caught her. She hung limply and prayed
she'd be carried to the Infirmary—and that Wilhelm would
lose interest in a weak female.

"Let's get her to Josie at once,'' Rose said. "Wilhelm,
I don't know how long this will take, and I'm sure you
want to get back to your work. I'll deal with this.''

Wilhelm grunted. Gennie was tempted to open her eyes
to see if he'd left, but she resisted. She let herself hang as
deadweight in Grady's arms until she heard Josie's alarmed
voice and felt herself being placed on a bed. Then she fluttered her eyelids. She almost went into a real faint when
she saw the thunderheads gathering in Rose's eyes, and she
knew she was in serious trouble when Rose sent Josie and
a protesting Grady from the room, telling them to close the
door behind them.

Rose sighed deeply and crossed her arms. Gennie sucked
on her lower lip, a habit she'd formed in childhood whenever she'd incurred Rose's wrath.

"The next time you feign a faint," Rose said, "remember to fall flat on your face. Don't tilt so conveniently toward someone's arms. It's a dead giveaway.'' She pulled
a visitor's chair next to the bed. "Now, tell me what happened to you. Have you been hurt in any way?'' Rose's
tone had lightened. Relieved, Gennie sat up and curled her
legs underneath her.

She shook her head. "Only my dignity," she said.

"I am more interested in the truth than in dignity,'' Rose
said.

A momentary sadness drifted through Gennie's heart as

she realized how far she had wandered from Shaker teachings. Dignity was, of course, a thing of the world. A Believer would willingly mortify herself if it truly glorified God. Pride was unimportant—or worse, it was a hindrance, since it could so easily spill over into hubris.

Gennie told Rose, in precise detail, about her night in the closet of the Medicinal Herb Shop. Rose's expression grew puzzled, but she made no comment as Gennie described what she'd seen in the shop's journals. Nor did she share her thoughts when Gennie had finished. Instead, she stood and silently replaced the chair on its wall pegs. She gave Gennie a warm hug to show that all was well between them.

"Get some rest," she said, "and then go to the kitchen and tell Gertrude I said to give you a late breakfast. Then rest some more."

"But—"

"Rest, Gennie. I want you well and out of sight for the time being. Wilhelm has a great deal on his mind and may forget about you if you don't remind him with your presence. Then perhaps I won't be faced with the need to lie to him about your experiences."

"You would lie to him?"

Rose rubbed her forehead, as if it hurt. Blue-black circles underlined her eyes, and Gennie wondered if she had slept at all the night before. "May God forgive me, sometimes it is necessary." She gently brushed Gennie's cheek with her fingers. "I can't make sense of what has been happening these last few days, but I'm quite certain that something is wrong in the Medicinal Herb Shop. I don't know how dangerous it is. If what happened to Nora and Betsy is connected to the shop, then it may be life-threatening, and I want you to be safe. Do not work at the shop today."

"But I—"

"Make me a promise, Gennie."

Gennie sighed like a frustrated adolescent. "All right, I promise not to work at the Medicinal Herb Shop today."

*   *   *

Rose had missed breakfast, which was just as well, since it meant she also missed seeing Wilhelm. She decided that Patience had been fasting enough for both of them, so she stopped at the Center Family kitchen for some leftover brown bread. Gertrude and the kitchen sisters were cleaning when she arrived.

"My dear, how I wish you'd been at breakfast," Gertrude called to her as she entered. "You missed everything! Oh, haven't you eaten? No wonder you are much too thin. Here, sit and eat and I'll tell you what happened. You will be astonished." After years of kneading bread and wielding heavy trays, first as a kitchen sister and then as Kitchen Deaconess, Gertrude could move quickly and lift as much as most of the brethren. With one arm she snatched a wooden chair from a wall peg, then swept up a plate of bread chunks with the other. After pulling up another chair for herself, she took a deep breath and began speaking, her dishwater-roughened hands waving in excitement.

"If it had been any other day, I wouldn't have seen it, but wouldn't you know, today one of the kitchen sisters was ill, so I said I'd do the serving, since it's so much easier for me than for the others, who are so tiny I'm surprised they can lift themselves."

Rose waited. For once, she wasn't impatient with Gertrude's rambling conversation; it gave her a chance to chew.

"Well, I was delivering some more water pitchers to the sisters—everyone has been drinking so much water nowadays, what with this dreadful heat. I'd already brought more to the brethren, so I thought, well, I'd better do the same for the sisters. I'd just set a pitcher down next to Irene, and I heard her whisper, which, of course, she shouldn't have been doing at mealtime, but I could understand why, what with that woman never eating anything at all, and how can she keep that tall body of hers going, that's what I'd like to know."

Rose swallowed quickly. "Patience was at breakfast, then?"

"Yea, that's what I was saying. And I'd have known she was there even if I hadn't seen her myself, because I've gotten so's I can recognize her plate when it comes back. She just takes a little bit of everything, you see, and then she cuts it in tiny pieces and mashes it around the plate so it looks like leftovers, but I wasn't born yesterday. I know my leftovers!" Gertrude leaned back in her chair with an emphatic nod.

Rose, as usual, was confused, but rather than worry about it, she sought the right question. "And you saw something having to do with Patience?" she asked.

"Indeed I did. Patience and Irene. Irene leaned over and whispered to her, and what with me being so close, I could hear. Irene was concerned—she's such a sweet girl, isn't she? She saw that Patience was only pretending to eat, and she was worried, so she whispered to Patience that she knew it was awfully hot but to try and eat even a little bit, even if it didn't taste very good, just to keep up her strength. And that's when it happened. My heavens, I nearly dropped my last water pitcher, and what a mess that would have been. Patience jumped up from the bench so fast she jolted everyone else." To demonstrate—or, Rose suspected, simply to dramatize—Gertrude jumped to her feet, and her chair scraped behind her. The other kitchen sisters had paused in their work to watch the show.

"Then she held out her arm, like this, and pointed her finger right at Irene's face, no more than an inch from her nose, and then as loud as could be, she shouted at the poor girl. She said, 'Harlot!' A harlot, she called her. Little Irene. Anyway, she said, 'Harlot! You have sinned and sinned again! Not one but two!' " Gertrude sat down and leaned toward Rose. "What do you suppose she meant by that?"

"I don't know," Rose said.

The kitchen phone rang. Gertrude jumped up to answer it before any of the other kitchen sisters could get to it. The telephone was, after all, an instrument for gossip.

Rose leaned back to consider the implications of Gertrude's story. "Not one but two," Patience had said. Irene seemed so content as a sister. Could she really be breaking her vows with both Thomas and Benjamin? Or could the sins refer to something else in Irene's past—or present?

A cry from across the kitchen jolted Rose out of her thoughts. She turned her head, as did the other sisters, to see Gertrude hang up the phone receiver and put her face in her hands. Polly ran to her and guided her to a chair. Rose and the others gathered around. They waited in silence as Gertrude sobbed, knowing they were about to hear bad news, and willing to avoid hearing it for a few more moments.

Finally Gertrude lowered her hands and wiped away her tears. Polly pulled a clean hankie from her apron pocket, which Gertrude used noisily. She gulped to steady her voice.

"That was Josie," she said. "Hugo slipped away while we were eating our breakfast. She thought he seemed better yesterday and this morning. She left him alone to get some herbs from the Herb House and then come here and eat. When she got back, he was gone."

FIFTEEN

ROSE WENT DIRECTLY FROM THE CENTER FAMILY KITCHEN to Agatha's retiring room.

"If you are still hungry, please do finish my breakfast," Agatha said as Rose entered her room. The former eldress sat in her rocking chair, a light blanket covering her knees, despite the heat. She was sipping tea, but most of her breakfast was still intact on a tray on the table next to her.

"Are you not well?" Rose asked, placing a hand on her forehead as Agatha had done with her many times when, as a child, she had caught a fever and taken to her bed. Agatha's forehead was too cool, as was her hand when Rose took it, as if her blood had thinned to nothing.

"Oh, I'm fine, my dear, just rather upset about losing Hugo. Josie just sent word to me. I know it's best for him, but I will miss him. I suppose it brings to mind my own final journey. Oh now, don't you fret," Agatha said, as she saw the stricken look on Rose's face. "I'm not packing my bags yet. Now tell me, have you come to talk of Hugo's burial? Josie said it must be done soon because of the heat. I suspect Wilhelm will arrange something very soon."

"I'm sure he will," Rose said. "To tell the truth, I wanted to talk with you about some other issues, but if you are feeling too sad . . ."

"Rose, sit," Agatha said, with her old sternness. "I am

133

merely indulging myself. To be honest, I would rather be distracted. Tell me these issues of yours.''

Since Agatha had missed breakfast in the dining room, Rose began with Patience's denunciation of Irene, then told her about Gennie's night in the Medicinal Herb Shop, and her discoveries there. Finally she described her own night spent watching Patience's odd ritual on the hill. Agatha was the only one she could trust with such information. Moreover, if anyone could offer any insights into these happenings, it was Agatha, who had been a Shaker for nearly eighty years, thirty-five of them spent as eldress.

Agatha frowned into the distance for a few moments after Rose had finished. Then she lifted the blanket off her knees and reached for her cane, hooked over the arm of her rocking chair. Instinctively Rose reached over to help her, but Agatha shook her head with a show of impatience. Rose sat back and watched with combined concern and pride as Agatha pushed out of her chair and limped over to a small bookshelf that hung from several wall pegs.

Her last stroke had paralyzed her right side. With Josie's help, she had regained use of her arm and leg, but both were weak. She managed her cane with her right hand and did most everything else with her nondominant left hand. But Agatha was a tiny woman, and the bookshelf was too high. Rose understood.

"Is this the book?" Rose asked, casually, so she did not draw attention to Agatha's weakness.

"Yea, the hand-bound one," Agatha said. "Bring it to the table. I've something to show you."

Rose pulled both their chairs up to the table and placed the book in front of Agatha.

"When I was a young sister, the Society was very different than it is now," Agatha said, turning the fragile pages with care. "Mother Ann's Work was done, but it was not just an old story passed from sister to younger sister. I worked many rotations with older sisters who had experienced the Manifestations, some of whom were chosen instruments. I heard so many wonderful stories.'' She smiled and smoothed her hand over a page filled with a young, firm version of her own handwriting. ''I was so fascinated that I began to write the stories down at night, in my journal. I was lucky enough to share a retiring room with two girls who didn't report me for writing past bedtime, when there was moonlight.'' She turned a few more pages. ''Here, this is what I wanted you to see,'' she said, squinting at her writing. ''At least, I think it is. Read it, Rose. Read the beginning of it out loud, so I can be sure.''

Rose slid the book toward her and began.

''I was doing my rotation in the weaving room today, and Sister Beatrice entertained us with the most astonishing story. She was a young sister at New Lebanon—I doubt she'll ever get used to calling it Mount Lebanon—during Mother Ann's Work, in the 30's and 40's. She told us of a very special feast day, one which no one honors anymore, that arose during that time. Holy Mother Wisdom would visit from time to time, causing great joy and celebration. On one visit, the Believers were instructed to designate a holy hill, a secret place, never to be noted on a map, wherein a sacred fountain would reside, visible only to true followers of Mother Ann. Twice a year, they would march to the holy hill, sisters in one line, brethren in another, singing at the tops of their voices. Thousands of angels would hover above and send messages through their chosen instruments. Once, Beatrice said, Mother Ann sent each of them a tiny gold cross to protect them from evil. Sometimes they received baskets full of sparkling jewels and yards of fine silk. The angels delivered dish after dish of celestial food—grapes and succulent chickens and rare sweets, of which Believers would gratefully partake. They drank sacred water from the holy fountain and heavenly wines sent by the angels. For hours, often

a whole day, they would march and sing and laugh and receive holy messages.

"Later I asked Beatrice if North Homage Believers had celebrated these feast days, too. She said, 'Yea,' but then went back to her task. I pressed her, asked if we, too, had a holy hill and a heavenly fountain, and she grew irritable. Finally, she told me I must wait to know these things, that the name and location of the holy hill are secret and only if I signed the covenant would I be allowed to know. Though I promised that I longed to sign the covenant as soon as possible, Beatrice would not budge."

Agatha interrupted Rose's reading. "The rest is another topic," she said. "I was only sixteen, and I had to wait for what seemed an interminable length of time before I could sign the covenant."

"And now I can barely stand the suspense," Rose said. "What did you finally learn?"

"I suspect that you will not be surprised," Agatha said.

Rose nodded. "So the hill on which I watched Patience was North Homage's holy hill?"

"Yea, it was. No one speaks of it anymore, and it is not shown on any map of our village. I should have told you long ago, especially when we began to see your calling to be eldress, but I simply never thought of it. Until Wilhelm came to us, our ways had changed so that the feast on the holy hill seemed more like a story. After all, even I am not old enough to have witnessed it." She closed her journal and held it against her frail chest. "But once it inspired me so . . . I should have remembered. I should have prepared you more thoroughly."

"Agatha, no one could have been a better teacher for me. Even now, you are teaching me." These moments of self-doubt worried Rose. She wanted Agatha to look back and see what an extraordinary life she had led, and be certain that Mother Ann would welcome her someday. Though not too soon.

"Tell me more about this feast," Rose said. "What is the name of our hill?"

"Ah, the secret name. You must promise, of course, never to reveal it to outsiders."

Agatha seemed serious, so Rose answered with equal seriousness. "Of course."

Agatha nodded. "It was named the Empyrean Mount. I was told that we celebrated the feast for only two years before it fell into disuse. The Manifestations were quite exhausting, you see, and rather hard for the Ministry to control. So many instruments of the angels emerged that the feasts would go on all day and into the night, and Believers were dropping from exhaustion. And from hunger." Agatha gave a hint of a smile. "The celestial food was perhaps not as hearty as that in our own cellars. Anyway, the Ministry began to designate which instruments were to be heard, and they were always those who kept the worship shorter and calmer. It was the only way. The world derided the Society more and more for its strange rituals, all of which threatened our sales and therefore our financial survival. One must be practical, after all. Living like the angels does not require us to worship to the point of collapse and ruin."

Rose relaxed. This was the old Agatha, with her clear-sighted spirit. "Patience's behavior sounds as if she knew of this feast and was repeating it. But for what purpose?"

"Indeed," Agatha said. "For what purpose?" She shuddered, despite the heavy air in the room. "A part of me longs to believe that she is truly a chosen instrument, sent to us by Mother Ann to renew our faith and deepen our understanding. But something is not right here. I wish I could say what it is. I have watched her at worship and listened to the stories, and I am convinced she is not pretending. Her actions are true and yet not true."

"Do you sense a sickness of the mind?"

"The mind or the soul, I do not know. Or something else, perhaps another influence, an evil one in our midst. Has anyone any influence over her, do you think?"

"She seems to associate closely with no one," Rose said. "In fact, she has accused nearly everyone else of something evil, including myself. I doubt that anyone has the slightest influence over her. She sneers at Wilhelm, though her actions seem to support his hopes for us."

Agatha leaned back and rocked herself gently. Her eyes closed, and Rose felt a prick of guilt for tiring her.

"I should let you rest," Rose said.

"Nay, this is far more important than my naps," Agatha said in the stern voice that Rose remembered. "This picture or design you mentioned, the one Gennie saw," Agatha continued. "Have you seen it?"

"Nay, I've been waiting for a time when the Medicinal Herb Shop is empty."

"Don't wait any longer," Agatha said. "Go now."

Rose deposited Agatha's breakfast tray in the kitchen and discovered preparations under way for the noon meal. It was the perfect time to follow Agatha's urging to take a look at those designs; it wouldn't take long, and she'd still be able to race back to the Ministry House and change for the afternoon worship service. She helped in the kitchen until everyone was seated and served. When the activity had settled down, she peeked into the dining room and saw everyone from the Medicinal Herb Shop, except Patience. Never mind, if she ran into Patience at the shop, she'd simply send her off to eat. Surely she wouldn't openly defy an order from her eldress.

A kitchen sister laden with a heavy tray of cold soup reached the door to the dining room, and Rose held it open for her. No sooner had she allowed the door to swing shut and turned toward the outside door than the sound of sniffling stopped her. She followed the sound to the open pantry. Inside, Gertrude stood in front of the shelf holding the partially used jar of peppermint jelly she had fed to poor Hugo. Her shoulders shook, and she patted her cheeks with her apron.

"Gertrude, are you ill?" Rose asked softly.

Gertrude spun around, gulping air. "Oh, Rose, nay, never you mind about me. I'm fine, truly, it's just . . ." Pain contorted her features.

"Is it Hugo?"

Fresh tears spilled over Gertrude's lower eyelids and cascaded down her cheeks. Yet she said nothing. "I'd best get back to work," she said, the words catching in her throat.

"You are in no condition," Rose said, taking her elbow. But Gertrude wouldn't be cajoled out of the pantry. She slid from Rose's grasp and stepped farther back into the small room.

Rose was puzzled. She'd had no idea Gertrude had been so fond of Hugo. Unless . . . "Gertrude, Hugo was dear to us all, a very special brother. I hope you know you needn't feel guilt if you miss him deeply. There is no shame in love of the heart."

Gertrude let out a soft wail and pushed past Rose. She ran through the kitchen and out the back door, as all the kitchen sisters and Rose watched in confusion and dismay. After a few moments' hesitation, Rose hurried after her. Gertrude was well into her fifties, but by the time Rose reached the door, the Kitchen Deaconess was nowhere in sight. The kitchen and medic gardens were empty. Rose picked up her long skirt, ran to the southeast corner of the Center Family Dwelling House, and looked around the front, but again she saw no one. Now deeply concerned, Rose raced to the back of the building and toward the herb fields. None of the herbs was higher than her waist, so she could see that the fields were empty.

As she turned around to return to the building, she saw a flash of movement out of the corner of her right eye. She squinted toward the area containing the Empyrean Mount and was certain she saw the swish of a dark blue work dress among the trees. Gertrude must have gone there to be alone. Well, she wouldn't be for long. Rose headed toward the area, determined to pry Gertrude's troubles from her. But as she rounded the northwest corner of the dwelling house, Believers began pouring from the two front entrances and scattering toward other buildings to prepare for the worship service.

After her racing around in the noonday sun, Rose was dripping. She would need a quick sponge bath before changing into her blue-and-white-striped Sabbathday dress. As it was, she would have trouble being on time. She turned away and found herself walking toward Andrew, who stood on the unpaved central path, watching her. He gave her a quick, shy smile, which she returned.

"I'm surprised to see you," he said, as she approached him. "I thought perhaps you had eaten in the Ministry House." His brow furrowed. "You have eaten, haven't you?"

Rose shook her head and glanced away to hide the prick of pleasure she felt at his concern.

"You mustn't skip meals, you know," he insisted. "You need your strength."

"Believe me, it is a rare occurrence," she said, laughing to lighten the air between them.

"I wanted to be sure to tell you something," he said. "It may mean nothing, of course, but I know you have had doubts about Hugo's illness . . ." Andrew focused his eyes on a point in the distance and pursed his lips.

"Where did you hear that I had suspicions about Hugo's illness?" Rose asked.

Andrew's eyes refocused on her. "Ah. Well, it was something that Patience said. You see, I think someone was in the shop after hours a few weeks ago. Patience complained that Willy had been sloppy in his cleaning and had moved around some of her experiments, and Benjamin said he'd noticed the same thing."

"Have you asked Willy about it?"

"Yea, and he denied touching the experiments, but . . ." Andrew shrugged. "I'm sorry. I should have mentioned it to you earlier. Or to Wilhelm, of course."

"Of course, but . . ." Rose hesitated in confusion. "What did Patience say that linked this incident with Hugo's illness?"

To Rose's surprise, a faint flush colored Andrew's cheeks. He shrugged as if to dismiss the importance of what he was about to say. "Oh, she just remarked that with our medicinal herbs spread around the village, it was no wonder so many people were getting sick and you were so . . . suspicious." His halting tone told Rose that Patience had used far harsher words to describe her. She pressed no further.

"As I said, all of this may be completely unrelated to Hugo's or the girls' illnesses. But if someone has taken any of our medicinal herbs, well . . ." Andrew glanced toward the Trustees' Office, from which two brethren were emerging, dressed in their white Sabbathday shirts with blue vests and trousers. Because of the heat, Wilhelm had evidently told them to forgo their long surcoats.

"We haven't much time before the service," Rose said. "Thank you for telling me your suspicions."

Andrew nodded. An instant later, Rose was watching his back as he sprinted toward the Trustees' Office.

SIXTEEN

THE BRIEF SPONGE BATH BEFORE SLIPPING INTO HER SAB-
bathday garments made Rose hopelessly late for the public
worship service. She was certain to hear about Wilhelm's
displeasure later, but that did not concern her. For Believers, work had often been known to take precedence over
formal worship, so his disapproval would have little bite.

Horses and wagons and a few automobiles were parked
on the path outside the Meetinghouse, but from the number,
it looked as if the public was less interested in the Society
than it had been at times in the past. That was how Rose
preferred it, though she knew Wilhelm would be disappointed.

Rose slipped in the women's entrance and watched for
a few moments. Wilhelm had started without her, undoubtedly with glee, since he wanted Patience to lead the sisters
in the dancing worship. The sisters moved in a straight line,
their backs to Rose. Between them, she could see the
smaller number of brethren, in a row facing the sisters.
Though the large, two-story room was far from full, enough
people of the world had come that the benches were full
and a group of tall men stood in front of Rose, giving her
only a partial view of the dancers. She considered weaving
through them to join the sisters, but she preferred to watch.
Agatha must have stayed in her retiring room, and Gennie

was probably with Grady, because the sisters' benches were empty.

Rose eased along the wall until she came to a doorway leading into the remainder of the Meetinghouse, which held a number of unused rooms and an observation area that looked down on the worship from a window high in the wall of the large meeting room. She climbed the stairway to the observation room and slipped inside. Without turning on a lamp, she sat in front of the window and looked down on the dancers, now forming two circles, sisters on the outside and brethren inside. Fortunately, the far greater number of sisters kept the circles from coming close to each other.

The outer circle opened out and straightened again, led by one sister, who was, Rose soon realized, far too plump to be Patience. Elsa was leading the dancing. Rose examined each figure in turn and saw none that had Patience's tall, statuesque body, nor her natural grace. Elsa shook the room when she walked, but she was an adroit and often dramatic dancer. Still, she could never compare with Patience's intensity and fluidity.

One sister stumbled and lost her rhythm. She stepped back out of the line, looking lost. When she turned and made her way back to the benches, Rose saw that it was Gertrude, swiping at her cheeks with the backs of her hands. She sat down and hunched over in prayer. She must have moved quickly to have returned from the holy hill, changed dresses, and made it to worship on time. Or perhaps, Rose thought, it was Patience she had seen disappearing into the woods.

For the next few minutes, Rose forgot all but the spectacle below her. Unlike previous times when the service had been open to the public, the worldly visitors watched with apparent enjoyment. Some sat forward on their benches, straining to see every twirl and hop, while a few swayed with the music as if they wished to join in the dancing.

Though Rose could barely hear the a cappella choir of

two sisters and two brethren, it was clear that the dancers had moved from a march into a livelier song that gave the dancers an opportunity to match their movements to the words. She guessed they were dancing to "Awake My Soul," as they mimed awakening and then shook their bodies. The movements reminded her of Patience, dancing alone on the Empyrean Mount.

The dancers filed back to their benches, and Wilhelm strode to the podium, which was set between the women on one side of the room and the men on the other, to deliver the homily. Rose decided it was a good time to look for Patience. Wilhelm would be content to finish the service without her presence. She exited by a back door into the afternoon sunshine.

Entering the wild area of trees and undergrowth surrounding the Empyrean Mount felt like stepping into another world, from heat and blaring sun to damp shade, light to dark. The twitter of robins and rustle of dry leaves underfoot would have been soothing on any other day. Today Rose strained for the babbling, not of the small creek, but of prayers spoken in tongues. Beneath the earth sounds, she heard only silence.

She retraced the steps she'd followed yesterday toward the holy hill. Finding the trees she'd stood behind, she peeked around to see an empty hillside. No twirling or bobbing head appeared over the crest. She wasn't surprised; the silence had told her that Patience must have gone elsewhere. Yet why hadn't she come to the service? She'd known she was to lead the dancing. Surely she wouldn't have missed such an opportunity. Unless she had become ill. The fasting and trance-filled nights might suddenly have demanded payment in full. No longer concerned with stealth, Rose began circling the perimeter of the hill, at first following the small creek that ran next to it, then cutting around to the other side.

Patience was there, after all. As before, she lay facedown

on the ground in her position of humble prayer, her arms and legs spread out. Rose approached slowly. As she got nearer, she began to sense that it didn't matter if she gave warning of her presence. Patience was far too still. Her head was turned away, so Rose moved around to her other side. For reasons she did not immediately understand, Rose felt nothing, though she knew now that she was walking toward death. The slack lips did not move in prayer, and those dark eyes watched her approach without a blink or a flicker.

For Rose, as a Believer, death was bittersweet. It might mean the loss of a friend, but that friend was now with the Holy Father and Holy Mother Wisdom. Patience had not been a friend, yet Rose should have felt some joy for her. She knelt beside Patience and closed her eyes. It took several seconds for her to realize what disturbed her. The dead sister's gray-streaked black hair splayed out around her head; her white cap was nowhere in sight. As Rose leaned in close, she saw that the hair was matted in back. She touched the area lightly, certain that it would feel sticky. It did. Under the thick hair, the back of Patience's skull was smashed into a pulpy crater.

Feeling sick, Rose sat sharply on the grass and stared at the blood staining the ends of her fingers. *Dearest Mother Ann,* she whispered, *who could have done such a thing?* She half sobbed a prayer that Patience's soul be granted peace, and for the doomed soul of her killer.

A piercing shriek jolted Rose upright, and her heart lunged against her ribs. She twisted around to see Gertrude standing to her left, her hands held out in front of her as if warding off an attack. The Kitchen Deaconess paused to gulp in some air, then released another wail. Gertrude's screams had apparently reached the Meetinghouse as the worship service ended. Running figures emerged from the trees—people from the world, dressed in their Sunday best; panting brethren; and flushed sisters in their striped Sabbathday dresses. Grady and Gennie appeared as well, hand in hand. They all stopped and stared at the scene before them. One of the sisters shook Gertrude to make her stop screaming.

Wordlessly Rose held out her red-stained hand toward Grady. With a gesture, he told Gennie to stay where she was, but she followed behind as he rushed to Rose's side. He held two fingers to Patience's neck and then her wrist, but shook his head as he found no pulse. Rose pointed to Patience's head, and Grady peered at the damage without touching it. Then he raised questioning eyebrows at Rose, who was staring at her own hand. Gennie pulled a handkerchief from her pocket and wiped the blood from Rose's hand, then put an arm around her shoulders as if she were a child.

Rose took a deep breath and forced her teeth to stop chattering. "I found her like this," she said. "As if she were in prayer, but . . ."

Gennie tightened her arm around Rose's shoulder.

"What is the meaning of this?" Wilhelm's voice, at sermon strength, roared behind them. He looked through them at Patience, then at Rose and Gennie. "Is this thy doing?" he thundered, pointing a blunt finger at the two women.

"Now, hold on, sir—" Grady began, his fists tightening instinctively.

"Wilhelm, for heaven's sake—" Rose said at the same time.

But it was Gennie who silenced them all. She straightened her tiny body, put her fists on her hips, and said, "Wilhelm, don't you dare accuse Rose! She's had a horrible shock, finding Patience like this. You, of all people, should understand what it feels like for a Believer to come upon violence. Now, let Deputy O'Neal do his job."

Wilhelm's already ruddy face deepened in hue, but he couldn't argue. She was right, and he knew it. He turned abruptly and began to herd the others into two groups, male and female, at the base of the hill.

"Thanks, Gen," Grady said, without looking up. "Would you two back away a bit, too, please?" He was already examining the area around Patience on his hands and knees. Rose and Gennie cleared away but stayed close enough to hear him muttering to himself. He came to a large, flat rock, set in the ground with grass and dandelions poking up around the edges. After peering closely at the rock and the grass around it, he stood, ran a hand through his straight brown hair, and nodded.

"What have you found?" Rose asked.

He jerked his head toward her as if he'd forgotten he wasn't alone. "Might not be murder," he said.

"But such an injury . . ." Rose objected.

"There's blood on this rock. Looks like she slipped here on the grass and fell backwards. You said she'd been acting strangely, right? Fasting and going into trances and all? Reckon she just lost her balance while she was dancing around. Seems clear enough to me."

Grady looked toward the hushed crowd at the bottom of the hill. "Y'all can go on home now. It's an accident, couldn't have been helped. Nothing more you can do."

"Grady," Rose said, "don't you think Sheriff Brock ought to be—"

Grady put out a hand and almost touched her. "Leave well enough alone, Rose. There's no way to prove this wasn't an accident. You go getting the sheriff involved, and before you know it, the story'll get turned into the devil visiting a witch's coven. You know what Brock is like."

"He's right, Rose," Gennie said. "You know how the townspeople react when anything mysterious happens out here. It can get dangerous."

"Speaking of which, Gennie, I want you to come back to town with me," Grady said.

"I'm staying here."

"Gennie—"

"I'll leave when Rose no longer needs me, and not before. Besides, if this is just an accident, then there's no danger, right?"

Grady frowned.

Gennie squeezed his arm. "I'll call you tonight, as I promised," she said. "I'll be fine. You'll see."

"Grady, what about Patience's body?" Rose asked. "Should we send for a doctor from Cincinnati for an autopsy?"

Grady shook his head. "Doc Irwin's feeling real poorly still, and I'm calling this an accident." He shrugged, then continued in a casual tone. "I'll send for a doctor from Cincinnati to come tomorrow and take care of the death certificate." He took Gennie's hand. "If I don't hear from you every morning and evening, just as we agreed, I'm coming out here and taking you back with me."

"Agreed."

With a troubled heart, Rose watched him descend the hill and talk with the crowd, presumably to tell them his accident theory. He could easily be right, of course. She fervently hoped he was. But she knew he should at least have kept the suspicion of murder open awhile, long enough to have a doctor examine Patience and confirm his observations. Or perhaps he was more suspicious than he was willing to let on. He might be playing down the idea of murder to protect her and the Shakers—and Gennie, as long as she stayed here—from the unreasoning fury of a suspicious world. But it might not be the wisest move. He could be letting a killer believe he—or she—had escaped without retribution. If Grady hoped that Rose would drop the issue there, he was mistaken. However, it might serve her best to keep her own suspicions quiet. An overconfident killer was more likely to become careless.

SEVENTEEN

"WHAT DO YOU THINK?" ROSE ASKED. SHE SAT TENSELY IN a ladder-back chair, well back from the bed on which Patience lay, covered with a white cotton sheet. Josie had pulled aside a corner of the sheet to examine the wound on her head. She replaced the makeshift shroud and rubbed her several chins.

"A rock could certainly have caused such damage," Josie said. "But something bothers me. The rock Grady found was large and flat. Patience's wound seems concave, almost as if crushed by a smaller, more pointed rock. Though I suppose the bone could simply have fallen in on itself so as to make the injury look deeper than it really was . . ."

"Is that likely?" Rose asked.

Josie shrugged a plump shoulder. "Who can say? Thank God, I have infrequent experience with violent deaths." She tilted her head at Rose. "Do you suspect her death was more . . . well, more complicated than Grady deduced?"

"Perhaps." Rose frowned at the shrouded body, abandoned by its soul. "Let's keep this between us for now," she said. "Grady is right about one thing, at least—the hint of a murder in North Homage would be enough to set off the hatred of some of our neighbors. I'll do a bit of checking on my own."

"As you wish."

*   *   *

151

Rose cut through the medic garden to reach the Medicinal Herb Shop without attracting attention. Tramping through gardens had become a habit, she thought; she was hiding too much, and it made her uncomfortable. As a Shaker, she had accepted the importance of living her life in the open, in the company and full view of her fellow Believers.

She hesitated only a moment at the front door of the shop, while she formed a plan. Everyone had been instructed to gather in the family room of the Center Family Dwelling House for an impromptu prayer service for both Hugo and Patience. As prearranged, Gennie had called from the dwelling house parlor to tell Rose that Andrew, Benjamin, and Thomas were present. Willy Robinson might be in the shop, cleaning up, but Rose could always send him off on an errand.

Her plan proved unnecessary. The shop was empty. Quite cluttered, as well, Rose noted with disapproval. Aware that Willy might appear at any time, she shut the door behind her and headed for Patience's worktable, ignoring the crumbled leaves that clung to the hem of her long dress.

According to Gennie, she had returned Patience's journal to her worktable. Despite the clutter of stems and leaves and equipment, Rose could see instantly that the table held no books. She glanced underneath, but found nothing but more debris, which she scattered with her foot, just to make sure. She examined the broom closet, in case Gennie had taken it with her and forgotten. Nothing but thin lengths of wood and far too much dust, cleared in the areas Gennie must have slid against.

Patience might have come in after breakfast and removed the journal for some reason—perhaps to catch up on her notes during the short interval between the noon meal and the public worship service. Where might she have left it then? Her retiring room, perhaps?

Rose moved to the men's worktable, where she found

two journals on top of one another, just as Gennie had described. After glancing at one page and seeing columns of numbers, Rose tossed aside the top journal. She picked up the second journal and turned to the end. The pages were blank. She peered closely at the binding and saw jagged tears. Two pages had been torn from the journal.

Fragrant lavender needles brushed against Rose's ankles as she hurried through the herb fields. Not wishing to explain her errand to Believers exiting the Center Family Dwelling House after their prayer service, Rose had raced north from the Medicinal Herb Shop. Since no one was in sight when she reached the west end of the fields, she sprinted through the grass to the trees surrounding the holy hill. This time she wasn't worried about disturbing anyone as she crushed the undergrowth. She climbed partway up the hill and located the rock Grady had found. It was smudged with blood, though not much for such a deep wound. As she had remembered it, the rock was large and flat, with no protrusions.

Rose smoothed her skirt under her, sat on the grass in front of the rock, and stared at it. The more she stared, the less reason she found in Grady's theory of Patience's death. The wound seemed far too deep and destructive to have resulted from a fall on such a flat stone. And where was all the blood? Such a head wound would have bled profusely. She imagined Patience tripping, falling backward. Even weak and dizzy, she would instinctively have tried to break her own fall, wouldn't she?

Scooting up on her knees, Rose examined the ground carefully. Yea, a skid mark bore the imprint of a heel. An indentation in the ground looked like the poke of an elbow. The grass in front of her was smashed in spots, as if it had not recovered from being lain on. There seemed little doubt that someone had slid and fallen against the rock. Grady had squatted where she now was, peering at the ground. He'd seen what she was seeing, and he was a bright lad.

She would make a point of talking to him soon.

She pushed to her feet and slowly spun around, taking in her surroundings. She walked to the spot where she had found Patience, spread out facedown, her hair splayed around her bloody head. Her hair. Whatever had happened to her white cap? In the heat of July, Rose would not expect Patience to have worn her heavy palm bonnet, but a Shaker sister would never go outdoors without her cap covering her hair, not if she had any choice.

When Rose had questioned the other inhabitants of the Medicinal Herb Shop, they'd told her that Patience had left the shop in a disturbed state about midmorning, and she had surely been wearing her cap then. Rose could not imagine that she had gone back to her retiring room, removed her cap, and then come out here to pray. So somehow her cap had disappeared. Or, more likely and more sinister, it had been taken.

The evening meal was getting close, but Rose decided to explore as long as she could. Maybe the cap would show up. She walked to the base of the hill and began to circle counterclockwise until she came to the small creek that meandered along the west edge of the holy hill. Though the summer had been hot and dry, the creek, fed by an underground spring, gurgled along over clumps of sand and smooth rocks. She walked alongside the water, examining the area. She wasn't sure what she was looking for, except Patience's cap. By now, her thinking had pushed her into the suspicion of murder. The deliberate killing of another human being was horrible for her to contemplate, but she knew that it was a strong possibility. Patience had made enemies with her trance-induced denunciations. With a prick of anxiety, Rose acknowledged that she herself was one of those enemies.

She rounded a curve in the creek and saw something that puzzled her. A rock, about palm-sized, lay at the edge of the water, which flowed jaggedly over it. As far as Rose knew, this area had rested, untended and undisturbed, for decades—close to one hundred years, in fact. The children were never brought here for outings, since it was too wild. Patience, of course, had come for her prayers and rituals, but it was unlikely she would have spent much time by the creek, which had no holy significance. Certainly she would not have bothered with any of the rocks. So why was this rough rock lying among all the other, consistently smooth ones? Her heart picked up speed as she squatted, pulled her skirts back with one hand, and reached for the rock with the other.

"Rose? What are you doing here?" Andrew's surprised voice nearly sent Rose forward into the creek. She pulled her hand back quickly. Andrew's eyes traveled to her hand, then back to her face. She stood and brushed off her skirts.

"I might ask you the same question, Andrew," she said, as calmly as she could manage.

"Oh, I . . . Well, I thought I'd gather a few wild plants for our experiments. I saw some earlier when we . . . when all of us were . . . I suppose you must think me heartless, to have been noticing plants while Patience was lying there . . ."

"Nay, Andrew, I don't think you heartless at all." She glanced at his empty hands. "I'm just not sure I believe you."

Andrew followed her eyes and looked at his own open palms. "Ah, I see what you mean." Suddenly he grinned. "You won't tell Wilhelm that I fibbed, will you?"

She shook her head, though she wondered why she was so quick to reassure him. It was unusual for a Believer to show no remorse for an untruth. "But tell me why you are here, then," she added.

"I will if you will," Andrew said, still grinning.

This was a game Rose did not intend to play. "Andrew," she said, a quiet chiding in her voice.

He nodded, understanding that he had received a correction from his eldress. "I was not telling a complete untruth," he said. "I did notice a plant while we were waiting to hear about Patience. I saw it from a distance and thought I'd come back to investigate. If it is what it looked like, I'll be pleased to know it is growing wild around here. I haven't seen it except in the medic garden, and there isn't enough of it for our purposes."

"And the plant is . . . ?"

"Foxglove."

"Foxglove? Growing wild? It can, of course, but I'd be surprised that someone hasn't already harvested it into extinction. We actually use very little of it, since it is so powerful. Until you came, we had only Josie, and she isn't comfortable working with the more dangerous herbs."

"Shall we see?" Andrew led the way through a small wooded area into a glen that somehow had escaped the decades of encroaching undergrowth. Slivers of sunlight warmed the few tall plants in the area.

Rose gazed around in confusion. "I don't see any foxglove," she said, looking for the stalks of bell-shaped pink flowers with spotted throats.

Andrew walked over to a clump of green leaves growing in a rosette shape. He knelt over it and rubbed the leaves. "Come feel this," he said. When he did not move a safe distance away, Rose went around to the opposite side of the plant and lowered to her knees. Andrew ripped off a leaf and held it out to her. The tip of his finger brushed her hand as she took the leaf. He seemed not to notice. She decided to do the same, though her rising discomfort forced her to stand quickly. The leaf felt fuzzy.

"You see, I'm quite sure this is a first-year foxglove plant," Andrew said. His dark eyebrows nearly joined as he scanned the area around the plant. "The only thing that confuses me, though, is that foxglove is a biennial. It doesn't bloom until the second year, if you see what I mean."

Rose saw. "In other words," she said, "it is July, so why aren't there any second-year plants nearby, in full bloom?"

"Precisely," Andrew said, with a broad smile. "Where did the seeds come from, if not from an older plant?"

Rose felt an unwelcome flush of pleasure at Andrew's delighted reaction to her quickness of mind. It wasn't until later, after they had heard the dinner bell and settled into their silent places in the Center Family dining room, that it occurred to her to wonder how Andrew, milling around with the others on the northeast side of the holy hill, could possibly have recognized a first-year foxglove hidden halfway around the hill and beyond a clump of trees.

EIGHTEEN

Rose sat at the desk in the small library of the Ministry House, leafing through an old journal she'd pulled from the shelf. For the most part, journals were stored in spare rooms these days, but this one was special. Wilhelm's predecessor as elder, Obadiah, had been a medicinal herb enthusiast and amateur artist. The medicinal herb industry had been booming in his day. He had kept a close and interested eye on it and had recorded his many observations in his journals, along with drawings. During the year he had written the journal Rose held, he had made a study of each medicinal plant grown by the North Homage Society, recording where it had been planted, its growing patterns, and how it was used.

Not far into the book, she found what she sought— several pages devoted to foxglove. He had drawn the plant at several stages of development and carefully printed a description next to the picture. The first-year plant looked very close to what Andrew had shown her at the holy hill. Obadiah described a low mound of fuzzy leaves; Rose recalled lightly rubbing a leaf between her fingers and feeling the fuzz. She was irritated with herself for not recognizing the plant immediately.

Rose read through the rest of Obadiah's description. Foxglove had been planted in both the medic garden and in one field north of the Herb House, so he could keep an eye on it and keep the children away from it. The children. Could this be what Nora and Betsy had gotten into? Gretchen had found the girls between the Trustees' Office and the Center Family house, which were very close to the holy hill. She would ask Josie for more information about the symptoms of foxglove poisoning.

Questions nagged at her, though. Why would the girls be attracted to a first-year plant, without those tantalizing bell-shaped flowers? Were there more mature plants somewhere else in that same area, perhaps reseeds from decades-earlier plantings? She skimmed through the journal entry one more time. Nay, she had remembered correctly: Besides the medic garden, north of the Infirmary, the only planting Obadiah reported was in the far northeast corner of town. The holy hill was at the other end of the village. If they had simply grown wild, which was possible, surely she and Andrew would have seen a colony of mature plants nearby.

Rose leaned back in her chair. There was one more possibility, and she was not eager to consider it. Someone could have planted the foxglove in the spring, right about the time the Mount Lebanon Believers arrived. So it was also possible that Rose had just now interrupted Andrew as he checked the progress of his secret planting of a highly toxic plant. The thought caused a stabbing sensation in her heart. She slammed the journal shut and held it to her chest as she closed the room and climbed the stairs to her retiring room.

After placing Obadiah's journal with her own on the corner of her retiring room desk, she headed for the hall telephone. She was increasingly certain that Grady did not believe his own theory about Patience's death. It simply did not make sense to her that a sheriff's deputy with his skill and intelligence would dismiss so quickly the notion that the death might have been made to look like an accident. Was he investigating on his own? If he had a plan, she wanted to be aware of it.

"Rose, I'm sorry, I'm rather busy right now . . ." Grady said, after the operator had connected them.

Such distance was unusual from Grady, and Rose's suspicions deepened. "Merely a quick question," she said. "Did you take a careful look at Patience's wound?"

"Uh . . . What do you mean?"

"Well, I was wondering what you concluded from the depth of the wound, whether you still think she simply fell on a rock."

"I don't think we should be discussing—"

"Oh? I was under the impression that, since you believed the death to be accidental, there would be no investigation, so why can't we discuss anything we please?"

The line wasn't clear enough for her to hear it, but she was certain that Grady sighed. "Rose, listen to me. I want you and Gennie to stay out of this. Yeah, it could just be an accident, and it could be something else, but I don't want folks around here to get riled up, like they seem to do when anything happens in North Homage."

"So you do think—"

"Rose, are you listening to me?" Exasperation drove his normally gentle voice into a higher, more strident range. "Let me do the investigating. Y'all just go on with your lives like nothing's out of the ordinary. Understand?"

This time it was Rose who sighed. "I can't."

"Rose—"

"Nay, Grady, it isn't possible. You know that. There are undercurrents in this village that only I can bring to the surface, and my instincts tell me they are directly related to Patience's death. You are not one of us."

"That might be for the best, you know," Grady said, in a more reasonable tone. "I'm not so personally involved."

"Exactly." Rose was suddenly tired and wished she could simply turn the problem over to Grady. He would be able to seek out the truth with single-mindedness. His heart would not be weighted down with the fear that the killer might turn out to be a Believer.

Grady must have heard the inevitability in her voice. "All right," he said. "Let's keep in touch. Just be careful, Rose, okay? I can't control Gennie any better than I can control you, so keep her safe."

"I'll do my best," Rose said, with feeling.

"We have a flock of hungry stomachs arriving for breakfast in just over an hour, and not a sign of a Kitchen Deaconess. What are we supposed to do?" The aggrieved voice on the other end of Rose's telephone belonged to Polly, one of the kitchen sisters, though she hadn't thought to say so. Rose leaned against the hallway wall, not yet awake enough to handle yet another crisis.

"Have you checked her retiring room?"

"Of course, did it myself first thing." Polly's tone implied that her eldress was none too bright.

Polly was no more than twenty-one, and Rose was inclined to forgive her, at least this once. "Did you try calling Josie at the Infirmary?"

"What on earth for?"

"In case Gertrude became ill during the night, Polly." Rose's understanding was stretching thin. "Never mind," she said. "I'll try to find her. You get on back to fixing breakfast, and I'll send Gennie Malone over to help you."

The sun hadn't yet made its entrance, but the air drifting in Rose's open window brushed over her skin like steam from a kettle. She splashed her face with lukewarm water. As she pulled a fresh work dress over her head, the bell over the Center Family house rang to awaken the village. She tidied her room quickly, giving Gennie a few minutes to crawl out of bed and dress before calling her to the phone.

"Oh, Rose, this is just like old times, being sent to work in the kitchen," Gennie said, her voice slow and sleepy. "And you know how I hate it."

"It's good to have you back, Gennie."

"Uh-huh. Why do they need me, anyway?"

"Gertrude didn't show up this morning, and she isn't in her retiring room. You didn't by any chance see or hear her leave, did you?"

"No—I mean, nay, I didn't, but I'll ask around before I go to the kitchen. Rose, do you think this is related to . . . You aren't going to find another body on the holy hill, are you?"

"Dear Lord, I hope not."

Rose decided against calling Josie; the fewer calls she made from the Ministry House, the better, since Wilhelm might hear her. Best to keep him uninformed as long as possible. For once skipping her morning routine of cleaning and prayer, Rose raced across the central path to the Infirmary.

Josie slept at the Infirmary to watch over her patients, which meant that sometimes she didn't sleep at all. But she always seemed cheerful. This morning she was already scurrying around the waiting room, dusting the dozens of apothecary jars and tins she used to mix her tonics and teas. She looked up in surprise when Rose rushed in the door, breathless and already sprouting dots of perspiration around the edge of her white cap.

"Is Gertrude here?"

Josie shook her head.

"Has she checked in with you at all since yesterday?"

"Nay. Rose, what is this about?"

"I'll explain later."

Rose turned to leave, and Josie called her back.

"That doctor Grady sent came in very early this morning to examine Patience," Josie said.

"What did he say?"

"Nothing. He said absolutely nothing. Just as if I wouldn't understand." Josie pursed her lips in disapproval.

Rose wondered if there had been a different reason for the doctor's silence—such as orders from Grady—as she raced through the medic and kitchen gardens to the outside door of the dwelling house kitchen. She poked her head inside, and Polly squeaked and jumped backward.

"Rose, you startled—"

"Is Gennie here yet?" A sense of urgency consumed Rose. She feared there was no time to waste.

"She just arrived. Is this about Gertrude?"

Rose stepped inside, spotted Gennie lifting a copper pan from a wall peg, and called out to her. When Gennie turned, she seemed to understand instantly. Not bothering to deliver the pan, she ran to Rose. To avoid the now curious eyes of the kitchen sisters, they stepped outside and closed the door.

"Here's all I found out," Gennie said. "Sister Theresa said she thought she heard Gertrude's door open early this morning, before the wake-up bell. She didn't think anything of it, of course. Gertrude might just have been visiting the bathroom, but Theresa couldn't go back to sleep, and she didn't hear Gertrude's door close again. That's all."

"No sounds of illness?"

"No sounds at all except a little moving about in her room and then the door opening. No one saw her at all when everyone started to tidy up the dwelling house and do the brethren's mending. That's when I left. Does that tell you anything?"

"It tells me she chose to leave, which is a relief in some ways."

"And puzzling," Gennie said. "I gather she wasn't at the Infirmary?"

"Nay." But there had to be a reasonable explanation. Rose wished her heart would ease up so she could hear herself think. "Go ahead back to work, Gennie. I'll find Gertrude."

"Two of us could look twice as fast."

"You can't get out of kitchen work that easily. Put your hands to work, my friend."

Gertrude could be anywhere in or out of the village. Sisters and brethren had been known to desert the Society in the dead of night, sometimes with one another. But Gertrude? Nay, not possible. Clearly she had been struggling with some burden during the worship service, but for her to desert her kitchen responsibilities was almost unthinkable. She would put aside a mere personal problem until her duties had been completed.

Rose found herself walking west on the central path. Toward the holy mount. Try as she might, the best explanation she could think of for Gertrude's behavior was that she knew something about Patience's death.

When she had nearly reached the village entrance, she veered off to the right, found the creek, and followed it to the holy hill. She hadn't entered from the south before. A dense cluster of sugar maples led to a sunny clearing, then more trees at the base of the hill. The atmosphere was peaceful, idyllic. In calmer times the clearing would be a lovely place for a picnic, with clumps of woodland flowers dotting the landscape. She had no time for such thoughts now, though. If she did not find Gertrude here—and it was only a guess that she would—she'd have to comb the village as quickly as possible.

Rose split off from the creek and circled around the hill to the side where Patience had been found. As soon as she rounded the curve, she knew her hunch was correct. Two feet appeared, wearing the black cloth shoes of a Shaker sister. They lay on the ground, soles up. Rose's breath caught in her throat, and she ran toward the figure lying prone, arms splayed outward, facedown on the grass.

"Gertrude!" Rose cried, falling to her knees beside the sister. She reached out to touch Gertrude's cheek, and her hand was knocked aside. She sat abruptly on her side as Gertrude screamed and rolled over. It took several moments for Rose to comprehend that Gertrude was very much alive and terrified. They stared at one another, wide-eyed and openmouthed.

Rose recovered first. She grabbed Gertrude's wrists and pulled her to a sitting position, then threw her arms around the startled woman. "Dear Gertrude, when I saw you lying on the ground, just like Patience, I was so frightened," she said, choking on her tears. She sat back and held Gertrude at arm's length. "What on earth are you doing here at this time of morning?"

Gertrude's shoulders slumped and her face crumpled. "Oh, Rose, I've been such a fool," she said. "Honestly, it would be better if I *had* been dead."

"Nonsense." Rose took a large hand in her own and squeezed it. "Tell me everything."

"Could we consider this confession?"

"Of course."

"My back hurts," Gertrude said, wincing. "I'm not as young as I once was."

"Nor I. Let's walk while we talk."

Rose stood and helped the older woman. They walked in silence until they reached the shade of some oaks and maples. Decades of fallen leaves had matted some areas into the semblance of a path, which they wandered slowly.

"I was praying when you found me," Gertrude said finally. "I have broken my vow."

"Which one?"

"My sacred vow never to do violence to another human being." Gertrude's already prominent chin jutted out even farther; she was ready and willing to take her punishment.

"Gertrude, are you saying that you had something to do with Patience's death? I simply can't believe that. Why? How?"

"Well, I must have killed her, that's all."

Rose blinked, thinking she hadn't heard right. "Why must you have killed her? What are you talking about? Did you or didn't you?" She resisted the impulse to shake Gertrude by the shoulders; she seemed confused enough.

"I feel so terrible, Rose. I can't eat or sleep or work, and when I tried to pray, I just fell on the ground like Patience. It's all my fault. Even if I didn't mean for it to happen—and I didn't, Rose, you have to believe me. Even so, it's my fault, and I have to take responsibility."

Rose sucked on her bottom lip to keep herself from shouting in frustration. Gertrude needed to approach confession at her own pace; that was clear. Pressuring her would only increase her anxiety and slow the process.

They had reached the creek. Rose led the way, so they would not leave the privacy of the holy hill too quickly. Gertrude halted suddenly and stared into the water. "Patience was quite horrible to me," she said. "You have no idea. No one does. When Hugo got sick, she said it was my fault!"

"Gertrude, surely you can't believe you are responsible for Hugo's death. He had been failing for a long time; you know that."

"She said it was my cooking."

"Your *cooking*?" Rose said, forcing herself not to laugh. "And you believed her? What, in the name of Mother Ann and all the angels, could your cooking possibly have had to do with Hugo's illness?"

Gertrude frowned as if the question had not occurred to her before. "Well, I don't know, truly I don't. I mean, everyone eats my cooking, don't they? Except you and Wilhelm, of course, when you eat at the Ministry House. And none of you gets sick from it, do you?" She searched Rose's face with red-rimmed eyes.

"Of course not. Patience's accusation was ridiculous. I can't imagine why . . ." Rose frowned as her voice trailed off.

"What? Rose, what are you thinking?"

"I was just remembering the afternoon Hugo became ill. He came into the kitchen while we were talking. He had missed the noon meal and was looking for a snack." Rose laid a comforting hand on Gertrude's arm. "There was one item he ate that no one else has tried, as far as I know."

"Oh dear," Gertrude whimpered. "Not my lovely peppermint jelly."

"I'm afraid so. But perhaps it's just a coincidence," she

said as Gertrude's eyes blurred with tears. "When we've finished, we'll go get the jar and I'll see if I can find someone to identify its contents. Just to rule it out, you understand. Now, what else do you need to confess to me about Patience? Tell me more about her accusations."

Gertrude nodded and gulped. "She said I didn't know how to use herbs properly. Imagine! I've been cooking for more than thirty years, and I've always used herbs, ever since I was a teen cooking for my papa, after my ma died. Why, I used to collect herbs from the hills, such like my ma did and her ma before her, down the line. We dried them ourselves and used them for tonics, too. Many's the time we cured the ague with one of our herb tonics."

"So of course you are familiar with all sorts of herbs and their uses," Rose said, keeping her voice light and encouraging,

"Yea, of course. Patience had no call to say what she did about taking my herbs away from me. Who does she think she is! Was, I mean." Gertrude sagged against an oak tree.

"Patience wanted to take the kitchen herbs?"

"She wanted to take them all, right then. Never mind we were cooking evening meal and baking bread for the whole week."

Rose was puzzled. "What was Patience doing in the kitchen during the workday?" Ordinarily the kitchen was the domain of the kitchen sisters, and others were discouraged from dropping by without a mission.

Gertrude avoided Rose's eyes. "Well," she mumbled, "we weren't exactly in the kitchen. We were just . . . out."

Rose sensed that silence would bring the story out, so she did not prod. Gertrude grew agitated under her gaze. She pushed away from the tree trunk, walked to the bank of the creek. She yanked off a length of high grass and began to twist it.

"I followed her," Gertrude said finally, tossing the shredded grass into the water. "She'd dropped off some basil at the kitchen and made that remark about my cooking being responsible for Hugo's sickness, and then she just walked out, and I was furious, as you can just imagine, so I told the sisters I had a quick errand, and I just walked right out the door. She was heading off this direction, walking in the grass, mind you, so I followed her a ways. I didn't want to call attention to myself. When I saw her go into the trees, I figured, well, that's just the right place to have a private talk with that Sister Know-It-All, so I went right in after her.'' Gertrude's eyes looked inward at a memory that twisted her face in pain.

"Tell me what happened," Rose said in a gentle command. "I promise, you will feel better."

Gertrude nodded. "I followed her into the woods—you know, those trees back there." She pointed to the area from which Rose had first watched Patience perform her solitary ritual. "I didn't know about this being the holy hill, even though I'd heard about such things before, so I was mighty surprised when I peeked around the trees and saw Patience twirling around like she was in worship service. I was hopping mad, but I just watched her for a while because . . . well, because I figured there might be a chance of catching her with it. You know, catching her with one of her false spirits,'' Gertrude explained in response to Rose's puzzled frown. "I always believed she wasn't a true chosen instrument, but she sure enough seemed chosen by *something*, so it had to be a false spirit."

With great difficulty, Rose resisted pointing out the theological unlikelihood of actually sighting a recognizably false spirit communicating with Patience. Enough time had been wasted.

"Did you interrupt her trance?" Rose asked.

"Yea, she just twirled and twirled, and I got madder and madder, so finally I stepped out and called her name. She stopped right away, so it wasn't much of a trance, anyway. I told her she'd no right to take my herbs and certainly no call to accuse my cooking of hurting Hugo. I said I'd go right to Andrew and insist we got our herbs in the kitchen. Oh, Rose, she was just terrible. A Believer shouldn't be like that. She said I was a fool and a worthless Believer, and all sorts of horrible things, and . . .'' Gertrude began to nibble on a thumbnail and curl in on herself like a child expecting punishment. Rose prepared herself to hear the true core of the confession.

"I hit her," Gertrude said.

Rose struggled to hide her distress. She had expected to hear about harsh words or uncharitable thoughts, but not violence. Believers' vows of pacifism were so central to their faith that they had refused to serve in the Civil War and in the great World War, earning them the contempt of many of their neighbors. And Gertrude was hardly young and impetuous.

Gertrude searched Rose's face imploringly. "I didn't mean to, Rose, truly, truly. I just got so angry I slapped her, right in the face, just like my ma used to slap my pa when he came home liquored up." Her face brightened. "You don't suppose it was her false spirits making me act that way, do you?"

Rose's eyebrows shot up.

"Nay, I suppose not," Gertrude said. "I take responsibility, Rose. I killed her. I slapped her and she fell backwards and tripped. She fell on that big rock and hit her head."

"Why did you not come for help when you saw how badly she had hurt herself?"

"Well, I didn't know, of course. Goodness, if I had thought she would die, of course I would have run for help. But I didn't, truly I didn't. She knocked her head and looked a little woozy, but she got up and spoke to me, and she was just as mean as ever, so how could I guess that she had really hurt herself?"

"Was she bleeding?"

"Honestly, I guess I didn't look all that carefully, but I didn't see any bleeding or I would have been more worried.

I mean, she hit her head, but it didn't seem hard enough to kill her, with all that padding.''

Gertrude began to chew on her little fingernail. Rose waited.

"There's more I have to tell you," Gertrude said. She moved on to another fingernail. "I shouldn't have done it, I know, and even though it wasn't exactly breaking my vows this time, I wasn't exactly true to them, either.''

Rose nodded, keeping her expression neutral.

"Well, this wasn't the first time Patience had talked about taking all the herbs away from the kitchen. I didn't say anything at the time, and I know I should have, but right after she arrived I saw her wandering about in the kitchen garden just picking whatever she pleased! When I told her those herbs were needed for our cooking, she just smiled and said the Medicinal Herb Shop needed them more, and she was going to see about taking them away from us. Well, I told her we'd see about that! I told her to get back to her own work and leave those herbs with me, and she just smiled again and kept right on harvesting. She was taking all my peppermint!''

"It's understandable that you lost your temper with Patience," Rose said, patting Gertrude's arm. "I wish you had come to me. I would have told her to stay away from the culinary herbs.''

Thinking the confession finished, and eager to move on, Rose squeezed Gertrude's arm to convey forgiveness and turned to go.

"Well, I was so angry with her, you see," Gertrude said, barely above a whisper. "It was a wretched thing to do, but I was *so angry*. I just pray it wasn't what I did that . . .''

Rose turned back to Gertrude to see her features twisted in anguish.

"She had taken all my peppermint, you see, and I needed more to make my new herbal jellies. So one evening I sneaked over to the Medicinal Herb Shop. I went right after we'd served the evening meal, and I made sure Patience was in the dining room—she wasn't fasting so much in those days, you know—and all the brethren were eating, too. Then I sneaked over to the shop to get some of my peppermint back.''

"Is that all you took?''

"I . . . Well, I tried not to take anything else, but, you see, sometimes it's hard to recognize herbs once they've dried.''

"Peppermint is hard to recognize?'' Rose asked in disbelief.

"Nay, not when it's still hanging in bunches, and I found those right away, but I was still so angry, you see.'' Gertrude attacked her other thumbnail. "I wanted to take all her peppermint, the way she took mine.''

"I don't understand.''

"Some of it was already ground up,'' Gertrude explained, "and sitting out on the worktables in tins and suchlike.'' Gertrude stared at the ground as a flush spread over her face. "So I took pinches of everything and smelled it all, and I took parts of anything that smelled liked peppermint. I didn't empty anything,'' she said, as if hoping her consideration lessened her sin.

"You took ground herbs from the worktables of the Medicinal Herb Shop and used them to make the jelly that Hugo ate?''

Gertrude nodded miserably.

"Didn't you know that peppermint is often used to make medicinal herbs more palatable?''

Gertrude gulped back a sob. "We used to do that back when I was growing up, but I just didn't think about it until . . . until Hugo got sick and Patience started accusing me. She'd guessed I'd taken the peppermint. The brethren in the shop just figured they'd suddenly used it all up, and Patience didn't tell them different.''

"Why not?''

"She was saving the information,'' Gertrude said. "She was going to use it against me.''

"Oh, Gertrude. You know how this will look, don't you?"

Gertrude's misery shifted to horror. "Rose, I know I did wrong, and slapping her was a terrible, terrible deed, but I never thought that it would kill her."

"I believe you, Gertrude, but here's what you must do—you must stop crying around the others, and you must never again say that you are responsible for Patience's death, or Hugo's. Let me handle this from now on. Do you understand?"

Gertrude nodded. The breakfast bell rang in the distance, and both women began to walk toward the eastern edge of the woods.

"I'll eat at the Ministry House today," Rose said, as they emerged from the trees. They separated and had walked a few feet when Rose turned.

"Gertrude," she called out, "just one more question. You said earlier you were surprised Patience was so injured by her fall, and you said it was because of 'all that padding.' What did you mean by that?"

Gertrude hesitated, her mouth half open. "Well, it's obvious, isn't it?" she said. "I mean, she had all that hair pinned up under her cap."

"She was wearing her cap? You're absolutely certain you remember it that way?"

"Yea, I'm quite certain," Gertrude said.

"I see."

NINETEEN

AFTER A BUSY BUT UNEVENTFUL DAY AND A NIGHT OF MUCH-
needed sleep, Rose awakened before the bell and hurried
through her cleaning chores. Guilt pricked at her conscience
because she had done so little work lately. In the United
Society of Believers, all were equal, male and female, from
the Ministry to the newest members of the family. And all
worked, if they were able. Wilhelm labored in the fields.
Rose tried to help wherever the sisters were especially
shorthanded. She ought to check on the Laundry or the
kitchen to see if she was needed, but her mind brimmed
with ideas, and she wanted to sort them out on paper.

Before the breakfast bell, Rose made a quick call to the
Center Family Dwelling House and asked Gennie to meet
her in the Ministry library as soon as the sisters filed out
of the dining room. With Patience gone, Gennie could no
longer work in the Medicinal Herb Shop, but she could still
be very helpful.

Rose was out of breath as she slid into her chair at the
trestle table in the Ministry dining room. Wilhelm arched
one white eyebrow at her.

"Perhaps the awakening bell should be moved earlier for
thee," he said. "Thy morning work seems too burdensome
for the normal allotted time."

"Good morning to you, too, Wilhelm." Rose silently

congratulated herself on her growing ability to keep Wilhelm's barbs from piercing her composure.

"We must discuss our plans for Patience's burial service," he continued.

"I assumed it would be a normal one," Rose said. "Simple and private. Perhaps combined with the service for Hugo."

"Thy assumptions are wrong. Patience died to send us a special message."

Rose smoothed the creases from her white linen napkin, biding her time. Finally she looked across at Wilhelm. "And what message would that be?" she asked.

"She told us during the sweeping gift," Wilhelm said. "There are evil secrets in our Society. They have been piling up while we twiddled our thumbs. Now we must pay the price. We must purge ourselves of this evil." He took a serving-spoonful of applesauce and plopped it on his plate as if personally smashing the wickedness.

Despite the heat, the fine hairs on the back of Rose's neck bristled. She leaned over the table, her food forgotten. "Wilhelm, we mustn't have a public burial service," she said. "It could be dangerous. We can't risk it." Public worship services had a history of turning nasty when unexplained death had aroused suspicion among North Homage's neighbors.

"A purging need not be witnessed by non-Believers," Wilhelm said. "But all Believers must participate."

"I've never heard of a purging ceremony."

"We have always created rituals as we need them," Wilhelm said. "And we need one now. More than a confession. It must reach deeper into our souls to root out the sources of evil within each of us. We will debase ourselves, beat our breasts, and beg for forgiveness." Wilhelm waved his bread in the air, and crumbs flicked onto Rose's plate. "And then we will, each of us, announce our sins to the entire community. We will finally cleanse our hearts, as Mother Ann told us we must."

"Wilhelm, I understand the importance of public confession, but what you are proposing is something even more profound. It would be unwise to link such a service to Patience's burial, surely. Word would spread to the world."

"Let it."

"But it would give the impression that we Shakers have some terrible guilt to purge. The world might decide that we had something to do with Patience's death, perhaps even that we killed her."

"And didn't we?"

"What are you saying? Do you believe that one of us . . . ?"

"Nay, not *one* of us. *All* of us. We ignored the message she brought us. We should have stopped all work and purged ourselves instantly." He applied himself to his plate as if his argument had now been proven.

Rose stared at him for several moments as she considered her own position. She had no objections to new forms of worship, nor to confession in general, but Wilhelm's idea made her squirm. It didn't seem to make sense. Was he keeping some part of his plan to himself?

"I'm confused, Wilhelm," she said, ignoring the glint in his eye when she admitted a weakness. "How could instant and intense public confession have saved Patience's life?"

Wilhelm planted his fists, still holding his knife and fork, on either side of his plate. Sadness flashed across his wind-and-age-roughened face before it hardened again. "Patience wanted to save us," he said. "Nay, even more, she was *sent* to save us. She labored relentlessly at her task. Day and night, she prayed and fasted and worshiped alone. If we had listened to her, taken action at once, she would have fulfilled her purpose. She could have rested, gone back to work and been restored. She would not have been on that hill, trying once again to intervene for us."

Rose sank back in her chair. "Wilhelm, Patience may have been killed by a human being," she said. "If she was, and it was purposeful, the end would have been no different had she been elsewhere than the Empyrean Mount. Her killer would have found a way.''

"Nay!" Wilhelm slapped his hand on the table, which took the assault with only a slight shudder. "Not if we had purged ourselves first. It makes no difference *how* she died. It is we who are responsible for her death. By neglecting to purge ourselves, we allowed false spirits free rein. We left Patience to fight them alone until they killed her."

A stab of pain shot through Rose's head, signaling the onset of a Wilhelm-induced headache. She had lost her appetite, but she nibbled her food rather than continue such a fruitless discussion. For the remainder of the meal, Rose and Wilhelm were silent, as if they were dining with the rest of the family.

Wilhelm crossed his utensils on his empty plate and scraped back his chair. "I believe we should do the purging ritual in two days," he said. "In the evening, in place of our Union Meeting. That should give both of us time to prepare the others. And ourselves."

Wilhelm stood and leaned with his fists on the table. Rose watched him, another warning pain shooting through her head.

"I have noted thy loss of influence among some of the sisters," he said. "Therefore, I think it best if thy confession be made first." He straightened and left before Rose could even formulate her objections.

Rose tried to put the purging ritual out of her mind as she flipped apart the light curtains in the Ministry library and opened windows to exchange stuffy indoor for steamy outdoor air. She had already decided that she would try to find a way to prevent the ritual, even if it meant a battle with Wilhelm. She would go only so far as to concede a voluntary confession during Sabbathday worship. But no purging ritual. Too risky. Her greatest concern was that Gertrude would feel compelled to confess her meeting with Patience and be accused of murder. Rose pulled paper and pens out of desk drawers in preparation for her meeting with Gennie in a few minutes. The sooner they solved the riddle of Patience's death, the better able she would be to argue that the community-wide purging was unnecessary.

"I hope those are good thoughts you are lost in," Gennie said, as she closed the library door behind her.

"I'm afraid not." Rose pulled two chairs over to the desk and beckoned Gennie to join her.

"So is it Patience or Wilhelm weighing on your mind?" Gennie asked.

"Both together." Rose told her about Wilhelm's plan and Gertrude's argument with Patience.

"Then we must work quickly," Gennie said. "How can I help?"

Rose pushed a sheet of paper toward her and held out a pen. "Can you search your memory and come up with an approximation of the drawing you saw in Benjamin's and Patience's journals? Both diagrams had disappeared by the time I went to search for them."

Gennie grimaced at the blank page as her hand hovered over it. "I wish I hadn't ripped up the one I started to draw," she said. She drew a circle, then another, then crossed out the first. She reached for a blank sheet and repeated the exercise.

"I can't, Rose," she said. "I just don't remember."

"All right, then, make a drawing that comes close to what you remember, even if it isn't an exact replica."

Gennie nodded and began sketching. Rose, seated beside her at the double desk, used the time to make a list of questions for the two of them to explore. They finished at about the same time and exchanged papers.

Gennie read the list aloud:

"1. Are Hugo's and Patience's deaths connected in any way? (Check the herb jelly for poisonous herbs.)

2. What secrets did Patience know about other
   Believers? (Call Mount Lebanon. Talk to Irene
   again—Gennie?)
3. Where is Patience's cap, and why wasn't she
   wearing it when she was found?
4. Where are the duplicate drawings from
   Benjamin's and Patience's journals, and what
   do they represent?
5. What did Nora and Betsy eat that made them
   ill, and why won't they talk about it?''

"What do you want me to find out from Irene?" Gennie
asked.

"Anything you can about the medicinal herb group, especially while they were together at Mount Lebanon. I'm
still not sure what might be important, so use your best
judgment."

"Would Irene be likely to know anything?"

"I have a hunch she has kept an eye on her husband and
children." Rose folded Gennie's drawing and slipped it in
the pocket of her apron.

"What are you going to do?" Gennie asked.

"Make a phone call. And then I'm going to frighten two
little girls," Rose said, smiling.

"I was wondering when you would phone us," said Sister Lilian, one of Mount Lebanon's trustees. She had become a friend on one of Rose's visits to the remaining
eastern Shaker villages, and Rose knew her to be bright,
observant, and just a bit of a gossip. But first Rose had to
break the news of Patience's death. Lilian accepted the information with surprise but not deep sorrow. Rose spoke
in vague terms of the circumstances, giving the impression
that the death was assumed accidental. When she had finished, Rose asked, "Why were you expecting a call from
me?"

"I suspected the new Believers we sent you might cause
you some headaches," Lilian said. "I had my doubts at the

time about the move, but the Ministry insisted they knew what was best. They can be a bit too trusting, if you ask me, but nobody did. Not that I didn't have my say anyway, but nobody listened."

"You had doubts about sending Andrew here?"

"Not so much Andrew on his own. He wouldn't have been such a risk, I don't think, though there's a good deal I don't understand about him, despite working with him for the past year. Nay, it was the whole group I wondered about. There's no Believers I know of who could match them when it comes to creating cures out of herbs, but they never seemed to mix well with each other."

"Anything specific?"

"Hold on, let me shut the office door." Sister Lilian returned in a few moments. "Everyone else is out at their tasks, but I prefer not to be surprised. Now, where were we?"

"Your concerns about Andrew and his—"

"Ah, Andrew. A kind man, truly, once you got to know him, though not everyone got along with him. Some here said he joined us only out of grief and not genuine faith. He was something of a rebel; however, I could never believe the rumors about him—you know, about how he lost his family."

"I know very little about it," Rose said.

"Well, let me tell you." Rose could almost see Lilian pull her ladder-back chair near the phone and settle in. "I heard most of this in town and haven't told anyone here, of course, but somehow the rumors spread around anyway. Seems his wife and two young sons all died within a week of each other, in 1929, just after the crash. They'd all had the sniffles—you know how young children are—and Andrew was treating them with something or other, nobody knows what. He'd been working as a pharmacist, but the drugstore owner had all his money in the stock market, so Andrew had lost his job. Naturally, some of the townspeople said he'd cracked up and poisoned his family. Nonsense, of course.''

"I assume the police agreed," Rose said.

"Actually, I believe there was an investigation, but no charges were brought against Andrew. I don't know any of the details. He never talked about it, and I certainly wasn't going to ask him."

Rose had no such qualms, and she made a mental note to bring up the subject with Andrew very soon. She could not afford to let her growing fondness for him stand in the way of the truth. "Tell me about Patience McCormick," she said.

"Not a favorite among the sisters, I'm afraid. She kept to herself mostly. For a time I tried to supervise her medicinal herb work, but she ignored me. She knew so much more than I, you know. So Andrew took over, and that started more rumors."

"Linking Andrew and Patience?"

Lilian laughed. "Yea, it kept the monitors fully occupied at worship service, watching for special looks between them. They never saw a flicker, as far as I know."

"Do you know anything about Patience's background?"

"Very little. She joined us six or seven years ago. If she has revealed her past to anyone, it would be to the eldress in confession, but you'd have to ask her, and she's on a visit to Sabbathday Lake just now. All I know is that Patience, rest her soul, made me nervous. She'd watch everyone with those gray eyes, and I always felt she saw right into my mind."

"Did she know about medicinal herbs when she came to you?"

"I believe so, but she certainly applied herself and learned more while she was here. Rose, I'm afraid it's close to noon here; I'll have to go soon."

Rose was aware of the passing time, too, and her questions seemed to be multiplying. "What do you know about the others—Benjamin and Thomas?"

"Benjamin is ambitious, and I was quite astonished when he chose to leave with Andrew. He could have been trustee here, or at least in charge of the medicinal herb industry."

Rose suspected his decision had something to do with Irene, but she kept the opinion to herself. "What was his relationship with Patience?" she asked.

"Very tense. They seemed to be rivals." Lilian hesitated. "Rose, was there something, um, unusual about Patience's death? Is that why you need to know these things? Oh dear, there's the bell. I must run. Anything else I can help with?"

"Thomas?"

"Short-tempered, but a good salesman." Static on the telephone line obliterated Lilian's next sentence, and Rose thought she was signing off until she heard: "Strange about the girls, though."

"Sorry, interference," Rose said. "What was strange?"

"About the girls, his daughters, Janey and Marjorie," Lilian said. "He insisted they go with him to Kentucky."

"I assumed it was Irene who brought the children here."

"Nay, it was Thomas. Irene only went because the girls were going. An odd circumstance. Not the way we hope to see Believers behave, but the Ministry turned a blind eye. They probably figured it was the best way to keep both Thomas and Irene content. Anyway, they're your problem now. Good luck!"

TWENTY

FAMILIAR SOUNDS GREETED GENNIE AS SHE ENTERED THE Herb House doorway, open to encourage some air movement. On the ground floor, three sisters sang a march and timed their movements to its tempo. The noise of the herb presses drowned out the song for a few seconds, but the sisters continued singing, their mouths and arms moving in sync. Gennie smiled a greeting.

As she climbed the staircase to the second-floor drying room, she felt as if she were entering heavy clouds of damp heat. She wondered, as she had every summer, how the hanging herbs ever managed to dry. Then she entered the drying room, and the air lightened. Since Gennie had last worked in the room, the brethren had designed a system of gentle fans that pushed the hot air down from the ceiling and out the door and window.

As the air drifted past her, Gennie recognized the rich citrus fragrance of bruised lemon balm leaves. Irene must be hanging bunches of it. Lemon balm grew thick and fast, so it was harvested frequently throughout the summer. The room was already filling with limp and nearly dry herb bunches hanging from hooks and pegs along the walls and ceiling. Gennie wove through the harvest, resisting the urge to squeeze leaves to release their fragrance. Irene worked alone at the table under the east window.

Irene smiled uncertainly at her approach, and Gennie realized that she might not be sure who she was. "It's Gennie, isn't it? Rose's friend?"

Gennie hopped onto a stool and pulled a pile of lemon balm toward her. "Rose and I used to work up here together," she said. "She thought I'd enjoy doing it again, now that Patience . . ."

Irene's smile faded as she tied a piece of twine around a clump of stems. "There really isn't that much to do. But of course you can help if you'd enjoy it."

Moment after silent moment passed, and Gennie grew puzzled. She'd heard from several sisters how friendly and outgoing Irene always seemed. And why hadn't she responded to the mention of Patience's death?

"Did you know Patience well?" she asked. "I mean, from your days in Mount Lebanon."

Irene darted a glance at her. "Nay, not well at all. We . . . She worked so much on the medicinal herbs and didn't do the other rotations." She scooped up a pile of prepared bunches and disappeared, choosing to hang them from wall pegs as far away from the table as possible. Gennie squirmed on her stool. Much as she loved working with herbs, she had an assignment and little patience. When Irene finally reappeared with a handful of twine, Gennie had to count her breaths to keep from firing questions at her.

"May I ask you something, for myself?" Gennie asked after what seemed like interminable silence. Irene raised her gaze from her work, which Gennie took as assent. "What's it like to be a mother?"

Irene's eyes filled and spilled over with tears so quickly that Gennie froze, unsure what was happening. The tears stopped as suddenly as they had begun. Irene wiped her cheeks with the sleeve of her dress. "Why do you ask?" She cut a length of string and wrapped it around some stems.

"Well, I . . . As you know, I'm not a sister, and I'm thinking of getting married. My own mother is dead, and

Rose doesn't have children, of course, so I was just wondering.''

"You are very young," Irene said. "Wait. That's my advice, wait as long as you can. Marriage is heartbreak; being a mother is heartbreak. I lost two babies after I had my two little girls. Maybe it would have been better for them if I had lost them, too."

"What do you mean?" Too late, Gennie heard the shock in her own voice. Irene threw her untied stems on the table, and lemon balm rolled onto the floor.

"There isn't enough work here for two of us," she said. "I'd appreciate it if you would just go now. And tell Rose I can do this work by myself." Her normally warm eyes had hardened. Gennie felt her cheeks flush as she slid off her stool wordlessly and hurried away from what used to be her favorite place on earth.

"Rose! Could I speak with you a moment?" Andrew took the Trustees' Office steps two at a time and sprinted toward the central path, his long legs as gangly as a colt's. Rose had been about to veer off to the Children's Dwelling House, hoping to catch Charlotte while the children were napping, but she turned and waited for Andrew's approach. She tried to distract herself from the warmth she felt when he smiled at her, and from her worry when she saw his flushed face and the perspiration-dampened hair on his forehead. She tried, but she failed.

"Andrew, you could overheat so easily on a day like this. Please be careful," Rose said, reminding herself that she would feel the same concern for any Believer, whether brother or sister. They were her family.

"I'm not quite decrepit; I can survive a little heat," Andrew said, grinning. "But I thank you for your care. I wanted to be sure to catch you as soon as possible. About the jelly, I can help."

Rose stared at him. "Do you mean the herbal jelly? How on earth did you . . . ?"

"Gertrude told me. I know, perhaps she shouldn't have done so, but she feels responsible for Hugo's death, and she wants to help. She thought, rather than having to wait for a pharmacist in town to try to sort out what's in the jelly, perhaps I could. I'd be glad to try."

"What else did Gertrude tell you?"

Andrew laughed, then sobered quickly. "Probably too much. Yea, she does overtalk a bit, but her distress is genuine. I will assume she has confessed to you and so I am not betraying her. She also feels that somehow she is responsible for Patience's death, but I stopped her from saying more."

"Thank you," Rose said. "I believe she is not to blame, and I hope to prove it to her. And to anyone else she may confess to," she mumbled.

"Then let me help."

Rose hesitated.

Andrew's earnest look slid into a frown, and he paced in a complete circle. "You don't trust me, do you? That's why you didn't come to me. You think Patience's death wasn't an accident, and maybe Hugo's, too, and you think I might be involved somehow."

"Andrew, I just—"

"Rose, what have I done to make you disbelieve in me?"

"I don't disbelieve—"

"Whatever it is, just tell me, and I know I can explain it."

"Andrew, do please let me finish a sentence." She paused for another interruption that didn't come. Andrew nodded and said nothing. "I can prove nothing at the moment, and the police are not convinced any crime has been committed. I am anxious, though, to show Gertrude that her guilt is less real than she fears. Otherwise, I'm afraid the rest of her life will be spent in self-recrimination."

Andrew raised his eyebrows a fraction—just enough to convey skepticism. Rose tightened her lips in a grim line.

She had told only part of the truth, and he seemed to know it, but she would risk no more. No matter how innocent he appeared.

"If Gertrude is your only worry," Andrew said, "then there is no reason not to let me help you by taking a look at the herb jelly. If something from our shop got into it, either Benjamin or I might be able to identify it. Would you be more comfortable having Benjamin do it? Or perhaps both of us?"

"I'd prefer to keep everything as quiet as possible. Since you already know about Gertrude, I'll ask you to examine the jelly yourself, with me there."

"Good, then how about now? There's an unused room in the Trustees' Office where I do some additional research when I have trouble sleeping. We can be free from prying eyes and ears there."

"I'll get the jelly and meet you in your office in ten minutes." Rose turned to go toward the Center Family Dwelling House kitchen and saw a familiar figure with white hair, standing just outside the Ministry House, looking in her direction. As she stared back, Wilhelm pivoted back toward the front door.

"Have a seat, and I'll see if I can do this quickly," Andrew said, reaching to lift a ladder-back chair from some wall pegs. He placed the chair right next to his at the worktable, and Rose pulled it farther away. With careful movements, as if the jelly's secret might escape, he unscrewed the jar lid. He leaned over and sniffed the contents. A quick frown creased his face.

"Peppermint," he said. "And something else."

"What mixtures do you all make with peppermint in them?" Rose asked.

"Quite a few. We use peppermint to mask bitterness or an unpleasant odor which might discourage people from taking the medicine, especially if it's an infusion or in powder form."

Andrew poured a small glob of jelly onto a flat plate and spread it around with something that looked like a wide wooden butter knife. He sniffed again and shook his head. Keeping his face close to the plate, he reached out for a magnifying glass, which he slid in front of his eyes.

"There's definitely something else in here," he said. "Some of the herbs were thrown in without being crumbled, and presumably after the cooking was completed. There are some larger bits that I might be able to identify if I can rinse off the jelly. I think I even see what might be pieces of flower petals. I'd like to hold on to this for a while."

When Rose hesitated, Andrew lifted his gaze to her face. "What is it, Rose? You still don't quite trust me, do you? Why?"

Might as well tackle the topic now, Rose thought. "I spoke with Sister Lilian at Mount Lebanon a little while ago."

Andrew blinked several times but otherwise showed no reaction. "And?" he asked.

"And I'm well aware that I'm repeating gossip, but there are some issues you and I need to discuss."

"I see. Such as . . . ?"

"Such as your relationship with Patience."

Andrew laughed. "My relationship with Patience. Strained, I would have to say. Why? Do you suspect me of having something to do with her death? Wasn't it an accident?"

"That was the deputy's conclusion. But I was referring more specifically to Lilian's comment that some Mount Lebanon Believers thought there might be a special relationship between you and Patience."

"And did Lilian offer any evidence to support the rumor?"

"Nay, she did not," Rose admitted. "She sounded as if she did not believe it herself."

"Because it is unfounded. Patience was creative with

herbal cures, and I respected her for that, but she and I could not even be called friends. What else are you wondering about me?''

''I'm wondering how your family died.''

Pain seared across his face, and Rose instinctively reached out, then pulled her hand back in the same movement. ''I'm so sorry, Andrew, that was brutal of me, blurting it out like that. Please forgive me.''

''You have a right to ask,'' Andrew said. ''And if it will help you trust me, I will tell you anything you wish to know. As for my wife and sons, there was nothing mysterious about their deaths; only unnecessary. I know the rumors—that I used my pharmaceutical knowledge to poison them, either because I could no longer support them, or I'd gone crazy after losing my job, or, according to my less charitable neighbors, because I wanted to be free of them so I could start over. None of it was true.

''I was desperate to keep them alive and healthy. But when my job disappeared, I hadn't been paid for two months. I'd kept working, hoping things would turn around. We used up what little savings we had, and we had no other family to turn to. We were running out of food. Inevitably, Vera and the boys all got colds. I'd saved some herbs and other items from the drugstore, so I made up cough syrups and poultices and anything else I could think of, but it wasn't enough. By the time I'd begged a doctor to make a charity visit, they all had pneumonia. They died within days of each other.'' Andrew began straightening the tins and apothecary jars on the worktable as if neatness helped him make sense of his tragedy.

''I buried them,'' he continued softly, ''and then I really did go crazy for a while. I wandered the streets for days, barely knowing who I was, or caring. That's probably how the rumors started. More than once I blamed myself for not saving my family. To some it looked like I had a guilty conscience. But it was only grief.''

For the first time since putting her signature on the covenant, Rose deliberately broke one of the Society's rules; she reached over and lightly touched Andrew's hand as he stacked one herb tin on top of another. "I'm so very sorry," she said. Andrew's hand twitched as if she'd applied an electrical current. He raised his eyes to hers. She withdrew her hand, but not so quickly that she might insult him or take back her expression of sympathy.

"Thank you, Rose."

Rose nodded, but he had already busied himself with tidying the worktable. "You may keep the jelly as long as you need to," she said. After a few moments of silence, she turned to leave.

"You know, there is much I love about being a Shaker," Andrew said. Rose stopped but kept her back to him. "But I do miss the kindness of a woman's touch."

Rose closed her eyes. She sent herself deep into her own breath and watched it flow in and out of her lungs. It kept her still, which was her prayer.

"I will let you know what I find, if anything, in the herbal jelly," Andrew said, with a casualness that sounded forced.

"Thank you," Rose said, and she left.

TWENTY-ONE

IN NEED OF QUIET, ROSE HAD JOINED THE FAMILY IN THE dwelling house dining room for evening meal. She avoided glancing toward the brethren for fear of catching Andrew's eye. Instead, she ate slowly and prayed silently. She longed for the privacy of her retiring room. She reminded herself that one hundred years earlier, she would have had no privacy, even in her room. Privacy meant decline, so she supposed she was wrong to value it. Still, the yearning grew stronger as she piled her utensils and napkin on her empty plate.

But privacy would have to wait. Wilhelm caught up to her as she walked back toward the Ministry House.

"To bed so soon?" he asked. "I haven't noticed thee laboring in the fields. What is tiring thee so?"

"Is there something you wished to say to me, Wilhelm?" She did not turn her head to look at him, but she could sense his jaw tightening.

"The purging ceremony," he said.

"What about it?"

"There has been a change of plans."

"Oh?" She didn't dare hope he had decided to cancel or postpone it.

"I no longer wish for your confession to come first," Wilhelm said. "Andrew will go first."

Rose did not trust herself to speak.

"I'm sure his confession will be of great interest to thee." Rose could hear the smirk in his voice. "In fact, it may serve as a model for thy own confession."

As they approached the Ministry House, they split to enter through the separate doors. Rose hurried up her staircase to her second-floor retiring room without daring to glance back at Wilhelm.

Rose sat at her open window far into the night. She stared at the summer stars, imagined she saw Mother Ann's face among them, and prayed to her. Her emotions were in a jumble. She knew she had some serious thinking to do, but there wasn't time. Either Andrew had confessed already to Wilhelm about their touch, or the elder had guessed enough to order Andrew to confess publicly. Either way, the danger was great for both of them. Their sins were tiny, but much more would be assumed, and they might both lose their positions in the Society.

She could give up being eldress, she told herself, but she wouldn't let Andrew be humiliated because of her. She had touched his hand, not the other way around. Wilhelm was willing to use one of the brethren as a pawn to force Rose to step down; that was all this was about.

Well, she wouldn't let him. However, she had only one idea for stopping him, and she had no guarantee that it would work. As it was, if she refused to participate, or to let the sisters participate, in the purging, she would never overcome the suspicions. Even dead, Patience now had more respect than Rose. She could see only one way. She had to determine how Patience and Hugo died, even if it meant more danger of embarrassment—or worse—for Andrew. If she could show that Patience did not die a martyr and an offering for North Homage's sins, the purging need not take place. If Hugo's death was natural and Patience's nothing more sinister than a tragic accident, so much the better. They could all go back to their quiet lives.

Her decision made, Rose began to droop in her rocking

chair. She had very little time to accomplish her task, and she would need rest. As if she didn't have enough to confess already, she flung her work dress over the back of a chair, instead of hanging it on a wall peg, and she fell into bed without bothering with a nightgown.

The enforced silence at breakfast was grating on Gennie's nerves. Rose hadn't shown up, and everyone seemed nervous. She knew about the impending purging, of course, and had never been so glad that she had decided to leave the Society for life in the world. In the world, she could keep her secrets. Not that she had any in the world; for her, secrets began to collect, it seemed, only when she returned to North Homage.

Gennie wanted something to do, something helpful for Rose. She couldn't return to the Medicinal Herb Shop, and Irene wouldn't welcome her back to the Herb House. What was left? She racked her brain until finally the sisters, almost as a body, stood to leave the dining room single file. As she reached the women's entrance, Gennie glanced over at the brethren and noticed Willy Robinson step through the men's door. Of course, she thought, she could talk to him all she wanted, since neither of them was a Believer.

Rose had told her Willy's story. If he went to work in the medic garden outside the shop, perhaps she could engage him in conversation and fill in a few blanks about his past and his reasons for being in North Homage. Beyond that, she had no plan as she ambled through the kitchen garden, casually following Willy to the Medicinal Herb Shop. As she'd hoped, he walked past the entrance and into the surrounding herb garden.

Forcing herself not to look eager, Gennie zigzagged through the kitchen garden, stopping now and then to bend over a squash or peer at a bean. She walked to the northern tip of the garden, which brought her nearly to the herb fields. Then she cut through the grass around the back of the Medicinal Herb Shop, so no one inside could see her.

By the time she approached the herb garden on the east side of the Medicinal Herb Shop, Willy was on his hands and knees, pulling tiny weeds from around a flourishing sage plant. Gennie paused and watched him for a few moments. He bent close to each weed and pulled carefully, tamping down the dirt afterward. Stringy pale brown hair hung over his face, nearly covering it. She had stood for several seconds before she realized that he had raised his eyes and was staring up at her.

Gennie flashed a smile to hide her embarrassment and picked her way over neat rows of herbs to join him. He straightened as she approached, his head sunk into his shoulders as if he expected to be disciplined.

"Hello, Willy, I'm Gennie." She extended her hand, and he stared at it, then at her dress, his head sinking another inch. "I'm not a Shaker sister," she assured him. "I'm a hired hand, like you. Don't you remember seeing me in the shop, helping Patience?"

"You ain't a sister?"

"Nope," she said, purposely using worldly language. She was beginning to feel awkward with her hand stuck out, when Willy suddenly grinned and grasped it. His grip was powerful, and Gennie winced. Willy let go immediately.

"Sorry," he mumbled. "Don't usually shake hands with a girl."

"No harm done. Are you weeding?" Using her long skirt as a cushion, Gennie knelt beside the sage plant Willy had been tending. It was so much easier not to worry about keeping a proper distance.

"Do you enjoy this work?"

Willy nodded and bent again over the ground.

"You have a special feeling for herbs, don't you? I mean, I can tell by how careful you are not to disturb the roots. I love herbs, too, so it's nice to see them so well cared for."

She knew she was chattering, but she hoped to slide into

her real questions more easily once she'd lulled him into a sense of comfortable conversation. She needn't have worried. He glanced up at her and smiled shyly. Encouraged, she slid a few inches closer and reached for a small blade of grass that had invaded the territory around the sage plant. Imitating the movements she'd seen Willy perform, she smoothed the soil after removing the interloper. Willy's smile widened.

"You're pretty," he said.

Oops, she thought. *I tried a little too hard.* She slid back on her heels and left the weeding to Willy. "I heard that you know a lot about medicinal herbs," she said. "Why aren't you working in the shop? They could sure use you now that Patience is gone."

"Who told you I know about herbs?"

"Well, I . . . I guess I heard it from someone in the shop. Isn't it true?"

"Yeah, it's true, all right. Reckon it'd be better if I didn't know so much. Never did me much good in the end."

"I guess I heard something about that, too."

"Somebody talked a lot."

"Oh, you know how things get around in a small village like this." Gennie settled herself cross-legged on the grass. She felt a little guilty getting dirt and grass stains all over her skirt, remembering what it was like to scrub laundry, especially in the summer months. "I'm sorry for what happened to you. I'm sure it wasn't really your fault."

Willy's gentle weeding turned rougher, and bits of loam sprayed Gennie's skirt. "I never killed that man, and neither did my granny. Not on purpose, anyways."

"I'm sorry. Do you have any idea what really happened?"

"Maybe we made a mistake in fixing up the cure, maybe not. Granny was gettin' on, but she still knew her healin', and she'd made that tonic a hundred times. I never could figure what went wrong. Now Sister Patience is gone, I'll probably never know."

"You talked with Patience about what went wrong with your grandmother's recipe?"

"Yeah. She knew lots. She was experimenting to find out what the problem was. I remembered the recipe by heart, and I helped her get the ingredients. She said it was a good cure."

"You mean she didn't have the right ingredients in the shop?"

Willy shook his head. "I had to hunt them down. It wasn't hard, though. I'm real good at recognizing herbs in the wild, and I found everything right here in the village."

"Really? Like what?"

"Oh, you know, like deadly nightshade."

"You found that here? Right in North Homage?" Gennie squirmed to her feet in excitement. "Can you show me where?"

"Well, I dunno, I've got to get this whole garden weeded, and—"

"I'll help you later."

Willy shook his head, with obvious regret. "Andrew'd have my hide, and I really need this job."

"Okay, then, tomorrow morning, early. Meet me right here a half hour before breakfast."

Willy grinned his agreement.

With an effort, Rose put aside her unsettled feelings about her conversation with Andrew, and she headed for the woods behind the burned-out site of the old water house. A quick phone call had told her that Charlotte had taken the children to the secluded area for a cool outing. She was eager for the shade herself; today the air seemed to liquify as it touched her skin and clothing.

The children were easy to find. Despite the heat, they were giggling and running through the thick maple trees, pausing now and then to chase a rabbit or squeal at a garter snake. Charlotte sat on the grass, leaning against a tree trunk, watching with half-closed eyes. She had removed her cap, and her dark blond hair lay limp and flat against her head. As she saw Rose approach, she grabbed at her cap, and Rose laughed.

"Don't bother on my account," Rose said. "This heat is enough to try a saint. If my hair were short, I'd take off my cap, too." She settled down on the grass beside Charlotte. "Besides, I'm not here to check up on you."

"Is it the purging?" Charlotte asked. "Oh, please tell me it's been canceled."

"I'm afraid not."

"What will Wilhelm think of next? Self-flagellation? I'm sorry, Rose, that was mean, but you know how I feel about all this going back to the old ways. As far as I can see, living like the angels requires us to love one another, devote our lives to worship, and work hard. Must we torture ourselves, too?" Charlotte pushed her hair back into her cap and tied it at the nape of her neck. "As if this clothing weren't torture enough."

"Believe me, I sympathize. But I'm here for a different reason. I have a couple of questions about the children."

"Nora and Betsy have behaved themselves since their release from the Infirmary, I promise you. I make them nap in my retiring room so I can keep an eye on them."

"I'm glad to hear it. But I was really wondering about the Dengler girls."

"Janey and Marjorie? They've been getting into things they shouldn't, too, haven't they? I knew it."

"Have they been a problem for you?"

"Oh, not seriously. But they are just Nora and Betsy's ages, and the four girls often play together. When there's mischief being done, it's usually Nora and Betsy doing it, but now and then I've wondered about the Dengler sisters. Several times I've caught them munching on candied angelica root when I hadn't given any to the children. I thought they might have learned some tricks from Nora and Betsy, like sneaking into the kitchen during naps for snacks. And they do both still have a few problems with bedwetting, I'm afraid. They are fearful children. Look, there they are now.'' Charlotte pointed between two trees to a line of four girls, chasing each other. Nora and Betsy were in front, followed by two thin towheads.

''I'll just go speak to them, if you don't mind,'' Rose said, pushing to her feet. ''Would you distract Nora and Betsy while I do? I don't want them involved.''

''Certainly,'' Charlotte said, curiosity brightening her eyes. ''Just send them to me. Sounds serious.''

''We'll see.'' A distant roll of thunder underscored the sternness in Rose's voice.

She sent Nora and Betsy off to Charlotte and smiled down at the Dengler sisters, who stared at her, pale blue eyes opened wide. The girls were almost identical. One was an inch taller with a longer face; that would be Janey, the elder. Little Marjorie clutched a corncob doll to her thin chest. Rose held out a hand for each, and they shyly inserted their own small hands.

''Let's walk, shall we?'' Rose said. ''I just have a few questions to ask you, and then you can come back and play with your friends.'' As she led them out of earshot, both pale heads turned to look back.

Still holding their hands, Rose chose a shady spot and sank to the ground. The girls dropped down next to her. Marjorie began to suck her thumb, and Rose said nothing. The children were scared; that was clear. Perhaps she was more frightening than she realized. Well, that might be for the best. She had no wish to leave them terrified, but if fear made them open up more quickly, so much the better.

''You know who I am, don't you?'' she asked.

Both heads nodded.

''And you know, too, that something bad happened to Nora and Betsy?''

Janey's lip began to tremble, and Marjorie stuck her whole thumb in her mouth.

''I need your help to find out why your friends got sick, so no other children will get sick. Do you understand?

Good, then I want each of you to tell me everything you know about what Nora and Betsy were doing the day they got sick. Janey, you start.''

Janey stared at her, mute. Perhaps she'd been too stern. ''Janey, you aren't in any trouble, I promise you. I truly need your help. You'll be helping everyone, including Nora and Betsy.''

Rose heard a sucking noise and a few mumbled words. ''Could you take your thumb out of your mouth, Marjorie, dear? That's a girl. Now, what did you say?''

''They went to a tea party,'' Marjorie said.

''We weren't supposed to tell!'' Janey wailed. ''Now everybody will be mad at us.''

''Who is 'everybody,' Janey?'' Rose asked.

Janey clamped her mouth shut.

''Marjorie? Janey doesn't realize how important this is, but you do, don't you? It will help me so very much if you tell me who you think will be angry with you.'' Two sets of pale eyes exchanged glances.

''Are you scared of someone?'' Rose asked.

Marjorie's small chin bobbed in a tiny nod.

''Who? Who are you afraid of?''

''Don't tell, don't you dare tell,'' Janey screamed, and threw herself on her sister. Startled, Rose jumped back.

''All right, you two, stop it right now.'' She pried Janey off Marjorie. ''Janey, we *never* hit one another in this village. I want you to go back to Charlotte at once and tell her that you hit your sister. She will know what to do.''

A sulky Janey jumped up, tossed a stinging glance at her sister, and ran toward Charlotte.

''Your dress is torn,'' Rose said. ''Are you all right? Do you hurt anywhere?''

Marjorie shook her head.

''Okay, you don't have to tell me who you are afraid of, at least not right now. But what did you mean when you said that Nora and Betsy went to tea?''

''They do it a lot.''

"Where do they go?"

"You know, the woods and places."

"These woods, do you mean?"

A sudden gust of wind rustled the leaves above them and lifted Marjorie's fine hair. "I guess," she said. "All the woods, I think. They never took us along, even though we told them about the flowers. It wasn't fair."

"What flowers?" Rose asked.

"The magical flowers."

"Who told you the flowers were magical?"

Spots of color appeared on Marjorie's sallow cheeks, and she looked as if she were about to cry. "I'm not s'posed to tell," she said.

"You can tell me," Rose said gently. "It'll help keep Nora and Betsy safe and well."

Confusion and misery took their toll, and Marjorie's thumb went back into her mouth. She shook her head. Tears spilled down her cheeks and her hand.

"Okay, you don't have to tell, then. But can you tell me what the flowers' names were?"

Marjorie shook her head again.

"Do you remember the name 'foxglove'?"

Marjorie shrugged.

"Did you see any of the flowers yourself?" This drew a nod, so Rose asked, "What colors were they?"

This question seemed safer; Marjorie removed her wet thumb from her mouth and thought for a few seconds. "They were lots of pretty colors. Pink, and blue, and purple, and white."

"Were any of them shaped like bells?"

"Sort of," Marjorie said. "Those were the bad magic flowers." When Rose looked puzzled, Marjorie explained, "Mama told us to be careful of the bad ones and to remember that they were shaped like bells. If we ate them, a bad angel would come and take us away forever. We told Nora and Betsy, but Nora didn't believe us. She said Mama was just trying to scare us. She said flowers are good, so they have to be good magic.''

So Nora had served Betsy and herself a ''bad magic'' flower as a form of defiant experimentation. That certainly sounded like Nora, Rose thought. She was a bright child, who sometimes put too much faith in her own logical processes. By adulthood, she'd be cured of that—if she lived that long.

''So was it your mama who told you about the flowers, Marjorie?''

The thumb went back in the mouth, and the girl scooted backward. ''You said I didn't have to tell,'' she mumbled around her thumb.

''But you just said—''

''You said I didn't have to tell!'' Marjorie jumped to her feet and ran back toward Charlotte, where her sister had joined Nora and Betsy. Rose knew there was no point in pursuing her.

Rose got to her feet and brushed the grass and dried leaves off her skirt. Another roll of thunder, this time closer, gave her a comforting hope of at least a temporary cool-down. With luck, it would arrive by the next evening, so the purging, if it must take place, could be accomplished in more comfortable temperatures.

Rather than walking back through the group of children, and perhaps upsetting Marjorie again, Rose took a circuitous route through the trees. She circled, just out of sight, around the clearing where the children played. She could hear them laughing.

As she rounded a large maple, she heard something else, underneath the laughter. Someone was crying, somewhere to Rose's left. Walking quietly, she followed the sound and found a man in Shaker work clothing, standing in the shadows with his back to her, watching the children play. He wore the flat-crowned, wide-brimmed hat of the brethren, so she couldn't see his hair or the shape of his head. He raised his arm and wiped his sleeve across his cheeks as if clearing away tears.

Rose ducked behind a tree as he turned and headed east, toward the perimeter of the maple grove. As she saw his profile, she realized the man was Thomas Dengler. On his arm he carried a basket. Though she was too far away to tell for sure, the basket seemed to hold a pile of green stalks with flowers attached.

TWENTY-TWO

AFTER A TENSE EVENING MEAL, THE BELIEVERS WERE SENT to their retiring rooms for an early bedtime. The next day would be demanding—a full day of work followed by the evening purging service. Gertrude had picked at her food, clearly anticipating the anguish of exposing her episode of physical violence. If Rose couldn't come up with a solution fast, Gertrude would probably confess to murder, as well. Rose might lose her position as eldress, but that was nothing compared with Gertrude's potential loss.

Rose decided it was time to check in with Grady O'Neal. She closed the door to the Ministry library, hoping to keep her conversation private from Wilhelm. The Languor County Sheriff's Office told her Grady was off duty, so she put through a call to his home number. His people were among the wealthiest in the state, so Grady could afford telephone service, even as a young bachelor on a deputy's salary.

Grady answered quickly. "Rose? I thought it might be Gennie calling. It's about time."

"Sorry," Rose said. "I won't keep you long."

"Are you wondering if I've looked into Patience's death? Somehow I thought you wouldn't let go. Well, I have done some checking, and I'm beginning to think you were right. Besides, the doctor I sent over said there's a good chance Patience's wound came from being hit with a sharp rock. So I talked to the folks who were gathered around when we found Patience. Most of them had followed Gertrude's scream, and they were in full view of each other, so they all have alibies way back to their arrival at your worship service. There's others, of course, but I think I got most of their names, and nobody could think of a single reason why any of the townsfolk would hurt Patience. They hardly knew her, and she wasn't one to come into town and be friendly.''

"So you've got nothing?"

"I wouldn't say that. There was one young courting couple that no one saw at the service, but they appeared when Patience was found. When I questioned them, they admitted they'd sneaked off to the woods well before the service to do some smooching—sorry, Rose. Anyway, they heard a loud argument, and it sounded to them like it was between two women.''

"Did they check to see what was happening?" Rose asked, with misgivings. She could see the noose settling around Gertrude's neck.

"Uh, well, they were pretty occupied, I guess. Anyway, the arguing stopped, and they just forgot about it.''

With great reluctance, Rose had decided that she must tell Grady about Gertrude's argument with Patience. She took a deep breath to keep her voice calm.

"But it gets weirder," Grady said, before Rose could start her story. "After a while, they heard all sorts of odd sounds coming from close by. They said it sounded like someone was having fits.''

"I suppose they were too busy to investigate that, as well?"

"Yup. So we need to figure out what the 'fits' were and who was having them. Was Patience still alive and in a trance? Was she badly injured and crying out in agony? Or was someone else there, having fits over her body?''

"I think I can help with those questions." Rose told Gertrude's story. When she'd finished, Grady paused so long that Rose was afraid he'd broken the connection.

"I'm afraid," he said finally, "we still can't be sure what was going on. We only have Gertrude's word for it that she left Patience alive."

"But—"

"We have to be realistic, Rose. I don't want to arrest Gertrude, for heaven's sakes, but we have to cover all the possibilities. For one, we have to remember that there's no evidence that anyone from town had anything to do with this. So if Patience was murdered, and if Gertrude didn't do it, that means another Shaker probably did."

"I know," Rose said. "But we can't just let it drop."

"Nope, that we can't. So here's what I need you to do. Put together everything you've got about anyone who might have wanted Patience out of the way. I've got to be out of town most of tomorrow, but I'll try to get to North Homage by late afternoon, and we can put our heads together."

"All right," Rose said. "I'm afraid I'll be busy in the evening."

"Yeah, Gennie told me all about that purging thing. Sounds awful. I don't know what else to say."

"As little as possible," Rose said. "Just get here as soon as you can tomorrow."

Early to sleep was out of the question for Rose, but she did slip out of her work dress. The sun had nearly set, but as yet they'd gotten no relief from the sultry air. The occasional bursts of thunder had begun to seem like a cruel trick.

Rose sat at the small desk in her retiring room with paper and pen and began her notes for Grady. Collecting the names of Believers who had reason to dislike Patience was not a difficult task. Rose thought back to the sweeping gift and jotted down several names: Irene, Elsa, Andrew, and, she had to admit, herself. Benjamin and Thomas also belonged on the list. Gertrude, unfortunately. All Believers.

Were there no people of the world who might have wished
Patience dead? Willy Robinson? He certainly had contact
with her, as well as the strength and opportunity to kill her,
but Rose could think of no reason why he would do so.
His past was murky but had no apparent connection with
Patience. Perhaps she had found out something he wished
to keep secret?

Next to each person's name, Rose wrote a few notes,
giving reasons why he or she might or might not be a killer.
To get it over with, she began with herself. Patience had
accused her publicly of being unworthy to be eldress; she
had left the impression that she could reveal more, probably
hints of an illicit relationship between Rose and Andrew.
Flashes of shame and righteous anger left Rose with a deep
sense of foreboding about the purging ceremony coming up
in less than a day.

Patience had accused Irene of sinning twice. Was she
referring to Thomas and Benjamin and their apparent struggle for Irene's affection? Yet Irene herself seemed uninter-
ested in both men, or in any man, for that matter. So how
was she the sinner? Could the accusation have something
to do with Irene's two children?

Rose jotted down more detail about Gertrude's disagree-
ments with Patience, then moved on to Elsa. Wilhelm's
protégée, Elsa was ambitious beyond her abilities. She was
cunning rather than bright. Her spiritual gifts had been
overshadowed by Patience's, and she was in danger of losing her special place with Wilhelm. Elsa's will had been
thwarted before. This time, did it drive her to murder?

Benjamin was ambitious, arrogant, and apparently in
love with Irene. Yet if Rose saw all this, others surely did,
too. Had Patience had additional, more damaging information about him? Was it perhaps related to the odd design
drawn in both their journals?

It seemed that Thomas, too, might be overfond of Irene.
Given what Rose had witnessed in the woods, he was certainly attached to his daughters. He had a history of drunk-

enness and violence. Had Patience known about it?

Reluctantly Rose reached Andrew's name. Patience would, of course, have known about the deaths of Andrew's wife and children. According to Andrew, he had nothing to hide. Had he told the truth? Or was Patience referring, during the sweeping gift, to something else in his past, something no one else knew about? If she and Andrew had indeed had a special relationship, she might have such information.

Yawning, Rose pushed her notes aside and stretched. A gentle wind ruffled the paper, and Rose walked to her open window, which looked out over the north side of the village. The sky was moonless but lightened somewhat by the clouds moving in. Everyone must be asleep; the Center Family Dwelling House was totally dark, including the kitchen.

Remembering that she wore only her petticoat, Rose went back to her desk and extinguished her lamp, then returned to the window to enjoy what little breeze there was. She had just pulled forward her rocking chair when she looked out and saw a dim light appear almost directly north of her. At first she thought it must be a flash of lightning, but it didn't disappear in a few seconds. Then she knew she was seeing a lighted window. Given the location, it had to be the Herb House, which had small windows all around for ventilation. Someone had just turned on a light in the second floor of the Herb House.

Rose hesitated. Under ordinary circumstances, she would assume that one of the sisters couldn't sleep and had decided to catch up on some work. But Irene was the only sister working in the drying room right now, and she had told Gennie that she didn't have enough work to keep the two of them busy. If she couldn't sleep in this heat, why not sit up and read or write in her journal next to an open window?

It was enough to warrant investigation, especially given the possibility that Irene or someone else from the Mount

Lebanon group might be a killer. Rose pulled her work dress back over her underclothes and slipped into her cloth shoes. She debated leaving off her white cap since it might be too visible, but she had been caught without her cap before, and she was in enough trouble as it was.

Leaving the Ministry House without Wilhelm's knowledge was easily accomplished. His room, on the ground floor, faced south and was far enough away from the staircase and front door that she could slip out unnoticed. A quick look up and down the village assured her that all other windows, besides the one in the drying room, were dark.

To avoid being seen from the Herb House, she veered off to the right and hurried past the east side of the barn. It was a short run to the southeast corner of the Herb House, where she would not be visible from the window. She edged around the corner and along the front of the building until she reached the front door. Praying the hinges had been oiled recently, she opened it just enough for her thin body to slide through.

The ground floor was dark, the huge presses silent. The upstairs drying room door must be open because Rose could hear loud, angry voices from above her. She heard two voices, both too low to be Irene. She tiptoed to the staircase, wincing each time she stepped on a squeaky floorboard. The men were too involved in their argument to hear.

Rose had almost reached the bottom step when her hand brushed against a table piled high with wrapped packages of pressed herbs. One package, balanced precariously on the top, slid down the stack, hit the corner of the table, and plunked on the floor.

The arguing stopped. Rose held perfectly still, preparing herself for a confrontation, until she realized that another voice was speaking. A higher, softer voice. Then both men began speaking—or shouting—at once. Rose was desperate to understand what they were saying, but getting up the stairs without being heard seemed impossible. She ventured up one step, which squeaked loudly enough to wake the village. One of the men continued speaking, but Rose knew she couldn't risk going any farther. If the woman, presumably Irene, spoke again, her voice wouldn't cover the sound of a creaking board.

The men's voices were becoming more distinct. She was fairly certain now that she was hearing Benjamin and Thomas. She heard one man, possibly Thomas, say, "Over my dead body. You keep your hands off them. They're *mine!*" Rose guessed Thomas was warning Benjamin to stay away from his family. So perhaps Irene was, indeed, guilty of two sins—loving two men in a worldly way.

When Rose heard Irene say, "It's none of your concern," she realized why the voices had become easier to understand. They were moving toward the door of the drying room. Without waiting for a louder voice to offer cover, she jumped backward off the lower step and flattened herself against the side of the staircase. Feeling behind her, she realized there was an open space under the stairs. She backed into it, trying to avoid the brooms and dustpans leaning against the wall. They should have been stored on wall pegs. Some Believer had picked an inconvenient time and place to be lazy.

Footsteps clattered over her head. Rose prayed, fervently and silently, that the group would head for the front door. They did. She heard the door swing open, then a male voice said, "Just a minute. I forgot something. You go on ahead." Footsteps left the building, and Rose waited. Her own breathing sounded like a train engine to her. Surely she would be found out. All she could do was huddle in the shadows under the stairs and *pray*.

Benjamin walked past her hiding place. Even in the dark, she recognized him. She could have reached out and almost touched him. She held her breath, but he looked straight ahead, intent on a mission on the other side of the room. When he passed out of her view, Rose risked inching her head forward, but she still couldn't see him. She heard some scraping sounds, as if something heavy was being moved aside, then a rustling sound and the thump of something being dropped. Benjamin cursed softly. A repeat of the scraping sound indicated something being moved again, perhaps back into place.

Rose pulled her head back just in time as Benjamin passed in front of her again. She remained still, breathing quickly, for several moments after she heard the front door open and shut. Slowly she eased out of her nook. As soon as she had shaken the kink out of her back, she followed the path she assumed Benjamin had taken to the far corner of the room. She came to a dusty herb press that must have broken down and never been fixed. Just behind it was a small, badly damaged chest of drawers that looked as if it had been made before Hugo took over the Society's Carpenters' Shop.

Excited now, Rose pushed aside the herb press. Yea, that was the sound she had heard. The top two drawers of the chest were missing, and the bottom drawer hung halfway open. Ignoring the dust and ancient bits of dried herbs on the floor, Rose lowered to her knees and felt inside the drawer. Empty. She peered into the cavities that used to hold the other drawers. She saw nothing. Benjamin must have hidden something in the chest and stayed behind to retrieve it.

She had half a mind to roust him out of his retiring room, if that's where he'd gone, and insist on seeing what he'd taken with him. She pushed to her feet and twirled around to find herself two inches from a broom handle, aimed at her stomach. Gennie Malone, prepared for attack, clutched the other end of the handle.

"Rose! I thought it must be you, but I couldn't be sure, and I decided I'd better protect myself, just in case. I mean, anyone could dress like a Shaker sister and wander around the village at night doing who knows what."

"Gennie, you can put the broom down now."

"Oh. Of course. Sorry, guess I'm a little on edge. It's been an exciting evening—and afternoon. I have *so* much to tell you, Rose!"

"The first thing I want to know, Gennie Malone, is what on earth you are doing here at this time of night."

Gennie laughed. "I could ask you the same thing, you know."

"But instead you are going to answer my question, aren't you?"

"Well, okay, I was taking a short walk after bedtime, just to get some air, and I saw Irene leave the Center Family Dwelling House, so I decided to follow her. When she came here, I thought she probably just wanted to get some work done and I was wasting my time. I stayed outside for a while, wondering what to do, and I was about to leave when Brother Thomas walked right up to the door, and sneaking behind him was Brother Benjamin."

"And I suppose you followed them in, just like that," Rose said.

"I was fine, Rose, don't worry. I'm not foolish. I waited awhile to see if the rest of the Medicinal Herb Shop would show up. Wish I hadn't, though, because I missed a lot of what they said." Gennie leaned her broom handle against the wall and scooted onto a worktable. She swung her legs like an excited child.

"I couldn't hear them well," Rose said. "How did you figure out what they were saying?"

"Oh, I just sneaked up the stairs and into the drying room."

"You *what*? How on earth . . . ?"

"It was easy. I spent so much time here, I could find my way around in my sleep. I know every creak in every stair. I did hear you take a step, though. Scared me half to death. It's a wonder they didn't hear, but they were so busy arguing.

"Anyway," Gennie continued, "I'm pretty small, so I could crawl under that desk we used to keep the Herb

House records in, the one we pushed way over in the corner. You can't see it from the doorway or the worktable, so I figured they'd leave without catching me. And I was right.''

"Oh my." Rose melted onto a nearby stool. "Gennie, you took an awful chance."

"But it was worth it. I don't know how all of this fits together, but I've got some information for you. Benjamin wants Irene to run away with him."

"I suspected as much," Rose said. "Does Thomas want the same thing?"

"Well, I think so. At least, he didn't actually mention leaving with Irene himself, but he seemed determined to stop Benjamin from taking his family away from him. He said that if Benjamin tried to take them away, he'd send the police after them because Benjamin had broken the law, though he didn't say what law. Thomas said he'd claim that Irene knew about it and have her declared an unfit mother, so she'd lose her children. That's when I heard you step on a squeaky stair."

"Irene said something then, didn't she?"

Gennie hesitated. "Irene was hard to understand because her voice is softer, but she was really angry, so I caught some of it. She said something like, 'You'll never get your hands on those children.' I assume she was talking to Thomas."

"After that I heard them coming and ducked under the stairs," Rose said.

"Talk about taking chances," Gennie said. "Anyway, after that, Thomas and Benjamin mostly hurled insults at each other, but they did mention Patience. Benjamin said something about Patience having a nasty story to tell about Thomas, too. That was all I heard. Does it help?"

"Indeed. I can't put it all together yet, either, but I'm getting closer. A few hours sleep may help. Come on, to bed with you. I'll walk you home."

Gennie slid off her perch without argument.

As they parted at the door to the Center Family Dwelling House, Gennie asked, "Rose, what were you doing when I came up behind you back there?"

"I heard Benjamin move something heavy and then retrieve something. At least, that's what it sounded like."

"Any idea what?"

"That's one question I'm hoping sleep will help me answer."

Gennie yawned and trudged up the steps without another word, not even a "good night."

It was just as Rose reached the Ministry House door that she realized what Benjamin might have been retrieving. The only items she knew to be missing—Patience's journal and the last two pages from Benjamin's own journal.

TWENTY-THREE

As a visitor from the world, Gennie had no required chores in the early morning, so she was up, dressed, and on her way to the Medicinal Herb Shop while the sisters cleaned the brethren's rooms and mended their clothes. She hoped Rose would eat breakfast at the Ministry House and not notice if Gennie was late to the dining room. Rose and Grady both had a way of being overprotective. They just didn't realize that she was eighteen now and well able to take care of herself.

As he'd promised, Willy waited in the garden next to the Medicinal Herb Shop. He took off his grimy cap and grinned broadly at her, revealing a broken tooth. He really wasn't a bad-looking young man, Gennie decided, just badly cared for. He was smarter than he appeared at first, and he had a job, which was more than a lot of fellows could say these days. Maybe she could introduce him to some of the girls she was meeting in Languor.

"Ready?" she asked. "Which direction?"

With his cap, Willy pointed northwest, through the Medicinal Herb Shop. He led the way around the back of the shop and past the Center Family Dwelling House.

"Are we going back to the holy hill?" By now, everyone in the village knew about the Empyrean Mount, even the non-Shakers.

"Nope, up a ways, beyond that old cemetery. There's

some woods up there nobody seems to go to much. That's where I seen the herbs.''

"How did you think to look up there?" Gennie asked.

Willy pulled his cap over his head. "Well, it was really Patience told me to look up there. She said it just seemed like a good place for those plants to grow.''

"Really? I wonder how she knew that.''

"Dunno," Willy said, with a worried sideways look. "Didn't think to ask.''

"Don't worry, I was just curious.''

Willy stepped in front of Gennie as they entered the woods, stamping down a path for her through the brambles and brush until they reached a small clearing. He led her to the far edge of the clearing, where he stopped and pointed to a cluster of plants with dusky green leaves and purple, bell-like flowers. Gennie thought it looked familiar, but she didn't remember seeing it in the Society's medic garden.

"I don't recognize it," she said.

"That there's belladonna. I wouldn't touch it, if I was you," he warned as she reached out her hand toward the flower. "It's real poisonous. My granny said it was called deadly nightshade for good reason.''

"Deadly nightshade? I know for a fact that we never let that grow anywhere in the village, not since I arrived as a girl. Josie was always afraid a hungry neighbor child would eat the berries and die, and we'd be to blame. What's it doing here?''

Willy frowned with worry. "Dunno. Granny and I always just picked it wild, though we never let it touch our skin.''

"Well, I suppose it could have gotten going wild again, if no one has taken care to pull it out regularly," Gennie said. "This looks like a healthy little colony. This was in your grandmother's asthma recipe?''

"Yup. You had to be real careful about the amount or it'll kill a person, but it works real well.''

"I'll take your word for it. Did you find anything else?"

"She had pretty much everything else, but while I was here, I had a look around, to see if anything else might've taken root. And look here what I found." He pointed to another grouping of plants, about five feet tall, with reddish stems and greenish-white flowers. "That's pokeweed. Granny wouldn't use it, said it was too dangerous and there was lots of safer plants that did a better job."

"What was it used for?"

"To empty the stomach."

"Oh." In the distance she heard the breakfast bell, and though her appetite had just dimmed, she knew they had to hurry. It wouldn't do for them to walk into the dining room at the same time, both late.

"Is that all you found?"

"There's more, but it's along in the woods a ways. We could skip breakfast, and I could show you," he suggested. "We could look around for more, too." His hopeful tone convinced her it was time to leave.

"Maybe later. If we don't show up at breakfast, everyone will worry. Besides, I don't know about you, but I don't work well on an empty stomach."

Rose waited impatiently through breakfast with Wilhelm. Though the purging ceremony to be conducted that evening must be on his mind, he said nothing. Under other circumstances, she might feel anxious, but she had too much to think about. She escaped as quickly as possible and went straight to the Medicinal Herb Shop.

Thomas wasn't in sight, but Andrew and Benjamin looked up from their work as she entered the shop. She directed a formal nod at Andrew and approached Benjamin's worktable.

"Could we speak privately for a moment?" she asked. The purging was scheduled to begin in less than twelve hours. She had no time for niceties.

Benjamin shot an irritated glance at Andrew, who turned

back to his notes. Rose walked out the front door, and Benjamin followed. Since Willy was weeding in the herb garden, Rose beckoned Benjamin to accompany her to the edge of the herb fields north of the shop. He dragged behind, scowling.

"I won't mince words," she said, once they'd reached a field edged with succulent rosemary plants. "I want to know what you hid in the Herb House and retrieved last night."

Benjamin's frown transformed into frightened astonishment. "I don't know what you're talking about," he stammered. "You've got some nerve accusing me of—"

"I'm not accusing. I'm stating a fact. You secreted something in an old chest on the ground floor of the Herb House, and last night you retrieved it. I want to see it."

Benjamin's handsome features took on a mulish quality. He tightened his lips and kept silent.

"Patience's journal is missing," Rose said. "It contains all her records of her experiments, as well as something else, as I believe you know."

Benjamin said nothing, but a slow flush spread up his face.

"It is extremely important that I see that journal," Rose said. "There is more at stake here than you seem to realize." She did not wish to give him details, since she did not trust him, but she hoped sternness would sway him. It did not.

"I have nothing," Benjamin said. "And now, if you will excuse me, I am behind on my work." He turned on his heel.

"Do you wish me to talk to Andrew about this?"

Benjamin did a slow pivot back to her. "You and Andrew do seem to have a *special* relationship," he said. "Perhaps we should ask Wilhelm to be part of the discussion, as well."

Rose knew the tide had turned against her. Benjamin's threat was effective. Wilhelm would like nothing better than to demonstrate, just before the purging ceremony, another link between Rose and Andrew.

"You do not understand the seriousness of the situation," Rose said.

"Perhaps not," Benjamin said, "but then you will understand if I do not take it seriously." This time he swiveled around and returned to the shop in long strides.

Rose wasted no more time pursuing him. She would find another way. She cut through the kitchen garden in back of the Center Family Dwelling House and was heading for the Trustees' Office when she saw Gennie hurry toward her from the direction of the old cemetery. She stopped and waited. Gennie arrived, panting, auburn curls plastered to her forehead, but glowing with excitement.

"Rose, you must come with me instantly. I've got the most fascinating news, and I think it might help. Come on, this way." She began to sprint back toward the cemetery. Rose shrugged one shoulder and set off after her. Gennie veered off to the right and entered a little-used wooded area just north of the cemetery, and Rose followed her, regretting that she couldn't put her own plan into operation immediately. But when Gennie had shown her the plants Willy had found, Rose plunked down on the grass and began to piece together bits of information that had meant nothing individually. A pattern formed, and she knew Benjamin had not outsmarted her. Not this time, anyway. On the other hand, it would simplify her task if she could take a look at those missing pages.

"Gennie, I want you to do something for me."

"Anything."

"Go back to the Medicinal Herb Shop, help Willy in the garden, anything, just keep an eye on the shop. If Benjamin leaves, especially if he starts toward the Trustees' Office, run into the shop and borrow Andrew's telephone to let me know. You don't have to say anything specific; just your calling me will tell me Benjamin has left the shop and might be heading for the office."

"Where will you be? Where should I call?" Gennie asked as she hopped to her feet.

"On the second floor of the Trustees' Office, in Benjamin's retiring room."

Rose closed the door of Benjamin's room behind her and leaned against it, slowing her breathing back down to normal. Everyone was at work, and she thought she hadn't been seen as she'd approached the Trustees' Office from the west end of the village. It struck her how easy it would be to move unseen between the building and the Empyrean Mount.

She began her search. If Benjamin had not destroyed Patience's journal and the missing back pages from his own journal, he would probably keep them in his room. The Medicinal Herb Shop would be unsafe. If, as she suspected, he was using the information in the pages, he would want them handy but someplace where he would be likely to be left alone.

Rose knew the Trustees' Office rooms well from her ten years of living there. Secret hiding places were almost nonexistent. She checked the obvious spots—the drawers and storage area built into the wall, the thin mattress, desk drawers. She found nothing unusual.

Despite her urge to move quickly, Rose forced herself to explore the room with her eyes. The white curtains were too short and thin to hide anything. A Sabbathday suit hung from one of the wall pegs circling the room. She ran her hands over it and checked the pockets, but again found nothing. She didn't bother examining the broom, hanging from another peg.

The only other hanging object was a small bookshelf that hooked over two pegs, where Benjamin kept his old journals from Mount Lebanon. Of course. North Homage still did its own bookbinding, and she wasn't sure what Mount Lebanon did, but their journals would undoubtedly be different in some way. These volumes were all similar from a distance—bound in worn black coverings—but when she went closer, she could see that the middle volume was darker and less battered, as if it were newer. She pulled it off, along with the one next to it, and opened them. The handwriting was neat and precise in the newer one and barely legible in the other. She leafed through them both, and out of the neat one fell two sheets of paper, folded in half.

Tossing both journals on Benjamin's desk, she spread open the loose pages and laid them side by side. They formed a design similar to the one Gennie drew. Her hands shaking with excitement, Rose turned the sheets slowly until the design looked familiar to her. It was exactly what she had expected to see—a map of North Homage, minus the buildings. A line through the center represented the central path, and the only other areas drawn were placed right where all the wooded or uncultivated areas were located, including the woods she and Gennie had just visited. Rose pulled up Benjamin's chair and pored over the small circles and symbols drawn on the map. They were beginning to make sense to her. If she could break the code, it might just give her much of the information she needed.

After Willy's friendliness earlier that morning, Gennie hesitated to volunteer her gardening services as a way of keeping her eye on the Medicinal Herb Shop door. It might be safer, she decided, to invent an errand. The glint in Willy's eye as she approached told her to make her fib a good one. She was glad she was now of the world, where a little lie for a good reason need not torture her conscience.

"Hello, Willy. I hope you don't mind, but Rose asked me to pick a few samples of medicinal herbs. I think Josie wanted to do some studying or something."

"Want me to help? I could tell you what everything is," Willy said, taking a step toward her.

"Uh, I think Josie wants to see if she can identify them herself. Thanks anyway." Gennie positioned herself at the edge of the garden, in view of the front door of the Medicinal Herb Shop. She knelt beside a small plant that looked unfamiliar to her and pretended to examine it carefully. The sun beat down on her exposed neck. It looked as if that promised rain would never arrive. If Benjamin stayed at work, she'd have an unladylike burn by the time the bell rang for the noon meal in about an hour.

A shadow fell across the plant she was examining.

"You didn't bring a basket," Willy said, "so I brought you this." He held out a battered, grimy wooden bucket.

"Thanks." She put a sprig in the bucket and scooted over to another plant, but Willy stayed put. "I don't want to interrupt your work," she said.

"It'll keep," Willy said. "I was just thinkin' how you remind me of my granny."

"Really?"

"Oh, I mean you're much younger and all, but just the way you are with herbs. Like how you're touching that boneset leaf right now, like it was a baby's cheek. My granny used to do that." Willy squatted next to her. "Not with boneset, of course. She always said it wasn't worth its own name. It never did cure much of anything."

"Why are we growing it, then?"

Willy shrugged. "Dunno. I just plant 'em."

"What do you think of the rest of the plants in this garden?" Gennie asked.

"They're okay. A few are good. Most of 'em my granny'd pass by, but they won't make you sicker."

"So none of them are poisonous?"

"Nah."

"And the plants you found in the woods—are they all poisonous?"

Willy frowned. "Now that you mention it, yeah, all the ones I found could knock out a bear, if he was dumb enough to eat it."

"Did your grandmother use any herbs like the ones in the woods?"

"Well, yeah, but she knew the right way to mix a cure. She never would've—''

Out of the corner of her eye, Gennie caught a movement. She glanced up to see Benjamin emerge from the Medicinal Herb Shop. With long, quick strides, he veered to the right, a direction that could take him to the Trustees' Office. Gennie didn't stop to worry about what Willy might think. As soon as Benjamin had turned his back, she jumped to her feet and raced to the shop. It hadn't occurred to her before that Benjamin would move with such speed. Of course, he might not be heading for the Trustees' Office, but she couldn't take that risk. As she reached the shop door, Gennie took a gulp of air to hide her nervousness.

She started speaking as soon as she was in the door, before Andrew had a chance to question her presence. "I'm just here to use the phone for a quick call to Josie. She asked me to do something for her. You don't mind, do you?" She was halfway across the room before she realized that Thomas was standing with his back to her and with the phone receiver at his ear.

"He's taking some orders," Andrew said. "He probably won't be more than ten minutes or so, but it might be quicker if you just walked over to the Infirmary."

Gennie had heard some new and colorful language since leaving North Homage for the world, and it was all she could do to keep it to herself. She nodded and left, careful not to run until she had cleared the entrance.

In a way, Andrew had been right. The Infirmary was the closest phone. Gennie ran through the grass for the door. She plunged into the waiting area, where Josie sat at her desk, shaking a light brown powder onto a scale. As Gennie bolted past, Josie jumped back in alarm, setting her several chins quivering. The jar of powder slipped from her hand and shattered on the floor. A cloud of fine dust puffed into the air.

"Goodness, what has happened?" Josie asked, ignoring the mess on the floor.

"No time." Gennie grabbed the phone and dialed the Trustees' Office number, praying for the speediest connection ever made. The ringing seemed interminable.

"Come on, Rose, answer, please answer," Gennie whispered. She heard a click, and the ringing stopped. A man's voice answered. It was Benjamin.

Rose had figured out almost all the symbols on the map when she heard the phone ring in the hall. She realized she hadn't thought her plan out very carefully. If someone other than Gennie was calling, it might seem suspicious for Rose to answer. She decided to take the call itself as a warning and let it ring.

She replaced Patience's journal, with the map stuffed back inside it, on the bookshelf. As she turned to leave, she saw Benjamin's old journal still lying where she'd tossed it. She grabbed it and pushed it back beside Patience's. Aware she'd lost precious time, she ran for the door and clutched the knob just as the phone stopped ringing.

She had turned the knob and opened the door a sliver when she heard a man's voice. Benjamin stood a few feet away, his back to her.

"Hello? Hello? Impossible contraption." Benjamin muttered what sounded like a curse. "Hello, Gennie? What on earth . . . ?"

Not daring to click the door shut, Rose eased her hand off the knob, then flattened herself against the wall. He was too close; she'd never be able to sneak past him and down the stairs. Her only hope was that Gennie would find a way to convince him to leave without going into his room. She could think of no appropriate prayer for her situation, so she simply begged for mercy.

"Why would Josie need to see me?" Benjamin said. "Oh well . . . Yea, I probably am the best one to help her with that; Andrew isn't really up-to-date. What, right now? Can't it wait? Oh, all right. I'll be right there. Yea, right away; I said so, didn't I?"

Rose heard a tap as Benjamin hung up the phone, followed by his voice uttering something unintelligible but irritable. Then silence. Would he be considering whether he could delay long enough to complete his errand in the Trustees' Office? Finally Rose heard the patter of work shoes on pine stairs. She let her breath out in relief and crumpled to the floor.

She gave herself a few seconds to steady herself. Then she slipped into the hallway and listened. When she heard the outside door click shut, she crept down the stairs and watched out a window until Benjamin was out of sight.

The bell for midday meal would ring soon. Rose considered sneaking one last look at the map, but it wasn't worth the risk. She had a knack for memorizing maps, honed during her years as trustee, when she had directed the Shakers' small sales force and conducted real estate transactions. What she had in her head was enough to help her understand what had been happening in her village. She hurried away from the Trustees' Office before other Believers began emerging for the noon meal.

Rose returned to the woods north of the cemetery. This time she knew exactly where to look. Rather than tramp through the brambles, she circled around the far northwest edge of the woods. She slowed down and kept her eyes on the edge of the woods until she found what she'd expected—a stand of plants about three feet high, with large, white, trumpet-shaped flowers that had a pale violet tinge to them. Jimsonweed.

The rank smell brought back memories of Rose's childhood, when North Homage still grew some jimsonweed. Even then they were phasing it out. Though it had many medicinal uses, it was also highly poisonous, and Josie preferred to work with milder substances. Gradually the Society had eliminated both the cultivated and the wild plants. Rose still remembered Josie showing her the plant and warning her not to touch it and never, ever to eat the berries.

Rose was almost certain that Nora and Betsy had found this plant somehow and had eaten some part of it. Luckily, the fruit had not yet formed, so the girls had probably consumed flowers and perhaps leaves. The seeds would most surely have killed them.

As she cut back through the woods, Rose came upon a flattened area under a large maple. It looked as if some animals, or perhaps children, had spent some time sitting on the mossy ground. She examined the area, pushing aside undergrowth, until she found two cracked white cups and small plates under a pile of leaves. They were from the Shakers' tableware and must have been discarded when they cracked irreparably. This was where Nora and Betsy had their "tea."

Rose took the crockery with her and went directly to the Center Family kitchen, where the kitchen sisters were already serving the midday meal.

"Where'd you find that old stuff?" Polly asked. "Here, let me get rid of it for you."

"Nay, I have a reason for keeping it," Rose said, holding the cups and plates tightly to her chest. "But you could do me a favor. Go get Nora and Betsy from the dining room and bring them to me. Tell them I just need to talk with them for a minute or two."

Polly gave her a doubtful look, then shrugged and left. She returned with two wide-eyed girls, who had to be pushed toward Rose. When they saw what she held, they stopped, and Polly almost stumbled over them. She gave each of them a shove from the small of the back.

"Go on, girls. I'm short on kitchen sisters, and I don't have time for your silliness."

"Nora, Betsy," Rose called, "come on over. Don't be frightened. I'm not angry with you."

With a nervous glance at each other, the girls held hands and walked over to her.

"I found these cups and plates in the woods near the cemetery. That's where you had your tea, isn't it?"

Nora nodded.

"And you ate some flowers and leaves, didn't you?"

Both girls nodded.

"Was one of the flowers big and white?"

"I told you we'd get caught if we ate a bell, Nora, I *told* you." Betsy let go of Nora's hand and looked up beseechingly into Rose's face. "We weren't supposed to eat the bells. That's what Janey and Marjorie told us. The bells have bad magic, and a bad angel protects them."

"And who told Janey and Marjorie that the bells have bad magic?" Rose asked.

"Their mama, I think. But Nora wouldn't listen."

"I did, too, listen," Nora objected. "It's just that I thought they probably got it wrong. They don't know a lot," she said, with the smugness of a smart little girl. "I thought the magic was probably just stronger, not bad, so I made sure we didn't eat much, just one flower and a couple of leaves."

"Okay, for telling me the truth, you are forgiven," Rose said. "But these tea parties must stop. You must never again eat something if you don't know for certain that it isn't poisonous. Do you understand?"

Nora and Betsy nodded.

"All right, you can go back to your meal now."

The girls scampered off, and Rose glanced around the kitchen. Polly had said she was shorthanded, and Rose realized that Gertrude wasn't there.

"Oh, who knows?" Polly said when Rose asked where Gertrude had gone. "Probably up to her retiring room to have a good cry. It's all she seems to do these days. She's behaving more and more strangely. I think she must be getting really old or something. As she left, she told me I could be Kitchen Deaconess from now on. As if I want to."

"Come in," said a weepy voice, as Rose knocked on Gertrude's retiring room door.

"What on earth are you doing?" Rose entered to find Gertrude packing all her belongings in laundry sacks.

"Getting my affairs in order," Gertrude said. "I can't run from it any longer, Rose. My conscience is aching, and I must pay for my crimes. Gennie said that her young deputy will be here for the purging tonight, so after I confess my horrible sins, I'm going to turn myself in to him. Don't try to talk me out of it. This is the only way to atone."

Rose threw up her hands in a gesture of helplessness. "Gertrude, I am convinced that you did not kill Patience. If only you will wait and let me resolve this. Please."

"It's no use, Rose. I've made up my mind."

"All right, have it your way," Rose said. "But I intend to find out what really happened. I'll just work faster, that's all." She squeezed Gertrude's shoulder and turned to leave.

"Rose, I believe I should warn you." Gertrude held a clean white kerchief against her stomach as if stanching a wound. "There has been some talk going around of asking you to step down as eldress. I told my kitchen sisters never to repeat such nonsense, but they said several of the other sisters are saying it. Especially Elsa. She's been saying that you've broken your vow of celibacy. You haven't, have you?"

Rose unclenched her teeth long enough to say, "Nay, I most certainly have not! Thank you for telling me."

She took the staircase two steps at a time, moving fast to work off a portion of the anger surging through her. The rest of her fury would serve her well as she pushed to fit the pieces together before what she had come to think of as the dreaded purging.

TWENTY-FOUR

R ose left by the front door of the Center Family Dwelling House just as the sisters and brethren were filing out their separate doorways from the dining room. She waited outside on the path until Gennie reached her.

"We have work to do," Rose said.

Gennie nodded and followed in silence to the Ministry House. Once they had ensconced themselves in Rose's retiring room, Gennie let her curiosity bubble over.

"Tell me everything," she said. "Did you make it out of Benjamin's room without being seen? What did you find there? I heard rumors going into the dining room that Gertrude has confessed to murdering Patience."

"I wouldn't be surprised," Rose said, responding to the last topic first. "I'm afraid her conscience is finely honed. Anyway, we will have to let her suffer pangs of guilt until we can straighten this mess out. As for what I saw in Benjamin's room—and many thanks for giving me a way to escape—I found the drawings you saw in the Medicinal Herb Shop. They are maps of North Homage, showing the location of plantings of dangerous herbs which we Shakers no longer use in our cures. Someone is undoubtedly using them in some of the experiments going on in the shop. We can't be certain who planted them, or whether it was a group effort on the part of the Mount Lebanon Believers.

Until we know for certain, we can't afford to trust any of them.

"I also determined that Nora and Betsy found or were told about some of these plantings and that they were made sick by eating jimsonweed."

"Jimsonweed? That sounds familiar," Gennie said.

"It's also called angel's-trumpet. When I saw the symbols on the map, I began to understand. The 'horn' was supposed to be a trumpet, the cowl was for monkshood, and so on."

"Angel's-trumpet." Gennie rolled the words around and listened to them. "So do you think that when Nora mentioned a 'bad angel' . . ."

"Irene told the children not to eat any flower that looked like a bell because they were protected by a bad angel. Jimsonweed causes hallucinations. My guess is that Nora's guilty conscience created visions of a bad angel after she'd eaten a plant she'd been warned not to eat."

"So how does this help us know how Patience and Hugo died?"

"At this point, all I can do is speculate," Rose said. "My guess is that either Patience or Benjamin was responsible for the poisonous herb plantings, but certainly both of them knew where to locate each plant. And someone might have been experimenting with the herbs, disguising their presence in curatives with peppermint. Which, I think, might be how Hugo became ill."

"By accident?"

"Yea, by tragic accident. Apparently Andrew could not be sure what was in the jelly—at least, he hasn't told me, if he does know—but if we can convince Grady to have it analyzed, we might find evidence of one of those dangerous herbs."

"I'll convince Grady," Gennie said.

"If we are successful, he may need no convincing." A dark cloud passed across the window, sending shadows leaping through the room. Rose was reminded that she had only a few hours before evening.

"Do you have a suspicion about whether it was Patience or Benjamin who did the plantings?" Gennie asked.

"Benjamin. I think he wanted so much to show himself superior to the others that he was willing to take the chance of poisoning someone. Patience could easily have found out about the plantings while she conducted her personal rituals. Maybe she saw Benjamin actually plant seeds or check on his harvest. It's quite possible that she saw the jimsonweed and got the idea to use it to help deepen her trances."

"So her gifts were not real after all?"

"I don't know," Rose said. "I really don't know."

"Do you think her death was an accident, too?"

Rose leaned back in her chair and rocked gently. "Nay, I'm afraid I do not. I am more than ever convinced that someone killed her. Patience always kept her eyes open, and she knew a great deal about her fellow Believers." She pulled her list of suspects out of a desk drawer and handed it to Gennie. "Some of her knowledge was true, and some was merely conjecture. Either way, since the information came out most often during trances, it had the ring of truth to it, and that made her potentially dangerous."

"But we still don't know who might have thought her dangerous enough to kill her?"

"Nay, that is what we still must find out." Rose checked the small clock she'd brought in from her bedside. "And we don't have long to do it. The purging starts immediately after evening meal."

"What shall I do?" Gennie asked.

"I don't suppose you'd be willing to stay out of this?"

Gennie laughed. "Rose, you know that if you don't give me an assignment, I'll just create one myself."

"And that could be worse than my worst nightmare," Rose said. "All right, perhaps you could talk more with Irene. Confirm our guess that she warned the girls about the poisonous plants and try to find out how she and the children knew about their existence. But for heaven's sake, stay out of trouble."

"What if Irene killed Patience?"

"If you become fearful of her, use those wits of yours. Get away from her and find me immediately. Do you promise?"

"Of course, I promise. Where will you be?"

"Probably at the Medicinal Herb Shop, since I'm suspicious of everyone there."

"Are you accusing one of us of harming Patience? We would never do such a thing," Andrew said, hurt in his voice. Rose had decided that the quickest, safest route was direct confrontation, so she faced Andrew, Thomas, Benjamin, and Willy inside the Medicinal Herb Shop. She had hoped that the culprit would break down when confronted with his secret and the enormity of his crime. After all, she'd reasoned, three of them were Believers. They had vowed not to kill even for a just cause. Surely the guilt of knowing he had murdered another human being, and a fellow Shaker at that, must be nearly unbearable. But so far she had not seen so much as a flicker of remorse. She decided to recount what she had pieced together about Patience's accusations against each of them.

Andrew's story about his family and his denial of a special relationship with Patience remained unchanged. "As you well know," he concluded, "her information was often inaccurate."

"Not always," Rose pointed out. "Benjamin, she found out you were planting poisonous herbs, didn't she? That's what you had mapped out in the back of your journal, which Patience copied. Did she threaten to expose you unless you provided her with sufficient jimsonweed to enhance her trances?"

Benjamin's boyish features hardened. He shot a resentful look at Andrew and shrugged. "I could have done a lot of good with those herbs."

"They are dangerous," Rose said, "and it is illegal to put them in cures without revealing their presence."

"I know what I'm doing. Maybe they are dangerous in the hands of others, but not in mine. Patience was a fool. To tell you the truth, I suspected she would kill herself eventually, she was so determined to explore those gifts of hers. She actually thought Mother Ann had told her about my herbs just so she could have a supply of jimsonweed."

"But the jimsonweed didn't kill her," Rose said.

"Nay, and neither did I," Benjamin said. "Why don't you ask Thomas about his arguments with Patience?"

"We didn't argue."

"Yeah, you did," Willy said, ducking his head as if he expected to be chastised for speaking up. "I heard you from the garden a few days ago. Couldn't hear what you said, but you sounded plenty mad."

"I'd bet they were arguing about Irene," Benjamin said. "I mean, Sister Irene. He won't leave her alone."

"*I* won't leave her alone. Look who's talking." Thomas stepped forward, fists curling tightly. Benjamin rose to meet him.

Andrew touched Thomas's rigid arm. "Brethren, remember your vows," he said. "And ask yourselves how much extra confession time you want to fill this evening at the purging worship."

Both men relaxed and stood back. "Anyway," Thomas said, "I had no reason to kill Patience. Irene and I are finished. I only want my children to be taken proper care of, that's all. You and Irene can run off together for all I care, but leave the children here."

Rose was ready to jump out of her skin with impatience. Her conjectures were being confirmed, one by one, but she was no closer to learning who might have smashed Patience on the back of her head and killed her. Before she could turn her attention to Willy, the shop's telephone rang. Andrew answered, listened briefly, and hung up.

"We're all called back to the dining room," Andrew

reported. "Wilhelm ordered the evening meal moved an hour early, so we can gather in the Meetinghouse before the rain comes in."

Her time was up. She had failed, and Wilhelm would have his way. Rose had not felt such despair since Agatha's first stroke. The medicinal herb brethren went back to their various projects, so their work could be brought to a conclusion in the short time left before the bell rang.

Willy followed Rose out the door and did not immediately veer off to the garden. He walked along beside her in silence for a few moments, then said, "I know you're real busy, ma'am, but I was wondering if I could ask you something."

"Of course," Rose said.

"It's about Gennie. I know she's not a Shaker sister like you, but I wondered if she's promised to anyone."

His voice held a poignant hopefulness, and Rose wanted to be gentle with him. "Yea, I'm afraid Gennie is spoken for. But I know you'll find someone just as nice."

Willy nodded slowly, not showing great surprise. "She sure is nice," was all he said.

He continued to walk beside her as they neared the central path. "Willy," she prodded him, "was there something else you wanted to talk about with me?"

Willy stopped and faced her. He stuffed his hands in his pockets and kicked at the dry dirt of the path with one scuffed shoe. "Yeah, it's about Brother Hugo."

"I'm so sorry, Willy, I'd forgotten that you spent a lot of time with Hugo. You must have felt very sad when he died."

Willy nodded and kicked harder. "There's something been preying on my mind," he said. "I went to see him when he was feeling so poorly, you know, before he got real sick. He was telling me everything he could remember about my ma and pa, and he'd look in his old books, too, the ones he wrote in a long time ago, so's he'd remember better. He was really nice to me. The nicest thing he said to me was, I wasn't like my pa. He said I work real hard and I don't tell lies. All I remembered about Pa was, he used to haul off and hit me any time he got mad. But I still felt bad that him and Ma went off without me. I figured Ma didn't want me, neither. Hugo, he said Ma did the right thing by getting Pa away and leaving me with Granny. That way Granny could teach me to be gentle, Hugo said. He said sometimes mothers love their children so much they have to give them up to protect them.''

"Hugo was very wise," Rose said. She was aware of the moments flying by. "Was there anything else?"

"Yeah." Willy grimaced. "I hope I didn't do wrong. Hugo asked me to do it, and I figured anything Hugo wanted me to do was okay. But then Brother Andrew asked me if I'd been taking any of the herbs, which I never did, but I felt like I'd done something wrong."

"What? What did you do?"

"I . . . Hugo asked me to sneak into the Medicinal Herb Shop one night and get all the journals and bring them to him, just for a few hours. Which I did. And then I brought them back real quiet, so nobody would know they was gone."

"Why did he want to see them?" Rose felt her heart perk up with hope. "Did he tell you what he learned from them?"

"Not straight out, he didn't."

"Tell me exactly what he said, as best you can remember," Rose urged.

"Oh, I can remember, because it struck me odd. He said, 'Shades of Nathan Sharp.' I asked who was Nathan Sharp, and he said, no one I needed to worry about, just someone from long ago. Hugo said he'd be talking to Wilhelm about it soon, but he promised I wouldn't get into trouble."

"When was this?"

"Right before he got real sick. I don't know if he ever talked with Wilhelm. Did I do the right thing? Maybe I should've told you earlier."

"You did fine, Willy."

*   *   *

A quick and carefully worded call to Wilhelm from the
Center Family Dwelling House told her that Hugo had
never spoken with him about what he learned from the
journals. She cut off the conversation before Wilhelm could
ask any questions. Next she stopped in Agatha's room.

"Nathan Sharp is a familiar name," Rose said, "but I
don't recall the story."

"Ah, Nathan Sharp. That incident happened at least a
hundred years ago, but still new enough when I was a
young sister. He was a trustee at Union Village in Ohio.
One day he took off, absconding with cash and property
belonging to the Society. Others had done the same thing,
of course, but he always stood out in our minds."

Rose felt her legs lose strength, and she sank onto Aga-
tha's desk chair. A trustee who defrauded his Society. If
Hugo had examined all the journals from the Medicinal
Herb Shop, he must have seen Andrew's, too. Somehow he
must have seen evidence that Andrew was cheating North
Homage. It was tougher now that Shaker holdings were no
longer in the trustees' names, but it was not impossible.
She cursed her own heart that had not allowed her to view
Andrew as a serious suspect. Patience and Hugo must both
have known, and he must have killed them. He tried to
make both murders look like accidents, and it almost
worked.

A kitchen sister arrived with a tray of bread and cheese
for Agatha's evening meal. Rose had no time to waste; she
had to keep a close eye on Andrew until Grady arrived and
could arrest him. She tossed a distracted kiss at Agatha's
cheek as she hurried from the room.

The evening meal had already begun when Rose slid into
her seat. A quick glance at the brethren assured her that
Andrew was there, eating as if his soul were free of guilt.
She had solved what now appeared to be two murders,
saved Gertrude's reputation and conscience, and should be
able to put a halt to the purging ceremony, yet Rose found

she had little appetite. Luckily, the meal was light, and she managed a few bites before giving up. Josie tossed her a sympathetic glance, probably thinking she was upset about the public confessions to come.

Wilhelm stood first, and the brethren followed him. Rose led the sisters through their own door, and the two lines emerged from the building into an early night. Thick, inky clouds had spread across the sky, obliterating the last sliver of blue and the first hints of sunset. A drop of rain hit Rose on the cheek. Saving solemnity for the worship service, the Believers scurried toward the two entrances to the Meetinghouse.

Rose decided to let the service begin. Grady was still nowhere in sight, and it would be easiest to keep an eye on Andrew if everyone was together in one building. She frequently glanced over at him as she led her sisters to their benches. All the sisters were present except Agatha, who was too frail for such a vigorous ritual, and Charlotte, who was caring for the children in their dwelling house.

Lightning burst across one of the large Meetinghouse windows, followed closely by explosive thunder that rattled the glass. Rose was glad to be safe inside, despite the circumstances.

Wilhelm walked to the podium in the middle of the room and began a short homily about purging and confession, timing his comments perfectly with the increasing lightning and thunder. Rose paid no attention. Instead she kept her eyes trained on the brethren's section, so she could keep Andrew in her sight at all times. So that he would not catch her staring at him, she let her gaze wander across the rows of brethren, counting silently.

Someone was missing. She looked up and down the rows again. Willy wasn't there, but she didn't expect him to be. Nay, a brother was missing. She reached the group from the Medicinal Herb Shop and realized it was Thomas. Glancing quickly from side to side, Rose located Irene, so they had not run off together. And yea, Benjamin was still there, sitting next to Andrew. Would Thomas have sneaked away to avoid the ordeal of public confession? Wilhelm would be furious.

The homily ended and a gloom settled over the room that had little to do with the blackness outside. Wilhelm sat down. There was to be no music; the occasion was too somber. The rain became a steady battering on the high roof of the Meetinghouse and pounded against the west windows, driven by a ferocious wind.

Wilhelm bowed his head in silent prayer, and the brethren followed his lead. Rose understood that Wilhelm considered himself in charge of this service. He had not even consulted her about the form it should take. She bowed her head, and so did the sisters. For a full five minutes, the only sounds came from the storm, growing in velocity. Even Elsa made no attempt to converse out loud with the angels, which made Rose wonder if Wilhelm had planned the ritual with her instead of Rose. He might be hoping that this evening would be Rose's last as eldress. Elsa, his fervent supporter, could then step in.

Rose raised her gaze to see Wilhelm nod slightly at Andrew, who moved with obvious reluctance to the center of the room. He did not look at the sisters. Rose closed her eyes and prayed again—for strength, for hope, and especially for Grady to arrive. Until now, she had believed that she and Andrew were both innocent victims, facing punishment for crimes others had invented for their own purposes. Now she wasn't sure of anything. It occurred to her that he might try to avoid retribution by admitting to their imaginary wrongdoings and placing the blame entirely on Rose.

When she opened her eyes again, Andrew had dropped to his knees and raised his arms heavenward. He opened his mouth to speak. But his words disappeared in the whoosh of an opened door, followed by a slam. All eyes turned to the women's entrance, where Charlotte leaned against the door, gasping. The light cotton of her drenched work dress clung immodestly to her body. She had tried to protect herself by wearing her heavy palm bonnet, but she must have tied it too hastily, because it had flown back and hung from her shoulders. Her thin white cap had become translucent and no longer hid her damp hair, darkened by rain. Rivulets dripped from her bangs down her flushed cheeks.

Charlotte's frantic eyes searched the rows of sisters until she found Rose. "Janey and Marjorie," she said. "They are missing."

In an instant, Rose understood. Not Andrew. Thomas. When Hugo remembered the Nathan Sharp story, he wasn't thinking about the fact that Nathan had been a trustee; he was simply pulling to mind a Believer who betrayed his own people by stealing from them. Hugo had once been a salesman, so he'd known what clues to look for. Thomas, who was such a good salesman, controlled the sales accounts so that Andrew and the others could concentrate on creating new cures. That was what Hugo had seen when he examined the journals from the Medicinal Herb Shop—evidence that Thomas was skimming the profits, hoping to leave with enough money to take his children with him. He had chosen to execute his plan now because he was afraid that, after being exposed in the group confessions, Irene and Benjamin would leave together and take Janey and Marjorie. He had to get to them first.

Irene screamed and lunged toward the door. Two sisters grabbed and held her as she continued to struggle. "Let me go," she begged. "You don't understand. He'll hurt them. He says he loves them, but he hurts them. I had to get them away from him. I had to keep them safe."

Wilhelm was either dazed or hoping to go on with the purging, because he neither moved nor spoke. Rose took charge.

"Has anyone called the Sheriff's Office?" she asked, as she reached Charlotte.

Charlotte nodded. "I called Gennie over to stay with the

children, and she phoned while I did one last search of the Children's Dwelling House. She said Grady wasn't back yet, and the one officer left said the winds have uprooted trees along the roads. The officer will try to get here, but he didn't know how long it would take.''

"Sisters, brethren," she said, turning to face them. "We must find the children ourselves. Their father, Thomas, has taken them, and he is dangerous. It hasn't been long; they can't have gotten far, unless . . . Andrew, do you suppose Thomas might have taken the Plymouth?''

Andrew's mouth curved in something that, under less grave circumstances, might have been called a smile. "Certainly he could have, and probably did. But it won't do him any good. The Plymouth has a flat tire. I discovered it just before the evening meal and didn't have time to change it.''

"He might still have tried to drive it off, though. Or managed to change the tire himself in the storm," Rose said. "It would slow him down, though. We may have a chance. Sisters, start calling our neighbors, and—"

"Our phone lines are down," Charlotte said. "Gennie started to call around after talking to the Sheriff's Office, but the phone went dead.''

"Then we must do this ourselves, with God's help," Rose said. "I want groups of you to begin searching. No one should be alone, and at least one brother should be with each group. Spread out and search the whole village, starting with the buildings. They might have taken shelter until the storm passes. Leave on all the lamps as you go through the buildings. It will help light the village.'' She directed groups in different directions. To her surprise, Wilhelm willingly joined several Believers heading for the Ministry House.

When the last group had dashed into the storm, Rose removed her long Dorothy cloak from a peg and tied it around her neck. Thank goodness they had thought ahead and brought their outdoor garments with them. She snugly knotted her palm bonnet and reached for the door.

"I was certain you would violate your own rule and set out on your own," Andrew said from behind her.

"Andrew, I thought you'd . . ."

"You feel responsible for those children, and you will put yourself in danger to save them. I am going with you."

TWENTY-FIVE

RATHER THAN BE DELAYED ANY LONGER, ROSE AND ANDREW left by the same door, which the wind slammed shut behind them. The rain had turned to hail, which stung Rose's cheeks and blanketed the grass, turning July to midwinter. Andrew led the way down the muddy central path to the Trustees' House, where the Plymouth was kept parked. It was still there. One corner hung lower where the tire was flat. As Rose caught up, Andrew stooped down and picked something up. He held it out to Rose. A corncob doll, battered and drenched. Rose slid the doll behind the triangular kerchief that crisscrossed over her bodice. She prayed for the chance to return it to Marjorie.

"What now?" Andrew asked.

"Thomas was at the evening meal, and so were the girls. So it must have begun to rain just as they set out. They might have gone back to one of the buildings for shelter, but I think it more likely that he took them into the woods to wait out the storm. They are less likely to be found there, and it would be easier to get away from the woods than from a building."

The nearest wooded areas were the holy hill and the grove of trees north of the old cemetery. They agreed to try the holy hill first. As they ran around behind the Trustees' Office, lightning slithered directly over their heads, followed instantly by a boom, as if the sky had cracked loose and crashed to the earth. An unseen hand flipped a switch, and all the lights in the village went out at once.

Rose and Andrew kept running, though now the Empyrean Mount appeared only as a dark mass against a dark sky. They relied on the frequent flashes of lightning to show them how close they were to the perimeter of the woods.

Once they entered the cover of the trees, they were protected from the downpour, but they could no longer use the lightning to guide their way. Rose tripped over a tree trunk, and Andrew caught her around the waist, breaking her fall. As soon as she was steady, he released her waist but grasped her wrist to keep her from falling again.

"For the greater good," he said. "Saving human lives is more important than observing the rules." Rose did not argue.

They reached the holy hill without seeing anyone or hearing anything but the wind whipping the tops of the trees. The hill itself was open to the sky. The rain still pounded, running in muddy streamlets off the overdry earth. Surely no one would hide in such an exposed area, certainly not with young children. Rose imagined Janey and Marjorie, soaked and terrified.

"Come on," she said. "They won't be here. Let's try the woods on the other side."

Staying in the trees, they circled around, then headed into the deeper woods northwest of the hill. Despite the thick canopy of leaves overhead, the wind had become a roar, sucking the trees sideways first one way, then the other. Bursts of rain penetrated the woods as the wind created openings among the trees.

Andrew stopped with a suddenness that nearly threw Rose off balance. Then she heard it, too. A child sobbing. It sounded close by.

"I'll go on ahead," Andrew said, "and you wait a bit, then follow."

"Andrew," Rose hissed in his ear, "I am perfectly capable of helping to—"

"I'm well aware of that. I just think it safer if Thomas doesn't know right away that there are two of us. Then if he overpowers me, you can come to the rescue."

Though his tone had been matter-of-fact, Rose wondered if he was mocking her. He still held her wrist, and she snapped it away from him more sharply than was necessary.

"Go on, then," she said, with irritation.

He moved away, creeping from tree to tree, and pausing to locate the sound of the child's wailing. Rose waited, but only until he was just going out of sight, then she followed. Andrew must have moved faster as he neared the crying, because Rose did not regain sight of him. Instead, she listened herself and hoped she would follow the same path.

She continued slinking from tree to tree for what seemed like an hour but was perhaps ten minutes, without seeing Andrew. The crying, which ranged from howling to whimpering, grew louder. Rose even thought she could identify eight-year-old Janey's voice. Was anyone trying to soothe her, or was she being left to sob in terror?

Rose inched around a huge oak trunk, thinking she must be close, when the child screamed, a shriek of horror, which was repeated over and over again, then stopped suddenly. Rose was torn. Was Janey injured, and should she rush forward to help? Had Andrew reached her and convinced her to be quiet? In the end, Rose couldn't just stand there and wait. She tiptoed toward where she had last heard the sounds, determined to see but not be seen.

She gently pushed aside a tall bramble bush and saw Janey. She was sitting on the ground, streaked with mud, and bound to a tree trunk with what looked like vines. A gag was tied around her mouth. It resembled a sleeve from a brother's white Sabbathday shirt. Next to her, little Marjorie slumped against their restraint as if unconscious or asleep.

Rose felt paralyzed. Her impulse was to rush forward and release the children, but where was Thomas? And where was Andrew? For the first time, doubt slipped into her mind. Why had Andrew insisted on going ahead, then disappeared from view so quickly? It began to look as if he'd wanted to lose her.

Hugo had looked at Andrew's journal, as well as Thomas's. She had only Andrew's speculation that any potentially dangerous herbs might have been mixed with the peppermint that Gertrude had used for her jelly. Both Andrew and Thomas visited Hugo on occasion. Moreover, if Thomas had been skimming profits from the medicinal herb sales, was it truly reasonable to assume that Andrew would not have known about it? The two of them may have planned it together. Leaving the children tied up this way might be part of their plan, or a part that went awry.

Rose's mind rushed from idea to idea, but none of them helped her know what to do next. The children might have been abandoned and the two men already gone from the village. Or the girls might be a trap. Andrew knew that, at the moment, Rose was the only other person in these woods. If they could disable or even kill her, they might have plenty of time to escape.

Either way, Rose knew she had to rescue those children. It could be a very long time before any other Believers extended their search to these woods. In the meantime, Janey was terrified, and Marjorie might need immediate medical help. Perhaps if Rose circled around before going to the girls, she could discover whether the men had gone.

Before leaving the protection of her tree, Rose looked around and found a hefty stick. She had faced the possibility of violence before, and she had agonized, but now she felt resolute. She would do what was necessary to bring Janey and Marjorie back to the safety of the Society. She would atone for the rest of her life, if need be, but she would save those children.

Clutching her only weapon, Rose crept from tree to tree in a circle around the area where the children waited. The wind had abated somewhat, and she listened carefully to the sounds of the woods. Perhaps the animals had taken shelter from the storm, because she heard no chirping or rustling. Or perhaps they had been frightened off.

It was possible that the men were watching her, waiting for the right moment. To create confusion, she backtracked a ways into the woods and widened her circle. She had gone about two thirds of the way around and had come across no one. She decided to take a risk and move in again, closer to the girls. She moved slowly, watching her feet to make sure she did not crack a fallen branch, alert to any sound of movement around her. She was almost in sight of Janey and Marjorie again. Just a few more trees to go. She sidled around one tree and moved toward the next. As she glanced at the area just ahead of her, she froze in place. The dark sole of a man's shoe was visible just beyond the perimeter of a tree ahead of her. As she watched, the foot began to move. But something wasn't right. The foot was moving forward, but the sole still faced upward.

Rose steadied herself against a tree. She felt her aloneness as she never had before. Her Shaker family was very close, yet she could scream and no one would hear her over this storm. Whatever had to be done, she must do alone.

Staying close to the tree trunk, she crept forward, toward the place where the foot had been. At least the wind howling overhead and the rain splattering on the leaves would mute the snap of a branch if she stepped on one.

Rain had penetrated even this deep in the woods, and the dusty ground was turning molten. She came to the spot where she'd seen the foot and noticed streaks in the mud. Crushed undergrowth and broken brambles told her that a body had probably been dragged away. She followed the path, careful to keep her stick ready for a quick defense.

The blurred tracks led away from the girls and toward the creek. Before they reached the clearing near the creek, however, they swerved north into a densely wooded area that Rose had never been in. A crash of thunder jolted Rose, and she almost dropped her stick. No lightning pierced the thick canopy overhead, and the thin slivers of visible sky were still black as midnight. For a confused moment, Rose wondered if she'd been out there long enough for it to have actually become midnight. But nay, the others would have reached her by now if it were that late.

She moved deeper into the woods. She came to an area blanketed by leaves and fallen branches, and the tracks stopped. She had a vision of someone hefting a body onto his shoulders and carting it off, to be tossed into a ravine. She'd have to continue the search with just her instincts to guide her. With her stick pointed forward, she inched along through the leaves. She stepped over a rotting branch, and her foot came down on another branch, hidden by the leaves.

Losing her balance, she fell face-first into the leaves. The smell of decay assaulted her nostrils. She rolled over and sat up quickly, pinching her nose to avoid sneezing. As the danger passed, she opened her eyes and realized she'd tossed her stick aside as she'd fallen. On her knees, she reached over for the stick, and her fingers halted inches from it. A human hand protruded slightly from under the leaves, as if it, too, were reaching for the stick.

Rose could not stop the squeal that escaped from her throat. She sat back abruptly and waited for the worst of her panic to subside. Then she crawled toward the hand, reached out, and touched a finger. It was cool, but not ice-cold.

With a burst of hope, she frantically brushed aside the blanket of leaves and uncovered a long arm, wearing the sleeve of a brother's shirt. The hand was tied at the wrist to the other hand. Within moments, she had revealed a shoulder, and then the head. It was Andrew. He was bound and gagged and unconscious, but breathing.

With a fervent but silent prayer of thanks, Rose reached for his bindings, then stopped her hands. What if her speculations about Andrew had been correct? What if his condition was the result of a falling-out among thieves? If she released him, she might be even less safe than she was right now. But if she left him, he might die. Furthermore, if she was wrong, and if Andrew had truly tried to rescue the children, she would be cutting off her only support.

She could not afford to spend more moments arguing with herself. In the end, Rose decided to follow the teachings of her faith—and to be truthful, she wanted to trust Andrew. She could not doom him to death, even if by releasing him she risked endangering herself. She quickly undid his bindings, grabbed her stick, and disappeared into the woods before he might regain consciousness. Once she had rescued the children and returned them to the sisters, she would send the brethren to deal with Andrew—to care for him and, if necessary, to subdue him and hand him over to the deputy.

Staying as quiet and hidden as possible, Rose hurried back past the creek and toward the tree where she had last seen Janey and Marjorie. She still hoped to steal them away and avoid violent confrontation. When she arrived, her hopes were dashed. The girls were loosed and sitting on the ground with their father, who had his back to Rose. He seemed to be speaking to them earnestly, and their pinched, dirty faces gazed up at him.

Rose looked at her stick and knew it would not be enough to subdue him, even if he had no weapon but his own strength. The girls would be too terrorized and too bewildered to help. She scanned the area around her for an idea. She saw Virginia creeper twining around many of the trees around her. The vines probably had been growing for decades without disturbance. Thomas must have used some of them to secure his children while he—did what? Explored the woods? Met with Andrew? Never mind, Virginia creeper might be the answer for Rose, too.

She ripped off six lengths of vines and divided them into two groups of three. She worked quickly, blessing the heavens for the roar of the winds. Pulling out Marjorie's corncob doll and placing it under a tree, Rose removed her triangular kerchief and shredded it into long, narrow rags.

Finding saplings that were well enough established and in the right locations took precious minutes, but finally she had tied the lengths of vine a few inches above the ground and a few inches apart. She had twisted the vines together and stretched them between sapling anchors, to which she tied each end with some of her kerchief rags. The rest of the rags she stuffed in her apron pocket. She studied her work. It wasn't hemp, but it might just give her the advantage she needed.

Rose took a deep breath to steady her nerves, then positioned herself just in front of the stretched vines.

"Janey, Marjorie," she shouted. "Where are you? Come on out, it's just me, Rose, and I want to help you." She waited a moment, then another moment. "Janey? Marjorie? Are you all right?" Yet another moment of silence. Then, as she'd hoped, Thomas appeared in front of her. She ventured a sigh of relief. There had always been the danger that he could circle around in back of her, but she had hoped that by indicating that she was alone, he would choose the more direct route.

"Hello, Rose," Thomas said. Blood spotted his white Sabbathday shirt, and one sleeve was missing. "Janey and Marjorie are fine, and in any other circumstances, I'd just send you home, but now I'm afraid I can't do that."

"Why not, Thomas?"

"Oh, Rose. Patience was right, you really have no idea what goes on in your own village. Because, of course, we need time to wait out the storm and then get far away. So you'll just have to come along over and sit with us. Come on." He took a step forward.

This wasn't what Rose wanted. She wanted him to run. She took a step backward. "You won't hurt me?" she asked, letting fear color her voice.

"Of course not. Why would I hurt you? All we want to do is get away, like I told you."

"Why didn't you just go? You could have taken a horse and been in the next county by now."

"Not with everything I've got to haul along," Thomas said, with a laugh. "Besides, Marjorie is afraid of horses, and she's been frightened enough for one day." His voice became tender when he mentioned Marjorie. Rose wondered how he could love his children, yet terrify them so.

"What else are you taking along besides your daughters?" Rose asked. "Could it be the profits you've been skimming from the medicinal herb industry?"

Thomas stiffened. "Not so ignorant as I thought," he said. "Yea, but I didn't steal anything. It was my money; I earned it. I'm a good salesman, and I deserved a salary for my work. Besides, I needed money so I could get my little girls back and take them away to start over. Irene did everything in her power to take them away from me, even taking them to the Shakers. I thought I could get them back by taking them with me when we came here, but Irene came, too, and she watches me like a hawk."

"She tried to keep you away from your girls?" Rose asked, encouraging him to talk. She might as well learn as much as she could, and every moment brought the other searchers closer.

"She always seemed to be there, like a witch. I think Benjamin was helping her. But sometimes I outsmarted her. I got some candied angelica to my girls a couple times. They liked that. I needed for them to remember their daddy with love and not get poisoned by Irene's lies."

"What lies did Irene tell?"

Thomas's mouth worked in anger, and he clenched the large fists hanging at his sides. "She said I wasn't fit to be their father," he said.

"Because you hurt them?"

Thomas took another step forward. *Easy,* Rose thought, *don't rush it.*

"You were merely disciplining them, weren't you?"

Thomas's taut shoulders lowered a fraction. "Yea, that's all. I mean, I wasn't a Shaker then, and anyway, I don't believe in sparing the rod. I love those girls. I want them to grow up right.''

"And Irene? Did she have to be disciplined, too?''

"Irene.'' Thomas spat out the name with disgust. "She had a gift the Shakers never saw. Her gift was for making me furious at just the wrong moment. I swear, she waited until I was just relaxing with a few drinks, or I'd been out all day trying to find work and I hadn't eaten, and then she'd go at me. I couldn't help it. She just made me so mad. Especially when she was pregnant; then she had no sense at all.''

"You hit her when she was pregnant?'' Rose tried to hide the horror she felt.

"Look, I did everything I could to make sure those babies were okay. I always gave Irene some jimsonweed afterward, so she wouldn't lose the babies. Just a little bit; I knew what I was doing. I even grew it myself because it was hard to get hold of.''

"I see,'' Rose said. "But she lost the babies anyway.''

"It wasn't my fault. I wanted those babies, too.''

"And did you grow more jimsonweed when you got here?''

"Nay, that wasn't me, that was Benjamin. Patience and I both knew it, and it was helpful for quite a while. Patience wanted to have better trances, so she told Benjamin she'd keep his secret if he'd keep her supplied with the stuff. Everything went fine, until . . .''

"Until what?''

Thomas shook his head. "That's enough,'' he said, and took two steps.

"Until Hugo found out you were skimming profits, right? So you killed him. Then Patience figured out you'd killed him and why, and was planning to expose you— how? When? At the Sunday worship service, in front of the world? That would have been a trance to remember, wouldn't it? You would never have seen your little girls again.'' Rose stepped backward quickly but did not turn.

Thomas roared and ran toward her, his beefy arms outstretched toward her neck. The first vines tripped him and snapped. He stumbled and recovered his balance. Without looking down, he ran right into the next vine rope, which threw him flat on his stomach, on top of his fist.

He was winded, just confused enough to give Rose an opening. She ran to him and grabbed his one free arm, twisting it up toward his shoulder blades. It was the only move she knew. She had once witnessed a fight at the farmers' market in Languor, and this was how the sheriff had subdued one of the men. In that struggle, the man had simply let go and given up. Thomas was far too desperate to do the same. He squirmed as he regained his breath, and Rose felt her grip loosen. She threw herself on her knees in the small of his back, hoping her weight would pin him down. Still he struggled, twisting from side to side to throw her off balance. She hung on, keeping his arm tight up against his back.

Rose had no idea what to do next. She had hoped to use the rest of her kerchief rags to tie his hands together, but his one hand was still trapped under his diaphragm. Her best hope was to wear him out, so she focused all her strength on staying where she was. Suddenly he relaxed, and she wondered if she had won. Then she felt his muscles bunch underneath her. Too late, she realized he was preparing for one powerful push, which threw her sideways. She rolled off his back as he staggered to his feet, gasping for air.

There wasn't time to stand, so Rose scooted away from him as fast as she could, hearing the skirt of her work dress rip as she skimmed over sticks and thorns. Thomas lunged for her. As his red face lowered over her, his feet flew out from under him, and he landed, once again, flat on his stomach. This time Andrew leaped on top of him, pulling both the larger man's hands in back of him. Rose overcame her surprise in seconds and jumped to her feet. White-faced with exertion, Andrew held Thomas down as Rose ripped

TWENTY-SIX

"NOTHING BROKEN," ANDREW SAID, WITH A GRIN. "I'LL BE back at work within the hour."

"Nay, you will not!" Rose said. "I speak as your eldress, and I'm sure Wilhelm would agree with me. You must take at least, oh, let's say two hours. After all, you are badly battered. You might frighten the children."

Rose sat in a visitor's rocking chair, a respectful five feet away from Andrew's Infirmary bed. Josie busied herself at a small dresser, pouring rose water in a bowl to sweeten the air.

"I won't tire you," Rose said, more gently, "but I thought you would want to know that Thomas has confessed to the murders of both Patience and Hugo."

"Poor Hugo, too," Andrew said.

"Yea, Hugo was too experienced, and Patience, too observant. They both learned of Thomas's fraud. Hugo would have told Wilhelm, of course, so Thomas killed him."

"How on earth did Thomas poison the jelly?"

"He didn't. In fact, when Hugo first became ill, Thomas didn't realize he was even suspicious. Hugo made the mistake of confronting Thomas, to convince him to turn himself in.

"The peppermint jelly is probably fine. Not very appetizing, but not deadly. Benjamin examined every mixture in the Medicinal Herb Shop, and there was nothing that would have caused more than an upset stomach for Hugo, which is probably what happened. Because of his weak condition, he ended up here, and Thomas simply came to visit and fed him one of Benjamin's more toxic infusions. We'll probably never know how he got Hugo to consume it.

"Benjamin, by the way, has personally ripped out all his poisonous herb plantings. He worked on his concoctions at night—that's who came in when Gennie spent the night in the closet—and he'd been very careful never to leave any evidence of the herbs lying around the shop, but he made the mistake of noting the locations of the plants in his journal. Patience watched everyone and soon found out his secret."

"Good," Andrew said. "Of course, the medicinal herb industry will probably fail now."

"We'll survive," Rose said. "I would give up more than that to have Hugo—and Patience, too, with all her faults—back with us."

Rose leaned back and caught the breeze from the open window. Cooler air had arrived, at least for a short visit. It wouldn't stay long, this time of year.

"By the way," Andrew asked, "whatever happened to Patience's cap?"

"Oh dear," Rose said, "I was thinking you'd be better off not knowing. But you'd find out anyway, so you might as well hear it from me. Thomas had watched the argument between Patience and Gertrude. After Gertrude left, Patience took off her cap to examine the lump on the back of her head from her fall. Thomas attacked her with a rock soon after. But then he realized that the cap, which had only a drop or two of blood on it, was a clue that Patience had suffered a second blow. So he took it with him. The brethren found it in the leaves you were lying on top of while you were unconscious in the woods."

Rose lowered her voice. "And now I have a question for you," she said. "How did you really find that first-year foxglove near the holy hill? You couldn't have seen it from the area where I discovered Patience.''

"I've been found out," Andrew said. He gazed at Rose, his eyes sad. "Sometimes I just need solitude, to think and pray and mourn. I had discovered the holy hill on my own just two days earlier, though, of course, I didn't realize its significance. I never saw Patience there, so I thought it was my secret place.''

"I see," Rose said, satisfied. "I'll let you rest now." She left the rocking chair where it was, in case another visitor should come soon.

She had nearly reached the door when Andrew called to her. "I have one last question," he said.

Rose turned back to him.

"Those rituals Patience performed," he said. "They were very like the ones early Believers conducted on the holy hills, weren't they?''

Rose nodded.

"So if North Homage's Empyrean Mount was a secret even you did not know about, how did Patience know?'' He tilted his bandaged head in puzzlement. Josie stopped straightening the room and waited to hear Rose's answer.

"We don't know," Rose said. "Perhaps we never will.''

"I should not have allowed myself these feelings." Rose paced around the room. "I should not have let this happen.''

"Let me tell you a story," Agatha said. "For reasons that will be obvious, I did not tell you this before, but now I believe you need to hear it." Her weak voice took on some of its old power. Rose stopped pacing and leaned against the windowsill.

"When I was about ten years older than you are now— before you came to live with us—we lost our entire Ministry in one day. You may have heard about the incident from others.''

Rose nodded. "As I recall, the elder and eldress ran away together."

"The village was devastated," Agatha continued. "The Lead Ministry concluded that we had strayed too far from their control, and for a time it looked as if we might close our doors, or at best be sent new leaders from the East to discipline us until we had mended our wild ways."

"But that's when you became eldress, isn't it?" Rose asked.

"Yea, we had a supporter in Mount Lebanon who convinced the Lead Ministry to give us another chance. I'd been raised here from infancy and had shown no leanings toward worldly love, so I was appointed eldress. Brother Obadiah was sent from Pleasant Hill to be elder."

Rose noticed for the first time a gentleness in Agatha's voice as she said Obadiah's name.

"Obadiah was a fine Shaker and a fine man," Agatha said. "He could not have worked harder for us had he been raised here himself. We worked together to save the village. And we did save it, with God's grace and Mother Ann's intervention." Agatha released a sigh that seemed to deflate her tiny body. "In the process," she said, "we grew to care for one another deeply."

"I see," Rose said quietly.

"Nay, you do not. Not yet. Though you may, in the end. Obadiah and I worked side by side for twenty years and never touched until the day he died, when I held his hand as he left us. Josie watched and never said a word. I would not trade a minute of those twenty years, though neither will I lie and say it was easy. At times it was torment. You see, I believe we loved one another all the more because we would not break our vows for earthly love."

"That I do truly understand," Rose said. "Thank you for telling me. But I'm afraid I don't have your strength and clarity. I feel as if I have already broken my vows."

Agatha reached out with one thin hand, and Rose came back to her chair. "This is where Wilhelm and I disagree fundamentally,'' Agatha said. ''To him, all actions and feelings and thoughts are equally evil. I believe, certainly, that their potential for evil is powerful, but . . .'' She leaned back in her chair and shook her head. ''It is always a dilemma,'' she said. ''If you open the gates of your heart, an unexpected visitor may drop by. But if you close your heart, to keep it pure, you may shut out the angels.''

''Then I have not truly broken my vows?''

''Nay, but you have a choice to make.''

Rose walked to the open window and looked out over her village. The evening meal was approaching, and Believers had begun strolling toward the dwelling house. Two sisters, friends separated during the day by different rotations, fell into step beside one another and chattered, bursting suddenly into laughter. They waved to a group of brethren, returning from the fields. Companionable, from a respectful distance. Loving yet pure. Rose returned to Agatha's side.

''I made my choice a long time ago,'' she said. ''I make it again now.'' She sank to the floor and leaned her head against Agatha's side, like a child, and was comforted.